FIRE IN BONE

A JAKE PETTMAN THRILLER BY

WES MARKIN

ABOUT THE AUTHOR

Wes Markin is the bestselling author of the DCI Yorke crime novels set in Salisbury. His latest series, The Yorkshire Murders, stars the compassionate and relentless DCI Emma Gardner. He is also the author of the Jake Pettman thrillers set in New England. Wes lives in Harrogate with his wife and two children, close to the crime scenes in The Yorkshire Murders.

You can find out more at:
www.wesmarkinauthor.com
facebook.com/wesmarkinauthor

BY WES MARKIN

DCI Yorke Thrillers

One Last Prayer

The Repenting Serpent

The Silence of Severance

Rise of the Rays

Dance with the Reaper

Christmas with the Conduit

Better the Devil

A Lesson in Crime

Jake Pettman Thrillers

The Killing Pit

Fire in Bone

Blue Falls

The Rotten Core

Rock and a Hard Place

The Yorkshire Murders

The Viaduct Killings

The Lonely Lake Killings

The Cave Killings

Details of how to claim your **FREE** DCI Michael Yorke quick read, **A lesson in Crime**, can be found at the end of this book.

This story is a work of fiction. All names, characters, organizations, places, events and incidents are products of the author's imagination or are used fictitiously. Any resemblance to any persons, alive or dead, events or locals is entirely coincidental.

Text copyright © 2021 Wes Markin

First published 2021

ISBN: 9798720407186

Imprint: Dark Heart Publishing

Edited by Brian Paone

Cover design by Cherie Foxley

All rights reserved.

No part of this book should be reproduced in any way without the express permission of the author.

For Roger M – Never Forgotten

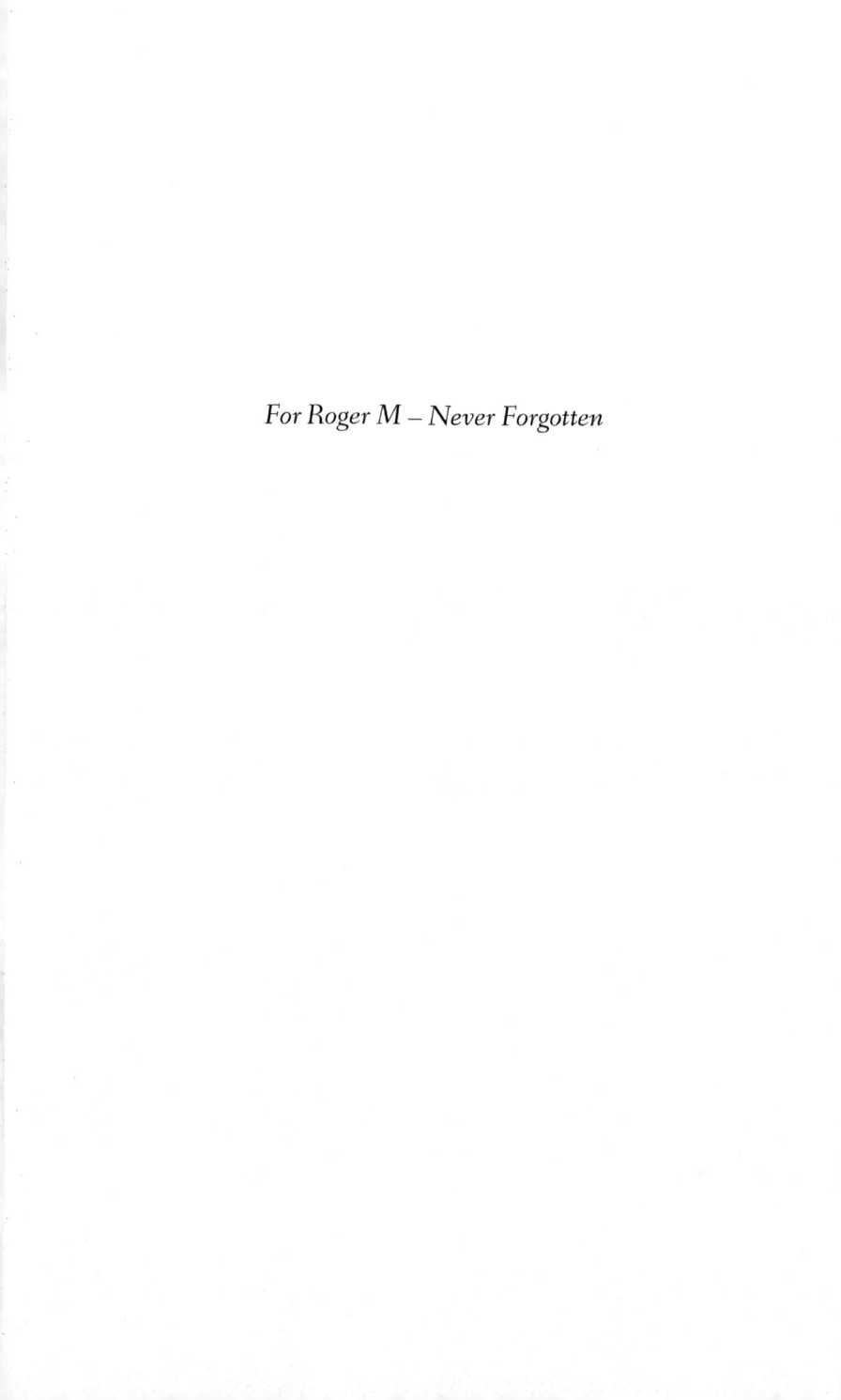

1975

THE HEAT PRESSED down on Charlotte White. "I don't remember it being anywhere near this hot last year."

On the other side of the table, Ryan let his spoon sink into his cereal bowl and laughed. "Your memory is letting you down again. In fact, I remember us having this very same conversation."

She undid the top button on her blouse. "Okay, so what was your suggestion then?"

His eyes widened. "Carry on with those buttons, and I'll give you a great suggestion."

She slapped his hand. "You've a teenage son upstairs."

"Did you have to remind me? Okay ... let me see, last year ... yes, we went on a long, cooling walk by the Stinson and had a picnic by the old Waterford Mill."

"I remember. It was fun, even with Bobby sulking over a girl."

Ryan rolled his eyes. "Can't say I recall. Didn't he spend his entire fourteenth year sulking? Personally, I remember the hum of fireflies and the gentle breeze over the lake …"

She squeezed the top of his hand. "Stop pretending to be a poet."

He turned over his hand and took hold of hers. "There's more of the poet in me than you'll ever realize."

"Go on then. Indulge me with this romantic side. Please. I've been holding out for it for seventeen years."

He grinned. "Well, let me get you to that patch by Waterford's, and I'll show you that side. If I remember correctly, the place was quite desolate last time round."

"With Bobby in tow? Please don't make promises you cannot keep. Especially those kinds of promises." She bit her lip.

"Bobby's in bed. He still will be by the afternoon. Do we really want to be heading out in the hottest part of the day with a grumpy teenager? Let's go now and pick up some supplies along the way. We'll probably be back before he's even up!"

She gave Ryan a long stare, wanting him to believe that she was giving his suggestion careful consideration. However, it was a bugbear of hers how long Bobby was spending in bed these days, and she'd been trying her best to knock the sloth-like habit from him, falling just short of violence. "It sounds fantastic, honey, but he might like to come."

"You *are* joking!"

"Well, maybe not *like*, but he'll definitely enjoy it when he's out with us, and you know how much I like it when we're all together."

Ryan wriggled his hand free of hers, and his playful expression fell away.

"Sorry, I do want us all to spend time together, honey. Just me and you. I'll make it up to you, I promise."

"Of course," he said, nodding yet avoiding eye contact.

She sighed. Ryan never dealt well with rejection. "Let me go upstairs and wrestle the argumentative little adolescent from his bed. Then I'll make us all coffee, and we'll put together a picnic." A knock at the door startled her, and she put her hand to her chest. "Do they always have to knock so damn hard?" She watched Ryan rise to his feet and approach the front door. Even after all these years, after all their ups and downs, and *even* after his brief affair earlier in the marriage, she adored him more than life.

As he opened the door, she slipped past him for the stairs.

She heard a deep, elderly voice. "Good morning. Carrs Deliveries."

"Jesus, what's in that?" Ryan asked.

"It's a big one, alright. Good thing we replaced the trolleys last week; I don't think the old ones would have handled it."

"There's no way that's anything I've ordered," Ryan said.

The delivery man laughed. "Wives, eh? You should see the shit that comes through my door!"

The sound of the conversation faded as Charlotte climbed the stairs and turned down the hallway for her son's room. He was a fifteen-year-old boy, so he required a courteous knock. However, he only ever got the one. If he didn't answer, she'd enter regardless.

She flattened the dogeared corners of the poster tacked to his door that read, *Unless you're delivering pizza, I'm busy!* as she waited.

"Pizza!" she said loudly.

Nothing.

Well, you were warned. She opened the door. "Sleepyhead, we have a plan—"

Every part of her body crumbled.

Ryan circled the three-foot-by-three-foot cardboard box. He paused, bent forward, and ran a finger over the thick wad of masking tape that sealed it. He straightened upright and tried pushing the box with his foot, but it didn't move. *What the hell have you bought, Charlotte?*

He went to grab a knife from the kitchen to attack the tape with. He heard the rumble of the departing delivery man's diesel engine. The company, Carrs Deliveries, had a reputation for being cowboys of the highest order; broken deliveries, products left outside to be stolen, and brushes with the law for so-called medicinal deliveries were just the tip of the iceberg. When Ryan had asked for the name of the sender, the delivery man had given a name he didn't recognize—Blake Marsh, owner of Marsh Properties. What could Charlotte have possibly ordered from a property company?

From upstairs, Charlotte called his name.

"Are you okay, honey?" he asked, splitting the tape on the box. Holding his knife in one hand, he reached for one of the flaps on the box to open it as he heard his wife bounding down the stairs.

"Bobby's not in his bed!"

He took a sharp breath through his nose and looked up at his stunned wife. He thought for a moment. "Henry's! That's where he'll be."

She shook her head. "No ... it's not like him. He'd have told us."

He felt a cold sensation starting up his hands. "He's fifteen. I pushed a lot of boundaries when I was fifteen. Call Henry's mom. He's there. I know it." But even as he said it, he didn't believe it. Not just because Bobby was very rule bound and would have told them, but because this entire situation was very peculiar.

Carrs Deliveries.

Marsh Properties.

He spied the box, and the cold sensation moved into his stomach.

"What's in the box?" She was no longer shouting, nor was she whispering. It sounded more like a hiss—the sound of something deflating.

With his cold hand trembling, he leaned forward, lifted back a flap, and looked inside. He jumped backward, holding the knife in front of him.

"What's happening, Ryan? What's in the box?"

"Someone ..."

"Who?"

Ryan slowly shook his head as the cold sensation squeezed his stomach, forcing his breakfast up.

"Who? Ryan?"

Once certain the person in the box was completely still and posed no threat, he eyed Charlotte on the staircase.

She'd slipped into a sitting position and was clutching the railings.

He opened his mouth to speak, but nothing came out.

"Oh god ... Is it Bobby? Speak ... please. Is it Bobby?"

"No."

"Thank god ... thank god!" Tears rolled down her cheeks.

"Someone with blond hair."

"Thank god ... thank god."

"They're wrapped in plastic." He felt his breakfast climbing his throat and into his mouth. "Who'd put someone in a box? This is sick ... *fucking* sick. Why here? Why bring them to us? Call the police. Call them!"

"I can't move." She closed her eyes and rested her head against the railing. "Where's Bobby? What's happening, Ryan? Please, tell me what's happening!"

He had no idea. He approached the box again. Despite the vise-like grip of the cold sensation that had now spread throughout his entire body, Ryan sweated hard. It ran down his face and back. He knelt, opened a flap, and looked in. "Jesus ... fuck." Ryan forced himself to stay there long enough to determine the person in the box was definitely dead.

The victim had been placed in a sitting position, hugging their knees. The head rested forward, so the face was hidden, but Ryan didn't want to touch the young man or the thin plastic he was wrapped in. He didn't need to. Ryan recognized the brown leather jacket and the tangles in the blond hair.

He turned from the box, put a fist to his mouth, and tried for a deep breath through his nose.

But it was too late.

His breakfast hit the floor.

CHARLOTTE BANGED her head hard against the railings, praying she'd wake. It didn't work. *Because this is real. Now, get control of yourself. It isn't Bobby, remember?*

Listening to her husband retching, she rose to her feet

and worked her way down the stairs. Her legs were shaky, but she used the bannister to steady herself. At the bottom of the stairs, she turned to Ryan. "Who is it?"

He wiped vomit from his chin, opened his mouth to speak, but then retched again.

"Who, Ryan? *Who* is it?"

"Henry," Ryan managed to squeeze out between retches. "It's Henry."

Charlotte put her hand to her mouth as her husband fought to a standing position, using the wall as support. She looked down at the box.

"No!"

She looked back up.

Ryan regarded her sadly. "Don't look in the box."

"Where is Bobby?"

"I don't know, but we'll find him."

She flinched and looked away. She took a deep breath, tried to ignore her heart as it thrashed against her ribcage, and fought the quivering in both her nerves and muscles to go for the phone sitting by the sofa. She dialled, then watched Ryan.

He nodded in her direction, clearly satisfied that she was calling the police.

Except she wasn't.

"Hello."

"Sylvia, I'm sorry."

"Char, is that you? What's wrong?"

Charlotte saw Ryan's look of surprise. When he realized what she was doing, he shook his head, wanting her to stop.

"Did Bobby stay over with Henry last night?" Charlotte asked.

"No. Not that I know of."

Charlotte spied the box again and turned her back to it.

"Why're you asking?" Sylvia asked.

"Bobby's not here. I got up this morning, and his bed's empty."

Silence. Immediately lost for words. Empathising with this dreaded experience. Every parent's worst nightmare, and she'd be desperate not to say the wrong thing. "I'm sure we can find out why. I'll go to Henry now."

But you can't, can you? Because Henry's in a box in our living room. But Bobby will be there, in Henry's room. Because he has to be. I don't know why, and I don't know how, but he will be. She steadied herself against the windowsill on which the phone sat.

Ryan came alongside her and put a hand on her arm. "The police, we have to phone the police."

She brushed away his hand.

"It's not right to phone his mother."

She glared at him.

She heard the clatter of the phone being picked up again and Sylvia's desperate voice. "Shit ... shit ..."

"Sylvia?"

"Henry's not there."

"Bobby?"

Silence. "No. Where are they? What are they up to?"

Charlotte tasted bile. *Henry's dead, Sylvia, but I won't tell you that. I couldn't hear those words, so how could I expect you to? It's not my place. But where's my son?* "Are you sure Bobby's not there, Sylvia?"

"Why'd you keep asking me that? If Henry isn't here, why would Bobby be here?"

"I don't know."

"They've been hanging around with another boy a lot recently ... what's his name? There's a van pulling up in our drive."

"What van?" Charlotte grabbed her net curtain, as if it was this house it had arrived at and not Sylvia's.

"Just Carrs. Another broken package, probably."

"*Don't* answer the door!"

"Char, it's just a delivery."

"Believe me, you can't open the door!"

"But Sean has already gone outside to help. So, do you have the number of that other boy's family?"

"Sylvia, please ... *stop Sean!*"

"Why? I don't understand, Charlotte. You're not making any sense. He's helping the delivery man, and jeez, it's a large parcel—heavy too, by the looks of it."

Charlotte screamed and dropped the phone. It bounced off the wall. Feeling her husband's hands on her shoulders, she collapsed to her knees.

Time passed. She wasn't sure how long, but when she recovered her senses, she was clutching the net curtain she must have torn from the railing as she'd gone down and was looking up at Chief Earl Jewell.

"Bobby?" she asked.

Earl opened his mouth to answer, but knowing what was coming, she didn't bother to wait and, instead, screamed all over again.

1

"THE SKWEDA," PARKER said, wading into the black river, "it translates to fire in bone."

"Fire in what?" Scarlett asked, sliding down her panties.

"Fire in bone. The Abenaki Indians named it." He dove under the surface.

"Prick." She tested the water with her toes and snapped her foot back. Too cold for her, but then, everything was too cold for her. Last year, the doctor had written it off as anaemia and had given her some iron tablets. They'd made little difference, much to the displeasure of her father, who really couldn't stand her costly interactions with the thermostat in winter.

She waited for Parker to break through the surface.

Nothing.

Prick.

When he did eventually burst out, dramatically gulping for air, she folded her arms. *Exhibitionist.*

He stood in the water to his chest, frowning.

"What's wrong?" she asked. "Was I supposed to start squealing?"

"Well, some form of compassion would be nice."

"Why? If you're stupid enough to drown yourself!"

"You're heartless."

"Or I'm just not like the women in those eighties horror movies you watch with your dad. I'm not turned on by macho men, and I don't need you alive to keep me safe."

He smiled.

"Now, fire in bone."

"What about it?"

"What does it mean?"

"Come in and I'll tell you."

"For fuck's sake." She waded in and folded her arms tightly against her breasts. It did little to warm her, and she shivered as the water reached around her thighs. No way she would do this normally, but she'd only recently started to have sex. Parker had assured her that sex in the water was the best thing ever, and she didn't want to miss out on the opportunity to try it out. "Is this the same spot you brought Sandra to?" It was dark, so Scarlett couldn't be sure if he blushed, but she suspected he did.

Sandra was his ex-girlfriend and Scarlett's ex-best friend.

"No." Parker brushed his long hair out of his eyes and pointed at the bridge that connected Blue Falls to Sharon's Edge. "There's a patch under that bridge that's real quiet too."

"You want to fuck there tomorrow night?" She wrapped her arms around him and was unsurprised and happy to feel his erection pressing into her thigh.

He kissed her neck.

"Now, fire in bone. What does it mean?"

He carried on kissing her.

She pulled backward, and he rolled his eyes. "I thought everybody knew this!"

She broke from his embrace and edged away. She was shivering quite hard but still managed to get her words out. "Clearly not everyone, shithead. Now, what the fuck does it mean?"

He waded toward her.

She smiled. The erection she'd felt under the water had shown he was ready, but she saw it just as clearly on his face. New to sex, she was really enjoying the education. Lust was interesting. It weighed so heavily on her, but yet also made her feel so light and happy when addressed.

"The Abenaki believe a fire burns deep inside us all."

She stopped and allowed him to approach. She let her hand close around his erection. "It's definitely burning in you."

He closed his eyes and sighed. "They believed the waters of the Skweda would best show you how to use that fire."

"Then how're you going to use your fire?" She stroked the end of his erection over her thigh, moved it gently toward her crotch, and lifted her leg up his side.

He moaned over the promise of what was coming. He leaned in to kiss her again, but she yanked away, laughed, spun onto her front, and swam farther into the river. "What are you doing to me?"

She turned, treading water. "Stoking the fire!"

"Very funny."

"I want you burning hot."

"I am. And your attempts at stand-up comedy are failing miserably."

"Come and get me then!" She raised her hands in the air and let herself sink under the surface. Unsurprisingly, it was pitch black under there, but it didn't bother her. Cold had always been the issue for her, not darkness. The swim had helped though, and she almost had the shivering under control. She swam around the silent darkness, holding her breath, enjoying the sudden deprivation of senses. Eventually, when she broke the surface, she whooped.

"Keep it down," Parker said, who had swum out to join her.

"Why? No one's here!" She whooped again. "You were under the bridge with Sandra! We're in the middle of nowhere."

"Still—"

"Still *nothing*." She dove under again and swam down a couple feet. She still couldn't see anything but could sense Parker's body close as he swam with her now. She reached out and stroked part of him, then turned and kicked hard with her hands extended to see if she could touch the bottom, although she had no idea how far away that was.

Her hand brushed against Parker again.

She reached in the darkness, searching for his hand. When she found it, she clutched it and—

She reeled backward. Terrified that the sudden impact of adrenaline would send her spiralling into the emptiness, she bolted for the surface and shouted Parker's name when she broke through.

"What?" Parker asked from several feet away.

"A hand. I touched someone's—*something's*—hand. It was small and cold, and hard. I think it was bone."

"Nice try."

"I'm *fucking* serious."

"Jesus!" Parker's eyes widened, and he pointed to her right. "What's *that*?"

Shivering again, and not from the cold this time,

Scarlett turned in the water. The smooth surface of a skull bumped against the top of her breast. She shoved the skeleton and screamed.

IN THIS MOMENT, lying among the tangled sheets with Piper Goodwin and still catching his breath, did Jake Pettman dare to feel optimistic? He was all too aware of how influential the chemicals in the brain could be. He'd experienced these rushes before—first with Lacey Ray, and then with his ex-wife, Sheila. And look what happened on both of those occasions. Yes, it was all too easy to ride that train of euphoria and buy into the false belief that things would turn out just great.

"Thoughts?" Piper asked, reaching up and stroking his face.

"Trying to avoid them." Jake ran his fingers down her damp midsection. "The most perfect moments don't need them."

She laughed. "I've either stumbled on the most romantic tourist or the most peculiar. Jury is still out on that one."

"So, I'm still just a tourist?"

"It takes more than a couple months in Blue Falls to lose that tag, even if you did help restore order to the place."

Jake looked away. Only two other people knew he'd been forced to pull a trigger on someone to make that happen, and neither of them were in the room right now. "I barely did a thing."

She turned his head to face her. "Besides, it's what you've contributed since then, in the last few months, that I value."

She was, of course, referring to the support he'd given her after she had discovered that Jotham MacLeoid, the man Jake had ended, had actually been her father. Discovering you were descended from such a vicious man would destroy most people.

"Don't credit me with that."

She shook her head. "You helped me through it. You're a good man."

He blushed. And there it was again. That contentment. A sense that maybe, just maybe, he was getting another chance at happiness. "Maybe we can drop the tourist for a day or two to see how it feels?"

Piper made a show of looking around the tiny room. "Jake, you're still living in a motel."

Jake shrugged. "I've grown quite attached to it."

"Have you grown attached to the cockroaches too?"

Jake laughed. "Not so much. Just the price, really."

"Until your medical bills explode. Which they will if you stay in this hole too much longer."

Jake removed some photographs from the bedside table and handed them to her.

"What are these?"

He shrugged again. "Because I love you."

She fell silent while she processed these words. It was the first time he'd said them, after all.

He was tense while waiting for the response but was unsurprised when it came.

"And I love you too. So, what are they?"

"They're of my son, Frank. I'm sorry I didn't tell you." He took a deep breath.

"How old is he?"

"Five." He could feel the tears threaten.

She kissed him on the cheek. "Thank you for telling me." She sat upright and looked through the photographs.

He watched her and observed the collision of his two lives: the old and the new.

"Beautiful," she said, looking at a photograph of Frank in a football shirt.

"Very. It's Southampton FC."

"Never heard of them. I was talking about your boy." She smiled at Jake "He looks just like you."

"Yes, I fear for him."

She stroked his chest. "He's a lucky man."

I hope so. He'll need all the luck he can get, descended from me. "There's something else ..." Jake paused and ran a hand through his hair. "I was lost for a time, Piper. And then ... And then I became involved with ... I ..."

She stroked his chest. "If it's not the time ..."

"It's the time. It would always be hard to say—"

Piper's cellphone rang. "Ignore it."

"Answer it. This can wait." *Because the story of Paul Conway, the poor boy caught in that car explosion because of my involvement with cruel people, will always be there.*

She reached for her cellphone and checked the name on the screen. "Hi, Sadie. Everything okay?"

Jake was certain he could hear crying.

"Slow down. A child?"

Jake sat upright.

As the conversation wound on, Piper's expression darkened considerably. "That's awful."

Jake edged closer to Piper to try to hear Sadie speaking.

"Drive to my parents', honey," Piper said. "I'll meet you there." After the phone call, Piper turned to Jake. "That was one of my best friends. She's panicked. It's awful, Jake. They've found a body in the Skweda."

Jake took Piper's hand. "A child?"

Piper nodded.

"How did she find out?"

"Driving back from work, she saw police vehicles in the road running alongside a small patch of woodland beside the river. When she got home, she called Tom, one of her close friends. He's a police officer here."

Jake rolled his eyes. "One of Gabriel Jewell's finest, no doubt. Relaying the events at a crime scene to a civilian, for pity's sake! Is anything done right in Blue Falls? Do they know who the child is?"

"I don't think so. The body is old. It's rotted. Jesus, this is awful."

"Anything else?" Jake asked, climbing out of bed.

"No. Where're you going?"

"Drop me a pin on a Google map where Sadie saw the vehicles and text it to me."

"You're serious, aren't you?"

He turned and raised an eyebrow.

"And ridiculous!"

Jake shrugged. "I just want a look for myself."

"Why? No! Actually, save it. I don't want that 'once police, always police' bullshit."

"Text it over please. It's a flying visit, I promise. I'll hang back. I just want to see if I can catch a word with Lillian, or even Gabriel himself. You know what they're like; they may need whatever help they can get."

She sighed and grabbed her cell to text him the map. "Sadie's worried. I'm meeting her at Mom and Dad's to calm her down."

"Good idea." Jake nodded. "I'll call you if I find out anything else."

2

THE CHIEF OF the Blue Falls Police Department, Gabriel Jewell, hadn't been surprised with the rapid response from the Maine State Police, nor had he been surprised when the Major Crimes Unit had contacted him immediately to issue a hands-off order on the body. They would see Gabriel's department as a dangerous entity—a potential source of evidence contamination and a hinderance—rather than a catalyst toward the truth.

Just shy of two hours later, the suited-and-booted Lieutenant Louise Price, tall and black, with energetic eyes, and hair pulled tightly into a bun, burst onto the scene, and Gabriel had been relegated to a gofer.

The first task Louise had given him had been to take detailed statements from the two young lovers who had unearthed the body, Scarlett and Parker. The lieutenant had made it sound like a crucial task, but was it? Really? The kids had gone skinny dipping in the Skweda—as thousands of young people before them had over the years—had dislodged an old body, which had then floated to the surface. Despite the shock, Parker had demonstrated some responsibility in pulling the skeleton to the bank rather than allow it to float downstream. That was it, really. It didn't matter how detailed the statements, there was nothing more to know.

Gabriel wrapped up the interview as quickly as he could. He thrust his notepad into his pocket and waved over Tom Wright, one of his younger officers who had bought into this recent trend of neatly clipped hair combined with excessive unkempt facial hair. He instructed him to see the skinny-dippers got home safely after their shock.

He crossed the road, weaving around the many vehicles. He hadn't seen so many vehicles at a police incident in his career; his world was one of domestic abuse, DUIs, and petty theft. This wasn't Gabriel's first body, of course, but it was the first one that wasn't a drunken lowlife with a rap sheet longer than his arm.

The medical examiner had already suggested that the body belonged to a young girl between the ages of thirteen and fifteen. *The same age as Collette when she disappeared.*

Gabriel was yet to see the body.

He maneuvered through a layer of oak trees and emerged on the sandy bank of the Skweda. He looked left then right and noticed the trees jutted farther onto the banks in those directions, hiding this little patch and providing an oasis for the horny teenager, as well as the murderer who wished to drown a victim or dispose of a body.

Portable lights that worked off one main generator had been set up. The medical examiner, with a white oversuit clinging to his portly frame, was using tweezers to pull evidence from the remains. After sliding samples into small plastic bags, he would hold them up with a gloved hand to his assistant, who would scribble on the bag and slide it carefully into a backpack.

Lieutenant Louise Price stood alone at the water's edge, staring at the distant, twinkling lights of Sharon's Edge, one of Blue Falls' two neighboring towns.

Nearer to Gabriel, whispering to one another, were two of Louise's officers. When one of them laughed, it forced Gabriel's top lip into a curl.

"What have you found out?" Gabriel called to Louise.

He expected her to turn. She didn't. Even her two officers ignored him and continued to whisper.

The ME looked in his direction and gave a sharp, asthmatic cough, which made his facemask billow. "Her neck was broken. I suspect this is what killed the poor girl. I hope they did it before they removed her teeth."

Gabriel took a deep breath. "What?"

"She had no teeth." The ME pointed at the skull. "They look like they've been pulled clean out."

"How long has she been under the water?"

"Too soon to say without testing. A long time."

"Thirty years?"

"It's possible."

Louise called out without turning, "Why do you ask, Chief Jewell?"

Because that was when Collette disappeared. Gabriel prepared an alternate answer, but the lie he formulated died in his throat when a frogman broke the lake's surface. Shielding his eyes from the sharp glow of the frogman's headtorch, Gabriel marveled over the resources available to the Maine State Police at a moment's notice.

The frogman tore out an oxygen regulator, and a deep female voice rose from the black river. "I found a small holdall loaded with rocks. A rope's tied to its handle. At the end of the rope is a small noose, a perfect fit for a child's ankle."

The ME coughed. "Makes sense. The noose would have lost its grip on the ankle as it decomposed. That teenager swimming could have accidently jolted the victim's remains, causing the foot to slip clean through."

Gabriel took several steps toward the ME and the body. He didn't expect to know if it was his sister or not, but now was the time for him to take his first look. He felt a cold tightening in his chest.

The skeleton's rags were a familiar dark blue.

"Is there a school badge on that clothing?"

Louise turned. "You can see that from there, Chief?"

No, he couldn't, but he could sense its presence. It was becoming more and more like a vicious nightmare he couldn't wake from.

The ME eyed him. "Yes. Blue Falls High School."

Whipped by sudden nausea, Gabriel stumbled backward.

The ME coughed again. This time, he couldn't stop himself, so he unhooked his facemask and let it dangle. "Sorry ..." he coughed again. "Pollen must be high here."

His assistant handed him an inhaler.

He sucked back the steroid.

Gabriel steadied himself against a tree. *Collette.*

One of Louise's officers, Ewan Taylor, put a hand on his shoulder. "Are you okay?"

Gabriel brushed it off. "Don't touch me."

"Easy," Ewan said. "Just trying to help."

Gabriel shoved him.

The officer stumbled backward into his colleague's arms.

"Don't *fucking* touch me. Did you not hear?"

"Loud and clear, *Chief*."

"Quit it." Louise said, coming up alongside her officers but fixating on Gabriel. "Show some respect to this poor child."

"Yes," Ewan said, staring at Gabriel with narrowed eyes.

Louise faced her officers. "*All* of you."

"Yes, ma'am," they both said.

Gabriel stepped backward toward Louise, who eyed him warily. "Her name is Collette, ma'am. She disappeared in nineteen ninety."

"And you know this because of the school uniform?"

"Yes ..." He looked down. "Among other things."

Louise stepped forward so they were now barely a yard apart.

He looked back, noting that she was almost as tall as him. He wasn't used to it, especially in the other gender.

"What other things?" Louise asked.

He felt like melting to the ground, but he also felt some overwhelming anger toward these aliens on his patch, so he used that adrenaline to remain dignified. "She's my sister, and if you tell me to show respect around her body again, you'll have to restrain me."

JAKE KNEW there was no point in getting too close. Not only would he be turned back, but he would make himself a person of interest. Neither situation appealed.

However, as an ex-detective sergeant, he knew the importance of getting a feel for the crime scene. Of course, he could argue that he still was a DS, as he'd never actually resigned or lost his job; he'd simply disappeared. How that would go down in a totally different country, never mind Blue Falls—a completely different world—he'd no idea.

He killed his lights and pulled over on the side of the road some distance away. It was busier than he'd expected. It was clearly a state issue now. Jake felt the weight leave his shoulders. The investigation of a young girl by an inept chief of police and his misogynistic cronies would have forced him into action. He sat on the hood of his hired Ford, watching the lights flash and listening to the steady hum of activity as the warm breeze played on his face.

After absorbing the bustling scene and having decided to return home to call Frank, Jake hopped down from the hood. It'd only been a day since he last called his son. He didn't like to make it a daily occurrence, because Frank would quickly start to expect it, and letting him down, as he'd done a few times already since arriving in New England, was a painful experience. However, after hearing about the death of a child, the desire to hear his boy's voice was overwhelming.

His cell rang. He was surprised to see Lillian Sanborn's name on the screen.

"Aren't you in the middle of this investigation?"

"Word travels fast round here."

"You sound surprised."

She laughed. "In Blue Falls? No. I'm also not surprised that you're interested."

He didn't mention that he was watching the crime scene and that one of the people he could see moving about in the distance may very well be her, pacing about on her cell. "Not really. This particular investigation will be in good hands, I'm sure."

"Yes ... sort of. But I'm worried still."

"What do you mean?"

"Well, even though the Maine State Police are involved and they've sent in their Major Crimes Unit, well, I don't know ..."

"Go on."

"Shit ... sorry, Jake, I really shouldn't be involving you."

"Who should you be on the phone to? One of your colleagues? First time I met you, they were shoving a G-string into your drawer and asking you if you were a pole dancer."

"Thanks for the reminder."

"Look, just reminding you that we've got each other's back. It certainly worked out last time. What are you worried about?"

"Fuck ... the chief, Jake. I'm worried about him."

"Concern over that man isn't healthy, you know that."

"Yes, and I'm full of it. He isn't going to stand down on this one and let the state run the show."

"He won't have a choice. Besides, if he can wash his hands of the responsibility, why wouldn't he? He's hardly the most proactive—"

"He thinks the body belongs to his sister."

Jake remembered Gabriel staring at the photograph of his sister on the mantelpiece; it had been part of the reason the stubborn bastard had experienced a change of heart—if he, in fact, had one—and offered his help in bringing down Jotham MacLeoid. Jake thought for a moment. "That won't be confirmed yet. How old would that body be if it's her?"

"She disappeared in nineteen ninety; however, she's wearing the school uniform she was last seen in."

Jake took a deep breath and shook his head. "Still, it'll need confirming."

"I get that, Jake, but I'm telling you now. There's no history of any other schoolgirls from that school disappearing. Who else will it be? The chief is not going to wait for an ID."

"No, you're right; he won't." Jake sighed. "Who's in charge of this investigation?"

"Lieutenant Louise Price."

"Warn her."

"Warn her of what? They're not going to lock him up, are they? Anyway, I think she's already witnessed first-hand how unstable he is. He almost lost it with a couple of her men apparently."

"Good. At least that will put him on their radar. Where's he now?"

"Louise sent him away."

"What?"

"Makes sense if it's his sister. He can't be involved in the investigation."

"Makes sense to them! In reality, they need to be keeping a fucking eye on him."

"But they won't, will they?"

"Probably not. They don't know what he's capable of. We can't let him jeopardize the investigation, Lillian. Go to the station and dig out the file on his missing sister. Price will want it off you anyway. Call me when you've looked at it, and if Jewell's there at the station, call me immediately."

She sighed. "Okay."

Jake climbed into the car and started the engine. He stared long and hard into the beating heart of the crime scene, worrying that, elsewhere, the investigation would be driving along at a much more furious and reckless pace.

3

THE SECOND SHOT of Jack Daniels slipped down easier than the first. Gabriel tapped the bar. "Same again."

Maggie, late teens, didn't move and chewed her lip instead.

"You're not going to tell me to slow down, are you, young lady?" Gabriel asked.

She sighed and reached for the bottle.

It was quiet in the Blue Falls Taps this evening, so he could see straight through to the young man admirably handling an acoustic guitar on stage, playing "Take it Easy" by the Eagles. Gabriel threw back the next shot. He winced, and his eyes watered. He sighed as his world blurred, and his demons quietened.

His mother's suicide, his father's fall from grace as chief of police, and Gabriel's dangerous desires all linked to that one moment when Collette had gone to buy a lighter for Chief Earl to satisfy his nicotine addiction.

Seen by two people at the top of Main Street on her way to the Rogers general store.

Not seen arriving.

Not seen leaving.

Never seen by Mason Rogers.

Or so he claimed ...

He tapped the bar again.

"Fuck you for bringing me to the place where my son died," Priscilla Stone said.

"I didn't bring you," Gabriel said.

"My chief of police drowning his sorrows in front of the whole town. You brought me, alright."

Gabriel shrugged. "Not drowning anything. Just getting ready." He turned to look at her. She was tall and dark with cheekbones like daggers. "And since when did you own me?"

"Since we chose you."

Gabriel laughed. "Charles chose me. Where is he, by the way? We keep having these little meetings, but last time I looked, your husband was the chief selectman."

"You know he's too ill now. I'm taking care of his affairs."

"Rumors are that you've always taken care of his affairs. What'll you do when he finally dies and someone else gets the gig?"

A ghost of a smile flickered over Priscilla's face.

"Figures," Gabriel said. "Let's hope they figure you out before that shitshow begins." Gabriel turned and threw back his fourth shot.

"That's enough. You need to go home now."

"That's my sister they just pulled out the Skweda."

"And who better to investigate than real police officers? Let's face it, it'll be more competent than that tinpot investigation your drunk father ran thirty years—"

Gabriel stood and kicked away his stool. He leaned over her.

"What you going to do, Gabriel? Make more of a show of yourself than you already have?"

"If you knew me well enough, you'd know I don't care what people think of me."

"That's a good thing! Public opinion has never been lower."

Gabriel pulled a handful of dollars from his pocket, counted some out, and threw them onto the bar. "Thanks, Maggie." He started to walk away.

"Stay out of this investigation, Gabriel. You've been told by them, and now you've been told by me."

He ignored her.

"Don't think I've forgotten about what happened outside Marissa Thompson's house. You didn't allow me justice."

Gabriel stopped. "You got your justice. And you got it the right way."

"You're on borrowed time, Gabriel. Don't make this any more difficult than it has to be."

Gabriel continued to walk away.

"And fuck you again for bringing me back to where my son died."

"See you in Hell, Priscilla."

"They won," Frank said.

"How many goals?" Jake asked.

"Mummy, how many goals?" Frank asked his mother in the background. "Three, Daddy! Can you take me next time?"

"I can't. But one day ... I promise."

"Didn't Grandpa take you?"

"Yes, those very same seats."

"Is this your shirt?"

"No. That's a new one. They look very different now. If you ask Grandpa, he may be able to dig out one of my old ones."

After the conversation with his son and while he was wiping tears from his eyes, Sheila said she wanted a word with him too.

"Of course," he said.

"No easy way to say this ... I've met someone else."

He felt his stomach constrict. "That's fair."

"Frank likes him a lot."

"Are you *sure* you're not finding it easy to tell me this?"

"Whatever, Jake. It just gets confusing for him. You must understand that!"

"Of course, but what are you saying *exactly*, Sheila?"

"I don't know. I guess he just wants a dad like all his friends."

"He's got a dad!"

"Yes, Jake, of course, he does."

"Listen. I'll be back. I just have to sort things first." *Promises, promises ... promises he surely couldn't keep.*

"When will that be?"

"I don't know, but—"

"You don't even send money."

"I *left* money. I told you where it is."

"No. I'm not touching that money. Not unless you tell me where it came from."

"Sheila, I ... The thing is—"

"Save it, Jake. Listen, maybe you should start calling less. Wean him off you a bit."

"Sheila, that's a bloody horrible thing to—"

"Better for him though, maybe. Like I said, he adores Sean."

"Are you worried about him, or are you just being nasty now?"

"Bit of both. Goodbye, Jake. Think about what I said."

"He's my son."

The phone went dead.

AFTER HER PHONE call to Jake, Lillian asked Lieutenant Louise Price if she should return to the station to dig out the old files on Collette Jewell.

Louise said that was a good idea, but she'd like to accompany her.

Most of the journey was spent in silence as Louise sent several long messages on her cellphone and scribbled in her notebook. Eventually, a couple minutes from the station, she spoke. "You handle yourself well, Officer Sanborn."

"Thanks, ma'am, but you can call me Lillian."

"Officer Sanborn will do just fine. I respect you. You know, I've been to a lot of towns like yours. I stop and stare if there's a woman officer or two."

"And why is that, ma'am?"

"I'm female, black, and bisexual. Let's just say, I'll always be fascinated with the rise of the minority—especially in the most patriarchal, homophobic, and racist of places."

"They're not all bad here. Not really."

"I never said they were bad. We are what we are. *All* of us. I simply pity those who find equality a bridge too far.

Anyway, I deviate. I just wanted to say I was impressed. They respect you."

"I'm not sure about that," Lillian said with a laugh. She glanced at Louise, who wasn't smiling.

"Yes, they do. And they fear that feeling, which is why they act out. Believe me, if they didn't respect you, they'd ignore you and marginalize you that way. And to me, that always feels a whole lot worse, Officer Sanborn. Enjoy the fact they are trying to intimidate you; it shows your strength."

"Thanks, ma'am." *I think*. She stopped the car.

"Tell me about your chief."

Lillian obliged.

"I'd love to say this wasn't common," Louise said. "Too often, in these forgotten areas, the most boisterous of men rise to the top. Anyway, under the current circumstances, we must consider your chief a wounded animal. Speak of the devil ..." Louise pointed out the window.

Gabriel stumbled down the steps of the police station.

Louise opened the door and stepped out. "Chief Jewell?"

Gabriel stopped at the bottom of the steps and turned in their direction. He nodded. "Lieutenant Price."

"I thought we'd agreed that you'd take some time off?" She closed the door and took several steps toward him.

"Yes, of course. I just wanted to pick up a few things first." He gestured at the backpack slung over his shoulder.

"What exactly?"

Lillian opened the other car door and stepped out. She nodded at Gabriel. "Sir."

He regarded her with narrowed eyes. "My laptop, my favorite cup, a couple of framed photographs ... You sound like you don't trust me, Lieutenant."

"It's not that I don't trust you. It's that I understand you, Chief. It must have been quite a shock back there, and if it does turn out to be your sister, you have my deepest condolences."

"It is my sister."

Louise nodded. "Do you mind if I take a look in your bag? Just to put my mind at rest."

Gabriel shook his head. "No, you may not. This isn't your town, Lieutenant."

Lillian looked down. The things she'd seen. The things she'd *done* with Gabriel and Jake. She suddenly felt very awkward.

Louise nodded and smiled. "Okay, Chief Jewell, that's fine. You should go and get some rest."

He laughed. "Are you not even going to try to force me?"

"And what would you do if I did that?"

"I'd report you to your superiors for intimidation."

"Precisely. Listen, Chief Jewell. We've gotten off on the wrong foot here, me and you. I'll do my best to find out what happened to that young girl by the river, and I'd appreciate your cooperation. It's standard procedure. If it's your sister, you're too close. We're not asking you to step aside for no good reason."

"Ah, I see. So, what is this good reason?"

"Protecting the integrity of the case. Protecting you, Chief Jewell."

"I see." He smiled and turned. "Make sure you wipe your feet before you go into my department." He walked toward his vehicle.

"The thing is, with a wounded animal," Louise said, when Gabriel was out of earshot, "if you can recognize them, then you can protect yourself." She faced Lillian. "And prepare."

IN JAKE'S DREAM, he was alone by the River Skweda, squatting over a tiny skeleton that wore a Southampton FC shirt—

A phone call ended his nightmare.

"Lillian?"

"Yes, I'm at the station with Lieutenant Louise Price."

Jake sat upright as sweat ran down his chest and stomach. "Are you with her now?"

"No, I'm outside smoking. She's in the chief's office."

"What's going on?"

"She just wanted access to the file on the Collette Jewell case, as you knew she would. She's reading the hard copies now."

"Okay. Can you access it in your database?"

"Yes. I've had a quick look. I've got the basics."

"Go on."

"First, you need to know he was here. The chief. Leaving as we arrived."

"And?"

"He had a backpack, said he was collecting his laptop and other personal stuff."

"Okay. Well, if Price is reading the file, he obviously didn't take that. Besides, he can view it all himself anyway, unless they revoke his access, but I doubt they've got that far yet. So, go on, the basics?"

"Collette Jewell, aged fourteen, left her house January twenty-fifth, nineteen ninety. It was approximately six p.m., so it was winter and dark. She headed to the Rogers general store on Main Street to buy a lighter and some milk. She was sighted at the top of Main Street by an elderly couple, who have since passed—Josie and Lincoln Bloom. No one else came forward to say they'd seen her that day, despite a sizeable reward offered and the case rumbling on for quite some time."

Jake sighed. *The Rogers general store.* Gabriel had gunned down Anthony Rogers, son of the store's proprietor, the night the three of them had worked together to end Jotham MacLeod's life. "So, that would have made Anthony Rogers's dad a suspect?"

"Prime suspect. Mason Rogers."

"And how did that pan out?"

"Uneventfully. Mason was adamant that Collette never arrived at the store. No evidence was discovered to the contrary. At first, Mason was vilified. Had a tough time by all accounts. But he's a nice guy, as we all know first-hand, including your good friend Peter Sheenan, who's his closest friend. So, people started to assume he was innocent. The file is just full of interviews. Mainly with Rogers. But that's as far as I got."

"What do you know about the case outside of that file?"

"I know the chief's mother committed suicide a couple years later, overdosed on painkillers. I also know Earl Jewell suffered from alcoholism, and the police department struggled for a while. He wouldn't buy that it wasn't Mason. He hounded the man until he was suspended. He did manage to pull himself together and return until he retired."

"And Gabriel stepped in?"

"Yep."

"How did Earl Jewell die?"

"Heart attack three days after retirement."

"Unlucky."

"Do you know any of Gabriel's thoughts on this investigation?"

"No. No one does. He's a closed book on that."

Jake nodded. "Wonder if he picked up where his father left off with that grudge against Mason Rogers?"

"If he did, he never mentioned it. Sorry, Jake, I have to go. Louise may be wondering where I've gone."

"Please call me as soon as you know anything."

"You know I will. What are you doing anyway?"

"Going back to sleep. First thing tomorrow, I'm going to do something I've been putting off."

"Oh, what's that?"

"I'm going to see a man about a gun."

4

DOWN ON HIS knees, sheltered by the woodland and the night, the old man used his binoculars to watch them bag the body. "There are so many of them. It was never like this thirty years ago when they were out looking for her."

"She's like a vintage wine," his older brother said. "Grown more valuable with age."

The old man glared at him.

"You never did appreciate my jokes."

"They've never been funny."

The irritating bastard smiled, exposing his toothless, swollen gums.

The old man turned back and watched the white-suited lawmen work.

"Of all the bodies that came to the surface, it had to be that one," his older brother said. "There was a time when the Abenaki brought their wrong-uns to the bank of the Skweda to wash away their sins, to allow the fire in the water to show them the true way. A fair few throats of the unrepentant were cut. It's a fucking graveyard out there.

Yet, out of all those bodies, up *she* floats. We should have tied the rope tighter—"

"Be quiet. I'm trying to think!"

"I know. I can hear your thoughts. They're like crickets in the grass—loud and chaotic."

"Jesus! Please *shut up!*"

"I warned you, little brother. I said it wasn't over. That the truth floats. It rises to the surface, and there it floats."

He glared at him again. "You're incessant! At least give me an idea. You must have an idea."

His older brother smiled again. "How many teeth do I have?"

"Not a single one."

"That's how many of my ideas you'll like, little brother. Not one. Not a single one."

AT ONE POINT, everyone had been looking for Collette Jewell.

In his basement, through a slot in the door, Gabriel watched the girl who no one had ever looked for—daughter of the now deceased Jotham MacLeoid, sister of the now deceased Ayden MacLeoid—Kayla. The world believed the MacLeoid children had fled into the sunset together to begin again. The story worked and so needn't be changed. But even though Gabriel owned her, his frustration grew daily.

Kayla had not spoken to him in a long time—ever since he'd slit her brother's throat in front of her, to be precise. For months, Gabriel had tried to sell her the beauty of her rebirth. Away from the poisonous MacLeoid legacy, with him, she could thrive. If only she could accept that. If only she could accept *him*.

Despite his demons, which filled him regularly and forcefully with lust for girls the same age as his dead sister, he'd never laid a finger on her—or any young girl, for that matter.

But she was stubborn, and even last week, on her fourteenth birthday, she'd refused to acknowledge his existence.

"I *need* you now, Kayla, more than ever."

She continued to read from *The Strange Case of Dr. Jekyll and Mr. Hyde*, one of the many books he'd given her.

"I can take your books from you, Kayla." But he wouldn't. It was an empty threat. He loved her too much for that.

She turned the page. Smug bitch was testing him. She knew how he felt. Sensed his longing and sensed the battle that raged within him.

He hit the door hard with the palm of his hand.

She flinched but didn't look up. She continued to read, or at least pretended to.

"They found her. My sister. They found her."

Kayla turned back a page to reread something. She nodded, then flicked back to continue.

"Someone broke Collette's neck and dumped her in the Skweda. She was fourteen, the same age as you."

She continued to scan the page.

"Kayla, listen to me. I just saw my sister's body. Someone broke her neck."

When she didn't respond, Gabriel slammed his palm into the door again. He laid his head against it. Useless. It always was—

"How'd she look?"

Wide-eyed, Gabriel lifted his head and looked through the slot. She appeared to be reading still, which made him wonder if he'd just imagined her speaking. "They were just her remains—a skeleton wearing her clothes."

"Not like a butchered animal, then?" She looked up with narrowed eyes. "Not like my brother."

Gabriel shook his head. He opened his mouth to speak, but nothing came out.

"That's something, then."

He took a deep breath. "You cannot compare, Kayla. Collette was innocent. Ayden wasn't. He was a part of what happened to that young girl, Maddie Thompson, and if you'd have gone with him when he came for you, your life would have been hell."

Kayla threw her book on the floor, stood, and outstretched her arms. "And what is this you offer me? Heaven?"

"This is temporary."

"No. You're a liar. You'll never let me out of here."

"That's not true."

She undid the buttons on her blouse. "Is this what you want?"

"No ... I mean, yes ... I crave it, of course ... but I won't let it happen. You mean too much to me."

She threw the blouse on the floor and stood there in her bra. "I hear you outside the room every night. I see you looking in as you do *those* things."

He looked away, ashamed.

"Every night."

"I've kept control. I will always keep control. I won't touch you. That is the right thing to do."

"And is keeping me here the right thing to do?"

"No, but you came to me. It was you who needed me."

Kayla shook her head. "I needed your help after I saw what my father and brother did." She raised her hands to gesture at her cell. "I didn't need this."

"At the time, Kayla, I thought it was the right thing, to protect you. And, even now, it still feels like the right thing."

"Once you lose control, once you do what it is you want to do to me, you'll kill me, won't you?"

"No, I could never—"

"You're lying. You're a *fucking* liar!" She started to cry and sat on the bed.

"I'm not. I'd never hurt you. For a start, you remind me too much of Collette. Your hair, your eyes, your temperament. And your innocence. I adored her, and I adore you. I will treat you no differently to how I treated her."

"Did you lock her up too?"

Gabriel sighed. "Please, Kayla. I saw her tonight. I saw her body."

"Did you lock her up too?" she screamed.

Gabriel turned from the door and bit into his fist.

Upstairs, Gabriel perused the old file he'd taken from his department. The paperwork had yellowed but was holding up quite well considering it was almost half a century old. No one would have touched it since the investigation had been closed. It was a cold case that no one in Maine had seen fit to reopen, because just like its place of origin, Blue Falls, it was better left in limbo, out in the middle of nowhere.

He ran his fingers over his father's handwriting as he reviewed the documentation. It was the closest he'd felt to him since he'd passed, and a few times, he stopped to wipe away tears, because it was almost like he was in the room, talking to him.

Gabriel read long into the night. Long before the loss of Collette and the alcoholism had begun, Earl, his father, had been a passionate policeman. It showed in the detail and the neatness of the scribe. Working through the file, Gabriel couldn't remember ever working this hard on an investigation, and he felt somewhat ashamed. It seemed no stone had gone unturned in hunting down the brutal murderer of two fifteen-year-old boys.

The two boys had suffered blunt force trauma to the front of their heads from a hammer. They'd been wrapped in plastic, boxed up, and taken to a delivery company called Carrs. In the report, Earl had meticulously detailed this company. Safety checks on packaging had been virtually non-existent, and little or no documentation had ever existed between them and the customer, making the company unhelpful in this investigation, as well as criminally incompetent.

Carrs Deliveries hadn't been able to provide any decent information regarding the identity of their client, other than he was male and that he'd left the boxes outside their premises overnight and conducted all the business by telephone. It'd also come to light that the client had offered a significant amount of money to send the parcels that day without a single security check. After Arran Carr, the owner, had agreed, a significant bundle of cash had found its way through his letterbox. Ironically, the company had been so bad that they'd even messed up the lucrative contract and conveyed each boy to the wrong parents.

Gabriel knew about Arran Carr's history. After the local scandal had destroyed his courier business and he'd served some jail time for his malpractice, he'd become a drunk and a thief until his death ten years ago, falling from the second-floor window of a house he'd been robbing.

In the early hours of the morning, Gabriel reached the end of the file, and he felt disappointment. It felt like an engaging book or movie with an ending suggesting it'd all been a dream. Because, despite the depth of his father's investigation, this brutal murder of two fifteen-year-old boys had been written off the same way that all unsolved crimes of this nature were written off—as being committed by 'someone passing through'.

And, in nineteen seventy-five this was a particularly easy sell. Tourism in Blue Falls had been at an all-time high, and these deaths had occurred in the heart of the summer season.

Unless the killer struck again elsewhere, with the same MO, it was a lost cause. Or at least that's what everyone had believed.

He scanned the autopsy reports of Bobby White and Henry Clark. All their teeth had been pulled out postmortem. He recalled the asthmatic ME hunched over his sister's body, describing how all her teeth had been removed.

SITTING ON THE RUG, bathing in the glow of a muted television screen and listening to his older brother's heavy breathing, the old man turned the small plastic Ziplock bag over and over, letting the loose teeth fall from one side to the other. He eyed his older brother on the sofa.

His lips were pulled back, and he looked as if he was in pain; his tongue darted between his empty gums.

The old man stopped turning the bag, and his older brother's lips settled, his breathing too.

The toothless bastard leaned forward and ran his fingers over the pliers that had assisted him in filling that Ziplock bag. "Everyone wants what they cannot have. *Everyone.* Yet, this is something they could never comprehend. But they will know that it was after, brother. *After*, and not before."

"But what difference would that make? They would still be disgusted by you. They would still call you sick."

"And you, brother. And you."

"We're different. I've never taken any pleasure from pain. And why would I? Having experienced so much myself, why would I wish it on others?"

"Whatever you say, brother."

The old man sighed. "We are wasting time. Now is the time for us to clean up, so do you want to touch them one last time?" He offered the Ziplock bag.

His older brother reached out. The tips of his fingers trembled as they neared. "No." His hand recoiled. "I've said my farewells. You're right. We shouldn't prolong this any longer."

The old man grabbed the mortar from the coffee table and placed it on the rug in front of him. He opened the Ziplock bag, emptied the contents into the ceramic bowl, and reached for the pestle. He pressed the heavy ceramic instrument into the teeth and rotated the grinder. It was heavy-going, and he sweated, but eventually, he achieved the powdery texture that would allow easy disposal.

He offered it to his older brother to throw it away, but he sadly shook his head. "I can't do it."

The old man nodded, stood, and headed to the bathroom to dispose of it down the toilet.

When he returned, his older brother was looking at that photograph again.

"Don't obsess, brother. Please."

His older brother looked up. "But it all started when he arrived. Everything. Do you not see that?"

He nodded. "But, brother, it doesn't matter how many times we say it; it changes nothing."

His older brother grabbed a pen and put the nib against the teeth of the smiling man on the photograph. "Maybe then, we should think about making those changes." He scribbled out Jake Pettman's teeth.

5

JAKE EYED THE assortment of handguns in the glass cabinet.

The proprietor, Mason Rogers, entered from his adjacent convenience store through a connecting door. Mason was a slim man with a weathered face and gelled-back white hair. He wore jeans and a denim jacket over a Grateful Dead T-shirt. "Can I help you, Mr. Pettman?"

Jake was taken aback. "Have we met?"

"I don't think you're a mystery to many people around here."

Jake raised an eyebrow. "I didn't think I'd made that much of an impression. At least, I tried not to."

"No impression goes unnoticed in a sensitive place like Blue Falls, no matter how subtle. Do you know who I am, Mr. Pettman?"

"Yes, I do, and I'm sorry for your loss. Please call me Jake."

Mason nodded. "For somebody who likes to keep their head down, you certainly know a great deal."

"I'm dating a resident here. She mentioned it, and again, I'm sorry for what happened."

"Anthony was a good boy."

Jake recalled Anthony training a rifle on him. He also recalled the young man's head snapping sideways under a cloud of blood and his eyes rolling back. "I'm sure he was."

"Yes, *was*. He made his decision a long time ago to go work for that bully, MacLeoid. It's not surprising they ended up in the same pit together. The truth is, I lost Anthony long before that. Still, if we continue this conversation much longer, you'll see an elderly man cry, and that has never been a good look. How can I help you, Jake?"

Jake pointed down into the display case. "I'm in the market for a gun."

"Never sold to a British tourist before."

"I'm not a British tourist. I have an American passport."

"Really? After the murderous Bickford mob fled to England, Uncle Sam kept their descendants furnished with the keys to the kingdom? Ridiculous, but typical, I guess."

"If the accounts of what my ancestors did are true, I'm nothing like them."

Mason opened the palms of his hands over the case. "Well, shall I just take your word for it then and open this case of goodies?"

"You needn't worry. I'm not buying today anyway. Just doing my research. I still have to get my Maine State ID, and I need gainful employment for that. Don't suppose you're looking for a hand in your store?"

Mason didn't smile.

Jake made a note to not attempt any more humour.

"What you after?"

"Just a no-frills handgun. I'm not going hunting. It's just for protection."

Mason did smile over this. "You figuring the place out quite quick then?"

Jake shrugged. "Feels like I'm the only person around here unarmed."

"One of the most popular handguns in the states for concealed carry is this Springfield." He pointed into the glass case. "You want a feel?"

Jake nodded.

Mason unlocked the glass case, grabbed a slim single-stack firearm, and offered him the butt.

"It's not loaded, is it?" Jake asked.

"Never made a habit of handing over loaded guns in this store, Jake."

Jake took the weapon. It certainly felt compact and looked sleek. He traced the words *Springfield Armoury U.S.A* with his fingers and practiced aiming it at the door that connected Mason's stores together.

"That is an XD-S Mod.2 OSP." He reached over and touched the top of the weapon in Jake's hand. "This milled slide makes it optic ready if you really want to focus on your target and is now available with the Crimson Trace micro red dot for just over a hundred dollars more."

"I like it. How much?"

"Five hundred and fifty. You want to look at some other options?"

"No, my heart is already set. Besides, I trust your opinion."

"There's a reason that it's one of the most popular in the US. So, now you need to hurry up and find that job, Jake. Stop leaving yourself vulnerable. You never know who may have it in for you."

He handed the gun back to Mason. "You're right. Should be fine at the moment though; there's a lot of police presence in town." Jake observed him for a reaction. He didn't get one; the elderly salesman was too preoccupied with carefully replacing his wares into the display case.

"Seen it before. They never stay long. They quickly lose interest in small-town crimes. I think they're happy to leave the pond life to feed on itself."

"They seem quite serious this time. Piper has a friend in the police department."

Mason locked the case. "Is there something you'd like to ask me, Jake?"

"No. What makes you say that?"

Mason looked up and took a deep breath. He seemed like he was going to respond, but then didn't.

A moment of silence ensued, but Jake was patient and waited for Mason to comment.

A bell tinkled in Mason's adjacent store. "That'll be Mrs. Hindley for her husband's newspaper." He checked his watch. "Like clockwork. Five past ten. He's bedbound, you see. Five years this August, every single day. Without fail. I've been telling her to have the paper delivered, but she just won't. Every time, she tells me that she has no family, so the day she stops collecting the newspaper will be the day I know both her and her husband are gone, so they won't be left to rot."

"Practical, I guess."

"People around here can have a funny way of seeing things."

Jake nodded.

"Goodbye, Jake. I must go to Mrs. Hindley." As he reached the connecting door, he turned back to Jake, who was heading to the exit himself. "Yes, I know they've found that little girl, Collette Jewell. I mean, who doesn't? And it's a wonderful thing that she can finally be at peace. Yes, it'll drag suspicion to my door again." He extended a hand in Jake's direction. "Case in point. But, you know, fuck you, and fuck them. My son died this year, and I'm a lonely, old man with nothing but an unprofitable general store and a failing gun shop, so what do I care? Let them come and rake up old cobwebs."

He turned and left, leaving Jake feeling rather guilty.

"Seriously, who has whipped cream on their coffee?" Jake asked.

"Me," Peter Sheenan said, wiping some off the end of his nose.

"It's bad for your teeth."

Peter smiled, flashing him a row of shiny, white teeth. "Are you worried about them because you paid for them?"

"Not really. Just don't want you crying to me when your gums ache."

Peter laughed. "They ache all the damned time anyway!"

Peter Sheenan was Native American. At seventy-three, he was still going strong and put it down to the rich Abenaki blood that coursed through his veins. However, despite his healthy appearance, he harboured his fair share of pain. After serving with the K9 Corps in Vietnam and developing a close bond with his Lab retriever, Prince, he'd been forced to watch the American Government leave thousands of these loyal canines behind as *surplus equipment* in Vietnam. Such pain never left a man like Peter, and after learning how badly Jotham MacLeoid was treating his American pit bull terriers, he'd decided to rescue them.

After Jotham had smashed his teeth with the butt of his rifle, Peter had been left to the mercy of three of Jotham's pit bulls and forced into the unthinkable: using a concealed knife on the kind of animal he cherished most in this world.

"I'm still going to repay you for the surgery."

"You are doing it already," Jake said, pointing at his mug.

"Going to take me a long time to repay you in coffee."

"We best drink quicker then."

They sat in Crowther's Coffee Cabin on Main Street. It was one of the few businesses still thriving in the difficult economic times, so Chase Crowther opted to keep his place looking shabby and lowkey despite the significant funds at his disposal. It would have made good business sense to make his café stand out from the several boarded-up properties alongside his, but he felt it would have been a little bit crass.

"Tell me about Mason Rogers," Jake said, trying to stop himself sinking too deeply into an old sofa with worn springs.

"And here's me thinking you just wanted to catch up."

"We catch up nearly every day. Conversation is getting stretched thin now."

Peter smiled, but then shook his head. "You know he's one of my closest friends, don't you? And before you remark that I don't have many friends, just let me remind you of the limited options in this town. I'm sitting with you, for example."

Jake smiled this time. "Listen, I'm not after ammunition. I just want to know a little more about the man."

"His son just died, Jake."

Jake nodded. "I know."

"So, you wouldn't need ammunition if you went after him anyway. He would crumble quite easily, especially after the last time."

"They went after him hard last time, did they?"

"Well, the father of the missing girl was the chief, so what do you think?"

"I can only imagine."

"At one point, some of the locals had him on the street at gunpoint. Ironically, it was Earl Jewell who got them to stand down, not out of concern for him, of course, but because he *believed* he knew where his daughter was. If he died, then she'd never be found."

"So, how did they clear him?"

"Not sure they ever really did. The investigation just moved on. To Portland. They released the photograph of Collette Jewell throughout Maine, and several witnesses from that area came forward to say they'd seen her with a young couple. I remember seeing the facial composites. They were everywhere at one point. They yielded nothing though, and neither Portland nor anyone else, reported any more sightings of Collette Jewell."

"Because she was at the bottom of the Skweda."

Peter nodded sadly. "Strange that sudden burst of witnesses from Portland."

"Yes, sounds like a diversionary tactic. I went to see Mason this morning."

Peter's eyes widened, and he shook his head. "He's innocent."

"I never said he wasn't. I was shopping for a gun."

"Bullshit."

Jake took a mouthful of coffee. "Well, it was one of the reasons I was there."

"And the other reason would have broken that man's heart. He'll know he's back on the radar."

"You don't think he knew that even before I walked through that door?"

Peter sighed. "Mason is salt of the earth. I've lost count of the number of times he's been there for me. His wife, Lorraine, died of cancer over ten years back. Anthony was only twelve or thirteen at the time, and it hit him hard. Mason did everything he could for that boy, but he rebelled every step of the way. He'd lost that boy long before his body was found in that pit."

"How long have you known him, Peter?"

"I moved to Blue Falls fifteen years ago. As you know, most of my people are in Sharon's Edge, but I needed a change. This town is not the most welcoming place, as you've discovered yourself, but I remember the first time I visited that store. Mason was fitting a new refrigerator. The old bastard was making a right mess of it, so I gave him a hand. He rewarded me with a six-pack, which I then drank in his company. Nobody can throw back a can like that man. Mind you, after his experiences in ninety, he's probably had a lot of practice."

"What was his wife like?"

"A quiet woman. She always looked worn out, and her hair was white and unkempt. They'd married back in eighty-five, and I guess the experience of living with the prime suspect in a child abduction case took its toll—"

Jake's cell interrupted them. "Lillian?"

"Hi, Jake. Can you meet me at Lookout Corner?"

"Yes ... why?"

"I know what Gabriel is up to, and I think he's about to go gung-ho."

"See you in fifteen," Jake said, already on his feet. After hanging up, he shook Peter's hand. "Later, okay?"

"Of course." He lifted the coffee cup to his mouth. "I'll have a few more of these and add them to your tab."

Jake smiled. "Just go easy on the cream."

LEANING AGAINST A BOARDED-UP STORE, the old man watched Jake Pettman leave Crowther's Coffee Cabin.

"Big boy, isn't he?" his older brother said.

"He reminds me of Earl Jewell and his son—men who like to make an entrance."

"Yes, like a herd of fucking elephants," his older brother said. "But don't you worry. Noise is temporary, while silence is forever."

"Very profound, brother."

"And what would you have said? 'The bigger they are, the harder they fall'?"

"Something like that."

His older brother opened his jacket, revealing the handles of the pliers poking from his inside pocket. "Are we ready, then?"

The old man raised an eyebrow. "You're insane. Isn't there enough heat on us?"

"You always did move too slow."

"No, I'm just careful."

"Ponderous."

"Listen, brother, killing this man will achieve nothing."

His older brother smiled. "Are you sure about that? Jesus, look." He pointed across the road at Peter Sheenan as he emerged from Crowther's Coffee Cabin.

6

AFTER LOOKING THROUGH the spyhole, Charlotte White's initial reaction was to back away, but, following a deep breath, she regained control of herself and opened the door to her visitor. "You're the spitting image of your father."

"So people say," Gabriel said. "They don't often tell me he was a good man though, but he was."

"In his own way, yes." Her voice was hoarse; Gabriel wasn't sure if this was the emotion or the eighty years of wear and tear on her vocal cords. "Earl never stopped trying for the truth."

"No, he didn't. I read the files. My father gave everything he had, Mrs. White, to finding the person who murdered your son."

"But came up empty handed."

Gabriel nodded.

"Are you here to tell me that you finally found someone?"

"I'm afraid not."

Her eyes lowered. "Forty-five years and twenty-six days

is a long time to go without the truth."

Gabriel nodded again. "But I do have *something*, Mrs. White."

She looked back up. "What?"

"It's probably better if I came in."

JAKE CONTACTED Piper on his cell. "I missed you last night. I thought you'd come back."

"I was up late with Sadie at Mom's. She was shaken up by the news, so we had a few drinks. Before we knew it, neither of us were in a fit state to drive."

"I hope she's feeling better."

"I think she is. We didn't get up until late, and she only just headed off. Anyway, what happened last night?"

Jake ran through the events of the previous evening and what had happened regarding Gabriel, Louise, and Lillian.

"What does Lillian think of this Louise Price?"

"Strong-willed and capable."

"She'll have to be, to keep Gabriel at arm's length."

"Yes, which is the reason I'm off to meet Lillian. She's found out something about Gabriel. No idea what yet."

"Where're you meeting?"

"Lookout Corner."

There was a moment of silence.

"What's wrong?"

"Nothing ..."

"Could have fooled me."

"Just a strange choice of place to meet, that's all."

"I guess she just chose somewhere out of the way so we aren't seen talking. I don't think she's going to do me in."

"It's not that ..."

"Go on, then."

"It's nothing."

"*Piper?*"

"Just a bit eerie."

"I'm waiting ..."

Piper told him, and his mouth fell open.

The River Skweda curved sharply at Lookout Corner.

Lillian was already standing on the raised platform overlooking the river.

Jake climbed the steps to join her by the plaque: *Captain William Ross, 1710 - 1765, Just like the Skweda, you will always run through the heart of our town.*

Lillian faced Jake. "Founding Blue Falls was one of the last things he ever did."

"Yes, I heard. Drank himself to death, I believe."

"He was a war hero, and probably went through hell. They didn't really recognize and treat PTSD back then, so I guess you had to find your own medicine."

Jake nodded. "Strange spot to have a memorial—out in the middle of nowhere."

Lillian turned to look over the river. "When he was awarded Rosstown Plantation in seventeen sixty-five, he stood on this very spot and declared this the heart of his new land."

Jake stood alongside her. The water was calm today, but he could still hear it hiss as it stroked the banks.

Lillian pointed at a large rock that jutted a foot from the water. "When the river flows fast, the water smashes into the rock, torrents high into the air, and cascades down the other side. On a particularly sunny day, the waters can appear a deep blue. So, when he saw this, Ross named the first of the three towns on the Skweda, Blue Falls."

Jake smiled. "Why did you bring me to this place, Lillian?"

She shrugged. "The privacy?"

"What about its infamous history?"

"I don't follow."

"The Bickfords?"

She paused, then turned her widened eyes toward him. "Ah, shit, Jake. I didn't think."

Jake continued to smile. "Don't worry about it. I'm not sentimental."

Jake's ancestors, the Bickfords, had founded the Blue Fall Taps in the early nineteenth century and, according to the history books, had run it as a brothel. They'd then, according to which version of history one bought into, stolen children from local towns, such as Sharon's Edge, to staff it. After the Bickfords had been run from town and fled to England, the bodies of five children had been recovered. Two of the dead children had been cast aside in the undergrowth here at Lookout Corner.

"They wanted those bodies found," Jake said. "They knew their time was up, and they were getting ready to run. Scattering the bodies of those poor kids was their final fuck you to the town."

Lillian grimaced. "Sorry, Jake. I feel awful now."

"Why? I've learned something new today because of you. Besides, I'm still holding onto the hope that way back somewhere in my family tree someone was adopted and that I'm not descended by blood. Anyway, back to more pressing issues, especially the one about Gabriel going gung-ho."

"We have cameras in the police department on a forty-eight-hour loop."

Jake's heart rate quickened. "So, you've seen why Gabriel returned to the station last night?"

Lillian nodded, smiling. "He went into storage, which is also monitored. He pulled an old file. Glad he used the light and not some dying torch, like in an old movie; the clarity was fantastic. I managed to zoom in. I got the case number, Jake."

Jake's eyes widened. "And that record also exists in the database?"

"Do you want to tell this story for me? Yes, it exists. Which is kind of fortunate, really. The case is from seventy-five, and it wasn't too long ago that we brought in some admin staff to scan in the old files."

"You're a flipping genius, Lillian."

"Compliment accepted, but you can't be my biggest fan; someone else beat you to that accolade."

"Who?"

"Lieutenant Price. She told me in my car last night. Anyway, do you want to know what was in the casefile?"

Jake nodded and, holding tightly to the railing that would stop the unsure of foot from taking an early bath in the Skweda, listened to the story of Bobby White and Henry Clark.

"The file is long, Jake, and I haven't printed any of it, as I don't want anyone to notice at the department, but that's the gist of it. So, what is it about this unsolved double murder that has Gabriel in a tizzy?"

"Don't know, but there must be some connection to the body of his sister, because it wasn't long after seeing her that he went to collect that file."

"Yes, but they died in different ways. The boys from

blunt force trauma, and then delivered to the parents—wrong ones, I might add. The file suggests the courier service made a mess of it. Collette died from a broken neck and was weighted down in the river."

"There must be something else. Was there anything else in the autopsy report?"

"I don't think so, but I did read it quickly." She pulled out her cell. "I wasn't going to risk print-outs, but I took a few snaps. Let me see ... yes, here it is."

Jake let her read. He stared across the river—a river that had taken its name from the Abenaki. *Fire in Bone.* How many bones were at the bottom of that river that the Abenaki had worshipped? How many fires had been extinguished by the water that had so fascinated Captain William Ross?

"There it is." She spoke quickly. "Awful ... grim ... but there it is ... a connection. Both boys had their teeth removed post-mortem. Collette also had her teeth removed, but we'll have to wait for the lab results before determining if it was done was post-mortem."

"Maybe they were taking souvenirs?" Jake sighed. "I've seen something similar back home. This certainly could be the same person."

"These crimes are fifteen years apart!"

"Is that really so long a time when you consider these crimes were in the same town?"

"So, does the killer live here, or did they return for a second time?"

"I don't know, but I do know this'll have been enough to spark Gabriel into action."

Lillian's brow furrowed. "I need to speak to Louise Price."

"You do, but first, we need to anticipate Gabriel's next move."

"And shut him down."

"Maybe. Maybe not."

"You're the last person I would expect to say that! You've made no secret of your feelings for—"

"Listen, Lillian. An old colleague and friend once told me to carefully watch the behavior of the obsessed. They can lead you to the truth faster than anything else can."

"Did he also tell you that they could also destroy it faster than anyone else?"

"There's always a risk, I guess. Let's check out his next move and take it from there. Price will be busy with the autopsy now. Let's do them a favor."

"So, what's the chief's next move, Jake?"

Jake watched Ross's famed rock glow in a sudden burst of strong sunlight and thought. "Well, my next move would be the surviving relatives of the two boys. A lot changes in forty-five years. Things that were blurred then can be clearly remembered. Truths about people they knew and trusted may also have come to light."

"There is only one surviving relative. Charlotte White. Bobby White's mother. She's eighty."

"Well, we need her address, because I'm absolutely certain Gabriel is already there."

Peter Sheenan knocked on the door of the Rogers general store.

No answer. Strange. He'd never known him to close during the daytime.

He shimmied along to peer through the store window. It

was light in the store, but no one was at the checkout or on the shopfloor. Noticing movement at the back of the store, he shielded his eyes from the sun and squinted. He saw a door opening, and then Mason exiting his small apartment tacked onto the back of his store.

Peter waved through the glass, and Mason waved back. He then sidestepped to greet his friend after he'd opened the door. "Not like you to lock up during the day, old-timer."

"These bones aren't what they once were. I was taking a nap." Mason leaned out the shop and gestured down both sides of the street. "Hardly rush hour anyway. Mind you, never is these days. Come in." Mason clapped him on the shoulder and led him past a row of sealed boxes. "Just in time to help me with a delivery."

Peter laughed. "Was renovating your shop not a favor enough?"

"I'll make it worth your while." Mason led him to the refrigerator. He reached in for two cans of Stinson IPA.

"No wonder you're taking daytime naps. Bit early for me."

"You're retired, you grumpy, old bastard, and well, Mrs. Hindley's already collected her morning paper, and I probably won't see another customer until midday."

"Jesus, things that bad?"

"Yes. So take the damn beer."

Peter obliged.

"Camden and Dominic Davis have opened a new store on Slant Street. They've worked pretty hard at undercutting nearly everything I sell. They'll be taking a loss, I bet, but they're only doing it to ruin me." He opened a can and handed it to Peter. "It's working."

"Why would anyone shop from those knuckle-draggers?"

"People have short memories when it comes to saving a buck."

"Jesus, Mason. Why didn't you say anything?"

"Been preoccupied." He opened his own can.

"Yes. I understand. But, buddy, you have to keep on."

"Save it, Peter. Also, don't tell me what Anthony would have wanted. That little shit threw his goddamn life away."

"Yes, he did, but you tried everything."

"So, that's about the size of it. The Davis brothers are going for the jugular! They just wouldn't let bygones be bygones."

"You've never told me much about what happened when you were a child."

"And I'm not about to now. It's water under the bridge as far as I'm concerned. If they want to dwell on it and drive me six feet under, then so be it." He opened his own can. "I'm losing the will to fight, to be honest."

"This doesn't sound like the Mason I know. Listen, I have some money. A partnership might be just what the place needs."

"The wolves are at the door again, Peter. My days are numbered. I'd keep your money out of harm's way." Mason drank back the IPA in one go. He belched and wiped his mouth with the back of his hand.

"Wolves?"

"Where have you been, Peter? Those who think I abducted a little girl. Strike that. Those who now think I *killed* a little girl."

"Things are different now with DNA and forensics. They'll be able to clear you in no time, I bet."

Mason snorted and reached in for another beer. "Yeah, we'll see."

Peter put his hand on Mason's shoulder. "Go easy on that, old-timer."

Mason nodded, pulled out another can, and opened it. "You weren't here the last time, back in ninety when they treated me like an animal."

"You told me about it."

"Did I tell you that the Davis brothers fucking revelled in it? You should have seen them then, full of piss and vinegar. That Earl Jewell was a nightmare and was convinced I was a monster, but those brothers ... well, they were playing a whole different ballgame."

"Probably not wise rounding on someone who owns a gun shop."

Mason chortled and took another mouthful, seemingly content to sip this one a little slower. "It didn't deter them any—even when I stood outside, waving a gun in their direction. The spiky little shit, Cam, strolled right up to me and told me that he wasn't armed and I should pull the trigger. That he'd happily die to see a child murderer behind bars. They beat the living shit out of me that day—Cam, Dom, and all their redneck friends."

"I'm sorry."

"Don't be, Peter. I got off lightly."

"It doesn't sound that way."

"I did. What happened to Lorraine was far worse." He took two successive gulps. "But I can't discuss that."

Peter drank too. He didn't want to push Mason on what'd happened. The man was struggling to hold it together as it was.

"One of our town's dirty little secrets," Mason said,

staring at his reflection in the glass of the refrigerator door. "I don't suspect it's the only one."

Peter heard a clatter from behind the refrigerators. "Did you hear that? It came from your apartment."

"Probably just the wind knocked over something. I left the kitchen window open to let in the air."

Peter walked alongside the line of refrigerators toward the door to the apartment. "We should check it out."

"It's okay, Peter. It won't be anything—"

Another clatter.

This one startled Peter into life. He moved quickly and went through the unlocked apartment door. "Who's in there?"

"Hey," Mason said from behind him. "I'm sure it's nothing, Peter. Let me go and check it—"

But Peter was already through the door and into the living room. He knew the layout well, having visited on several occasions. He could see why Mason had been hesitant about letting him enter. Dirty plates and empty bottles were strewn across the coffee table. A mound of laundry had collected on the floor, and a small pile of pizza boxes looked ready to topple. Peter eyed the closed door to his left, which led to the kitchen. "Hello?" He paused for a reply, but there wasn't one.

"There's no one here, Peter, I'm telling you. It's just the open window in the kitchen—"

Something smashed.

Peter's gaze moved to the closed bedroom door opposite him. "Someone's in there." He started across the room, reaching for the handle—

The floor rushed up to meet him, and everything melted away.

7

LILLIAN TURNED INTO Charlotte White's road. "Fuck, you were right. It's the chief's car."

"Keep driving," Jake said from the passenger seat.

Lillian drove to the end of the road, then pulled over.

Jake looked in his side mirror. "If Jewell exits this direction, we slide down, okay?"

Ten minutes later, Gabriel did just that. Although it was probably unnecessary—as he came past at such a ferocious speed he wouldn't have noticed them anyway—they slid down regardless.

Lillian shook her head. "You still think this is a good idea? Your obsessed man is going to kill someone before he leads us to any truths."

"That's one way of looking at it, Lillian. The other way is that something's just put a rocket up him, and I'd like to know what that was."

They exited the car and walked past a series of identical whitewashed bungalows.

"Eerie neighborhood," Jake said.

"Popular. Garnered the nickname Sleepy Hollow a few

years back, on account of them being our retired residents. They are also very wealthy. The board of selectmen put a lot of pressure on the Blue Falls PD to keep this a crimefree area, as many of these folks invest heavily in our town. There's been talk of turning it into a gated community."

"Best way to keep the riffraff like us out. Let's enjoy it while we still can."

They walked down a cobbled path lined with garden gnomes and found an elderly lady beside a patch of colourful rhododendrons. She wasn't gardening. She seemed to be just admiring the flowers and appeared lost in her own thoughts.

"Charlotte White?" Jake said.

Charlotte turned her whole body rather than just her head. She also winced. "Sorry, arthritis. Used to just strike in winter, now it sticks around all year."

"Sorry to hear that," Jake said.

"Nah." She dismissed his concern with a wave of her hand. "When you get into your eighties, you take what you can get. If you still want it, that is. Unfortunately, a lot of my friends have been giving up of late. Anyway ..." She used a walking stick to maneuver herself in her direction. "I've only just waved off one visitor, so is there a reason I'm high on popularity at the moment?"

"We come from the police department, ma'am. Chief Jewell sent us," Lillian said.

"Why would he do that? He was just here himself not ten minutes ago."

"He just told us to follow-up, take some notes. As you could probably tell, he's a busy man. He just wants to ensure he didn't miss anything."

"Still, I'm surprised he didn't mention you."

"He's had some difficult news and—"

"Yes, dear, he told me." Charlotte smiled. "But I wasn't born yesterday. You're worried about him, aren't you?"

Jake looked at Lillian, then back at Charlotte. "Yes, Mrs. White, we are. The discovery of his sister's body has thrown him."

"Yes, I could tell."

"We just want to be certain he hasn't found out anything that might lead him off the rails."

"I knew his father well. Earl Jewell, a hot-blooded man with a furious temper. He tried his best to get to the truth, but sometimes, the truth just isn't there, and sometimes you can cause more harm than good looking for it. You're both here because Gabriel Jewell is just like his father, aren't you?"

"Yes," Jake said. "I suspect he is."

"And when dealing with a dangerous man, you could do with all the help you can get, so come in, and I'll get you both an iced tea."

A YEAR OR SO BACK, Gabriel had thrown a young man by the name of Nile Waters into the tank for public intoxication. Nile was diagnosed with ADHD and had a bottle of instant-release Adderall on his person It clearly didn't mix well with alcohol—at least it didn't for Nile—so Gabriel had confiscated it before slamming the cell door. Nile had never asked for it back, so Gabriel had thrown it into his bedside drawer at home.

After spending a sleepless night glued to his father's file on the murders of Bobby White and Henry Clark, Gabriel had reached into the bedside drawer for some caffeine tables and had rediscovered the Adderall instead.

It woke him *right* up.

And then some.

During his meeting with Charlotte White, he'd worked hard not to grit his teeth and pace her living room. And had mostly failed. He must have looked a right state. Hopefully, she'd written off his peculiar behavior to his shock seeing Collette's body on the banks of the Skweda rather than drugs.

Anyway, the uppers were worth it. He had clarity like never before. And he didn't just feel focused, but he felt hungry for information, and every morsel Charlotte had provided had been nourishing.

So, after leaving the elderly woman, he'd popped two more Adderall and filled his mouth with gum. Now, he stared over the road at the old building and waited for the chemical to explode within him.

When the tingling began, he clenched his fists, and, with his teeth grinding gum, he marched across the road. The hammering of his heart and his fast, shallow breathing could, on another occasion, cause him great anxiety; however, now he felt unstoppable. The truth was at his fingertips, and he felt the strength to tear it loose. He barged through the door.

The bastard stared at him, wide-eyed.

This is for you, Dad, and for you, my dear Collette.

Darting forward, he reached for the monster's neck.

CHARLOTTE WHITE WAS PREPARED to discuss that day in 1975 with Jake and Collette, and she did so without shedding a tear. Jake was impressed; most people would have struggled to maintain composure when discussing a tragedy of this nature. Charlotte relayed the story of the grisly deliveries, then discussed the subsequent investigation. On a few occasions, her voice wavered, and she looked as if she might finally break, but she retained control.

"Half a century ago," she concluded, "and anything else about that time is so distant ... so hazy ... apart from those months. Everything is still as clear as if it happened yesterday."

"I'm so sorry for your loss," Lillian said. It wasn't the first time she'd said it since taking her seat on a sofa opposite Charlotte White.

Charlotte had opted for a rather solid-looking rocking chair. "If I sat on that sofa with my arthritis, I wouldn't be able to get back up."

"I'm in awe of you, Mrs. White," Lillian said. "The way you rebuilt your life."

"Thank you, dear. But you don't really have a choice in the matter, and you feel ever so guilty about it at the time, as if you're giving up on them. We had support with our grief, and we met others experiencing loss. One couple we met had to deal with a missing child. I remember thinking we were the lucky ones. Imagine not knowing if your child was alive or dead? How *could* you ever move on? At least, we had some closure. *Some*." She looked down. "And that closure was the elusive out-of-towner who never struck again."

"It doesn't sound like you believed it," Jake said.

"You're not from around here, are you, Mr. Pettman? But Officer Sanborn will understand what I mean when I say you never know what to fucking believe in this place."

Despite that Charlotte had lived twice as long as he had

and so could have easily sworn twice as much as he had in her life, the sudden profanity still stunned him.

"I read through the investigation, Mrs. White," Lillian said. "It seemed, on first look, very thorough. For the time. Forensic analysis wasn't what it is now. What made you question the findings?"

"Well, the same reason you're here questioning the conduct of Gabriel Jewell. Him and his father are cut from the same cloth. I won't question Earl's drive, not for a second. And, in a way, I am grateful to him for his compassion, but he was a hothead who led with his fists. Thought and rational behavior were an inconvenience to Chief Jewell."

Jake and Lillian looked at each other.

"Sounds familiar, doesn't it?" she said. "Like father, like son."

"So, what was it you think Earl missed in the investigation?" Jake asked.

"Everything, Mr. Pettman. Right now, you sit in the wealthy heart of Blue Falls. Every property around you, including the assisted living facility across the road, house the great and the good of Blue Falls. These people are the people who run the town today, and the town of yesteryear. Nothing happens in Blue Falls without their involvement. *Nothing*. Without that understanding, without the subtlety in your approach to them, there are no truths to be learned. That is why they always keep someone like Earl or Gabriel in charge of the police department. They're easy to predict and easier to control."

"With all due respect, Mrs. White," Jake said, "aren't you one of these people?"

"I got lucky with my husband's insurance when he passed. It's funded this retirement. A few like-minded individuals are dotted around here. I don't need many friends at this age."

"So, you really believe the town had something to do with what happened to your son?" Jake asked.

"I'm not saying that. I'm just saying any truths that fall outside their best interests do not exist. And it doesn't make for a healthy investigation. It has taken forty-five years for us to learn the killer struck again. It's hard not to be surprised. Would you be surprised if there were more victims?"

Jake didn't respond.

"You can be assured, Mrs. White, we have no time for their best interests," Lillian said. "We're here for the truth."

"Yes. I sense that. It's refreshing. Gabriel Jewell is also of the same mindset. He's a loose cannon, but I told him everything. The fact of the matter is I'd tell anyone who is prepared to listen." Charlotte White winced as she rose to her feet. Jake stood to help her, but she waved him away. "I'm convinced that if I accept help, I'll just get weaker. I see it as exercise."

Jake nodded and sat again.

Using her walking stick, Charlotte shambled to the mantlepiece to grab a photograph of a pale, smiling teenager with a mane of frizzy red hair. "You said before, Mr. Pettman, that I'm one of these people, and, to my great shame, I'm about to tell you that I am. I, like most of these bastards around here, have been economical with the truth. Nineteen seventy-five was a very different time, Mr. Pettman. A very different time. You see, my son was gay. And I genuinely believed the whole truth would do more harm than good. The look of surprise on Gabriel Jewell's face when I told him and the way he flew around the room, gesticulating, showed me that I had been wrong. He left my home with such purpose and intent. I think he knows. I think he knows who killed my son and his sister."

Jake leaned forward on the sofa so he was closer to Charlotte.

She stared smiling at her son's picture. "I wasn't embarrassed at what Bobby was. I could never be anything but proud of him. And now, these days, no one would even bat an eyelid ... so stupid. I thought if I told the police he was gay, they would lose interest in the case. That Earl Jewell would lose interest in his case."

"It was a very different time," Jake said, trying to reassure her.

"And his father ... his father, God rest his soul, never found out. He never needed to know. It would have broken him even more. How was I to know that what he was would have any part in what happened? I wanted people to care. I wanted people to be desperate to help find the killer, not turn up their nose in disgust when they read in the newspaper that he was gay and suggest it was in some way his fault."

Jake nodded at the photograph in her hands. "May I?"

"Of course."

Jake smiled. "He has your eyes."

"Yes. The hair was his father's fault."

He handed back the photograph. "What else did you tell Chief Jewell?"

"I told him I caught Bobby and Henry kissing. That's how I found out. Days later, they were both dead. I never told anyone until today." She sighed. "There's something else. Something really peculiar. And it was after I told Chief Jewell this that he left in a flurry."

"Go on."

"After I walked in on them kissing and they broke away

from each other, I noticed another boy. He was sitting in the corner of the room, staring right at Bobby and Henry. He didn't even acknowledge that I'd entered the room. And when I asked Bobby to show his guests out, this boy still didn't even look up at me."

"Did you know the boy?" Jake asked.

"Yes."

GABRIEL FELT Mason's knees in his balls and stumbled away, the world suddenly on fire. It took two gulps of air before he could steady himself against a shelf full of tinned veg. He felt some relief that Mason had struck; if he hadn't, he'd have squeezed the life out of the old shopkeeper, and he desired a confession before ending him.

After recovering, Gabriel reached for his sidearm, but Mason had managed to retreat behind his counter and was now holding a shotgun. Gabriel left his hand pressed against his sidearm. "Have you got it in you to kill the chief of police, Mason?"

"Don't you worry about that. Ever since your father-daddy cracked the fridge door with my head, I've dreamt about it. So, take your hand off the weapon."

Gabriel held his palms in the air. Temptation to charge at Mason picked at him, but he realized that was the Adderall's influence. Getting torn to pieces by buckshot before getting answers was unacceptable.

"I knew you'd be coming. But the truth is, I never expected you to come like this. Even your daddy started off with more decorum."

"He hadn't just found evidence it was you." Gabriel's

whole body shook now. He chewed hard on the gum, blinking as sweat ran into his eyes.

"Evidence?"

Gabriel stepped forward, pointing with a trembling finger. "Bobby White and Henry Clark."

Mason didn't speak and kept the gun trained on Gabriel.

"Cat got your tongue?"

"I want you to leave."

"You killed both of them and pulled their teeth right out, you sick fuck. And you did the same to my sister—"

"I said, *leave*."

"Tell me the truth." Gabriel inched closer.

"You wouldn't believe the truth, so I'll wait for some real police."

"The truth is you're a faggot."

Mason laughed. "Even if that was true, what would that have to do with anything, you narrow-minded prick?"

Gabriel was now only several feet from Mason. Every nerve in his body twitched, seemingly screaming at him to charge. "You were jealous of Bobby and Henry."

"Why would I be jealous?"

"The mother caught them kissing and saw you obsessing from a chair in the corner."

Mason curled up his top lip. "A different lifetime ago, Jewell. They were my friends, then they were murdered. I was fifteen. I wasn't some twisted killer. So, leave. Now. My life isn't worth shit. My wife is dead, my son is dead, and everyone in town is beginning to turn their eyes on me again for something I didn't do. You think I care about killing you? In jail or out of it, I'm rotting away."

Gabriel chanced another step. "Rotting? Like my sister?"

Mason shook his head. "One more step and I'll kill you. I swear it."

The urge to pounce was insatiable. Gabriel's head knew he wouldn't survive it, but his entire being craved it. He heard something behind him. He turned and looked down the short aisle at the door to Mason's apartment.

"Leave, Jewell."

Still watching the door, he extended a hand. "Shut up." He held his breath and listened. He could definitely hear something; it sounded like scratching.

"*Jewell!*"

"What's that noise, Mason?"

"I can't hear anything."

"How can you not? It's coming from your fucking apartment." Gabriel marched down the aisle.

"I told you to leave."

"Someone's in your apartment, who is it?"

"There isn't. Get out or I'll use this."

Gabriel reached for the handle.

The shotgun fired, and the world shook.

8

JAKE SAT RIGID in the passenger seat. He held his breath while clutching the grab handle as Lillian defied the laws of physics on the next corner.

"For a big man pumped full of bravado, sometimes you worry me."

"Just got a thing about speeding."

"Why?"

"I don't know." Jake paused to clench his teeth as Lillian overtook a worn-out Impaler. "With some people, it's spiders. With me, it's fast cars. You need any other reason?"

"I don't mind spiders."

"Piss off, Lillian, and just get us to Mason's store without killing us." As they neared Main Street, Jake said, "I hope we're not too late."

"The chief's on edge, but he's not stupid."

"He's just found out that the prime suspect for his sister's disappearance was involved in a case with a similar MO. I don't think his intelligence will be running the show anymore. Not that he ever really had any."

Lillian turned onto Main Street. "Louise Price needs to

be brought into the loop now, Jake. This has to be investigated properly."

"I agree."

"Maybe that's where we should be heading now. Let them handle this?"

"No need," Jake said, pointing out the window.

Lieutenant Louise Price was standing in front of her black BMW, flanked by two of her male officers. She was pointing at the Rogers general store.

"Capable police can sniff out trouble all on their own."

"Jesus," Lillian said.

"Just drive past. She's about to discover Gabriel's gone rogue. Last thing they need is to find out a civilian and the police officer she so admires for some reason are off working their own angle."

"What's not to admire?" Lillian said, following Jake's instructions.

"Ask me again when you're not subjecting me to your driving."

SINCE THE GUNSHOT, Gabriel had remained in a crouching position. He'd been told that if he stood, he was dead. It was an easy decision to make.

"It took every ounce of willpower to miss," Mason said. "And you owe me for it. A new set of shelves and a range of condiments."

Again, Gabriel heard the scratching from behind Mason's apartment door. "What's in there, you sick fuck?"

He heard Mason's footsteps grow in volume as he came down the aisle. "None of your business."

"You won't get away with any of this. You'll pay for your sins."

"If I'm a killer, why're you still alive?"

"Because killing me doesn't feed your fantasies."

"Jesus." Mason laughed. "If this is the way you start thinking as a cop, I'm glad I never chose that option."

The scratching at the apartment door continued.

"You know," Mason said. "If you'd just come here and asked your questions, I would have answered them. I may have even gone to the station with you to give any statement you so wished. But you, just like your father, have a habit of creating unnecessary situations—another animal who needed to be caged."

"Shame for you he wasn't. He sniffed you out."

"You crossed a line, assaulting me today, Jewell. Your father was lucky when he hounded me, because I had everything to lose back then. You, on the other hand, couldn't be any more unfortunate, because I have nothing left to lose. Blowing off your head doesn't faze me in the slightest. In fact, it excites me. You know, maybe I'll give you the truth. Why not? You won't understand it anyway. A man like you wouldn't be able to."

Gabriel felt the shotgun touch the back of his head.

"Go on. Stand up. Open that door. But control your anger, your frustrations, or I will end this."

Gabriel stood, took a deep breath, and reached for the handle.

"Go easy."

Gabriel started to push down the handle.

"Put down the gun!"

Gabriel recognized the lieutenant's voice. He didn't know whether to smile or curse. Even though his chances of survival had just increased a hundredfold, he wanted to know the truth of what was behind the door. He faced forward until he heard Mason deposit his weapon on the floor, then he turned.

Mason's hands were in the air while Louise and her two sidekicks had their guns trained on him.

"Thank god, Lieutenant," Gabriel said, inching forward.

"Stay where you are a moment longer, Chief. At least until you tell me what the hell is going on."

"Mason Rogers murdered my sister. I came here to arrest him."

"Bullshit! He didn't come to arrest me. He came to kill me!"

"Nonsense!"

"He had his fucking hands around my neck seconds after he came through the door! Look at his eyes. Look at the way he's moving. He's wired! If I hadn't pulled my weapon, I'd be cold on the floor by now."

"Is that true, Chief Jewell?" Louise asked.

"I won't dignify that with an answer."

Ewan, the officer who Gabriel had pushed the previous night at the crime scene, said, "You do look on edge."

Gabriel narrowed his eyes. "I saw my sister's body last night. Who wouldn't be on edge? Seeing the officers attending the crime laughing to themselves didn't help either. What was so fucking funny anyway?"

The officer looked away.

"Enough!" Louise said. "It's not the time to be questioning anyone's integrity. Yours, Chief Jewell, or my officers'. A violent altercation was happening in this shop, and a passerby called it in. We came because your name was given, Chief. You'd been asked to step aside due to your personal connection to the case, so I'm entitled to some answers." She nodded to Ewan, who went to Mason and cuffed him.

"What the hell?" Mason said.

"You had a shotgun pinned to the back of the chief of police's head. What did you expect?" Louise said.

"I was *defending* myself."

"We'll listen to your side of the story ... at the station."

The officers started to lead him from his store.

Louise holstered her weapon.

"Wait," Gabriel said. "Keep your weapon out. I think someone's back there." He pointed over his shoulder. "Someone has been scratching at the door, trying to get out."

She nodded and drew her weapon again. She turned to look at Mason, who was by the door. "Stop. What's back there?"

Mason turned. "I've done nothing wrong. You're leading me out in handcuffs, and you expect me to comply?"

"That's exactly what I expect, Mr. Rogers."

"Oh really. Well, fuck the barbarian over there, and fuck you and the horse you rode into town on. I'm an innocent man, and I've lived through this bullshit once already, and I'm in no mood to live through it again."

She nodded at one of her officers. "Keep him there." She refocused on Gabriel. "Open the door and step aside. I've got you covered."

Gabriel leaned forward and opened the door. It was dark inside and difficult to see anything of note except the outline of a television and a sofa. The Adderall was still coursing through his veins, so the urge to dive in and satisfy the curiosity was overwhelming. He shimmied to one side and clutched a refrigerator door to try to keep himself from doing anything stupid.

"What could you see?" Louise said.

"Not much. Curtains must be drawn. It's dark. I can go in."

"No. I will—"

A small dog padded from the apartment. It scanned the occupants of the store and whined.

"Try not to scare him," Mason said. "He's just a puppy."

"Jesus," Gabriel said, approaching the puppy and looking back at Mason. "It's a pit bull. Only one person around here ever had pit bulls."

"Yes." Mason said. "The night someone set Jotham MacLeoid's property on fire and released his dogs, I was part of the party who searched for them to round them up. I came across this little man all on his own. I didn't want him to end up in the pound like the others."

"Heart of gold. Careful, I might just burst into tears," Gabriel said.

"I told you that you wouldn't understand."

Louise approached the dog, shooing it.

"His name's Kyle," Mason said.

Louise continued to shoo it without using its name.

After Kyle had retreated into the apartment, she closed the door and nodded at her officers. "Take Mr. Rogers to the station."

"Can I at least lock up?"

Louise nodded.

Outside, after her officers had left with Mason, she turned to Gabriel. "Now, Chief Jewell." She pointed at the floor. "Last night, we were standing together, clueless, at a crime scene. Less than fifteen hours later, we are standing here, and you seemed convinced, to the point of ruining your life, that this man is guilty. Can you fill in the gaps please, and I'll see if I can save your ass?"

Right now, Gabriel couldn't care less about having his ass saved, but he filled in the gaps anyway.

ON HIS WAY up the path, Jake swooped for an empty cigarette packet and slipped it in the trashcan by the front door. Before he'd even knocked, the homeowner answered the door, holding an icepack to his head.

"Are you behind there, Peter?" Jake asked.

Peter moved the icepack, revealing a lump.

"Christ. What happened?"

"A pile of Mason's dirty laundry. Took my legs out from under me—"

"Hold up. You went to see Mason?"

"Yes, straight after you left me on my lonesome in Crowther's."

"Reckless." Jake slipped past Peter into his hallway.

"Come in," Peter said, turning and closing his front door behind him.

Jake sniffed and turned in the hallway. "Have you been smoking?"

"Yes. I'm seventy-three, Jake. Any more of my choices you want to question me on?"

"Just didn't know you smoked."

"I don't, but I used to, and the last couple of months have been hard."

"They'll stain your new teeth."

"Good. They stand out. Trying to make them look like the last set."

Jake sighed. "You shouldn't have gone to see Mason. I think he's dangerous."

Peter grunted and barged past Jake. "You're starting to sound like every other basket case in this town." He turned left into his living room and sat on his sofa. Keeping the icepack to his head, he reached for the packet of cigarettes on the arm.

Jake eyed him from the doorway.

"Fuck off, will you!" Peter said, leaving the cigarettes alone. "It's hard to fight this relapse with you here!"

"You say he's not dangerous, but look at you."

"I fell over his dirty fucking underwear."

"Honestly?"

"God's truth. I heard noises in his apartment, so I went to have a look. Next thing I knew, I went ass over tit and banged my head on a cabinet. The lights went out."

"Noises?"

"Turns out, he kept one of Jotham's puppies. Rescued it after Ayden released them."

Jake shook his head. "A pit bull? Do they actually start off as cute, little puppies?"

"Well, this one is. Woke up with the little guy licking my face. I tell you, Kyle won't be going down the same road as his kin, not with Mason looking out for him."

"Have you been to the hospital?"

"Now you sound like the old-timer himself! He was outraged when I said I wasn't going."

"He was right."

"I've been to war. I think I can handle myself."

"You're probably concussed, and that can be dangerous."

Peter pulled out a cigarette. "Jesus. You are turning my willpower to dust."

"I'm taking you in, or I'm calling an ambulance. You might want to opt for the least-embarrassing option."

Peter sighed. "Can I smoke this first?"

"You can smoke it in the car on the way to the hospital, and then we can also finish the conversation we had earlier."

Outside in the car, Jake let Peter enjoy his cigarette out the window. Afterward, Peter turned to him. "I've forgotten how slow you drive."

"Have you been talking to Lillian?"

"No, why?"

"Never mind. Anyway, we found out some things about Mason. I don't think you know everything. I'll tell you now, hoping you stay away from him. At least until these matters are cleared up."

After Jake had finished relaying about the circumstances surrounding the mutilation of Mason's two friends, Peter threw his second cigarette half-finished out the window. "That would be one way to help me kick the habit, I suppose. Jesus, I feel sick now."

"That could be the concussion."

"I think it's more likely to be your graphic description of what happened to those poor youngsters."

"You needed to know. If Mason did this—"

"Sorry, Jake, but you're definitely barking up the wrong tree. You and that fuckwit, Jewell. I've known that man a while now. As I said before, salt of the earth. The idea of him pulling teeth from the mouths of dead children? That doesn't sit right with me. And I've seen a lot of dark shit in my time."

"Me too. And you can never truly know what someone is capable of until you've seen it with your own eyes. And the fact that Charlotte saw him in the room with the two kissing boys, staring off into space, unresponsive ..."

"I think I'd probably respond in exactly same way if my two best friends started kissing in front of me. Although, to be fair, the one in the car with me right now is as volatile as they come, and the other, well, he's your friendly neighborhood serial killer apparently, so it would be a very peculiar situation."

"Too many coincidences here," Jake said. "Your judgement is clouded by your friendship with him."

They neared the hospital, which was larger than Jake expected considering the small area it served.

"Okay, Jake. I don't believe any of this for a second, and you'll struggle to change my mind. However, I'll tell you some things about Mason. You're bound to find out sooner rather than later anyway."

"Go on."

"Years back, long before I knew him, Mason's family had a bitter feud with the Davis family. Over what, I don't know. He has been a good friend to me, and he has chosen not to talk about these things, so I've chosen not to press him. I can tell you that the Davis family are bad news though. The two elders, Camden and Dominic, are trash. Both drove their wives into early graves with their drinking and womanizing. The fact they're in their sixties hasn't slowed them down much either, and the brothers are inseparable and live together at Forest End on the farming land they inherited from their folks. Rundown farming land, I might add. Looks more like a junkyard these days, and most people tend to stay away." Peter reached into his cigarette packet and sighed. "They don't live alone either."

"I thought you felt sick."

"I do, but the next part of this story will make me feel

even worse, so I'm hoping smoking may help with that." He lit the cigarette. "The elderly brothers live with Cam's son, Carson." He took a puff on his cigarette and blew it out the window. "Carson is married to an Abenaki girl named Felicity."

"Okay, I see where this is going. She's treated badly?"

"An understatement. There's something you don't know about me, Jake. Years back, I sat on a small council for the Abenaki community. As I'm sure you can imagine, many of our people don't get a fair deal in this part of the world. This council tries to even the scales. They tend to focus on helping some of the more vulnerable members of our community."

"And this council helped Felicity?"

"Yes, you follow correctly. Not one of the council's success stories, I'm afraid. She was sixteen when she hooked up with Carson. He was in his thirties. That was enough to put her on our radar. But what do you do when someone is in love? Or, at least, *thinks* they are in love? We're not heavy-handed people, Jake. We didn't meet fire with fire to take her back. We tried to convince her to come home, and I even tried to convince the Davis family, personally. I didn't get far with that discussion, believe me, and most of the conversation was around my heritage and how it was a blight on their town."

"Yet, they were happy to accept someone into their home from your community!"

"Brain cells are in short supply in that family. Besides, ignorance and racism doesn't work on a logical level."

Jake drove into the hospital parking lot.

"I've visited regularly over the last twelve or so years, Jake, to see how she is faring."

"And?"

"Not great. There's abuse, for sure, but she'd never admit to it. She's had two boys, and that has given her something to focus on. The eldest is autistic, the non-verbal kind. He takes a lot of her attention. The youngest, who is around ten, is already getting into trouble, stealing and bullying other children. Another chip off the old block, I guess."

"Okay, I've got the picture. We are adept at developing dysfunctional families back in the UK too. So, back to this rivalry. There is only Mason left from the Rogers family, and the Davis family continue, unfortunately by all accounts, to thrive. So, what relevance is this right now?"

"I'd have said nothing before today. But when I visited this morning, the things he told me made it seem very relevant."

Jake parked beside a BMW and looked at Peter.

"Cam and Dom have built a new store on Slant Street and are sucking the profits from Mason's general store."

"Have they done this intentionally?"

Peter shrugged. "Mason seems to think so."

"You think it's worth talking to the Davis brothers?"

Peter shook his head. "Bad news. I'd steer clear. It might rile them. Mason told me what happened back in ninety when he was public enemy number one. They beat him outside his store. They also did something to his wife, Lorraine, but he wasn't clear on what."

Jake nodded. "Thanks, Peter. I'll take this to Lillian and see if she can dig up some history on this rivalry, but right now, you're getting looked at."

"Okay, but I feel fine. I'll get a cab back."

Jake laughed. "Don't trust you. I'm coming in too."

9

KAYLA MACLEOID CLUTCHED her ears as her captor raged upstairs. The basement was soundproofed, so he must have left the door at the top of the steps open. Two smashes came in quick succession. *Was he in the kitchen, throwing the dishes?* Keeping her hands over her ears, she crawled into the corner of her room and drew her knees to her chest.

Pointless. There was no shutting out this sound.

His feet pounded on the floor above. There were several crashing sounds. He must have been lashing out in all directions, overturning furniture.

She rocked back and forth.

Everyone was gone. *Everyone.* Her mother from cancer. Her father from a bullet. Her brother from a knife. Dead. All of them. *And how would she join them? What was her fate?*

She sang to herself, desperate to drown out the rampaging monster above. It was no good. Her kidnapper's cries of anguish cut through, and she felt it piercing her insides again and again before ... silence. She stopped singing and wept. No one was coming for her. No one. *Ever.*

When the silence had lingered for a minute or so, she dropped her hands from her ears to her knees.

His footsteps down the stairs were loud and quick.

"No, no ..." She rocked harder. She heard him wrestle the key into the door and yank the door open. "Please ..." She squeezed her eyes shut. She thought of Morris, her toy monkey. How she longed to hold him right—

"Open your eyes, Kayla!"

It had been a gift from her dying mother.

"Open your fucking eyes, now!"

She felt his hands on her shoulders. He was shaking her.

"Now!"

She opened her eyes.

His twitching, sweating face was inches from hers. He shook her again. "You will talk to me!" He was chewing hard. His eyes were wider than she'd ever seen them. Sharp exhalations from his nose struck her like red-hot spears. "Talk to me now, or I'll *kill* you!"

"Are you going to arrest me for holding a shotgun on that prick?" Mason asked.

Louise narrowed her eyes and leaned forward in her chair.

Mason edged backward in his.

For moments like this, she liked being tall and intimidating. "I haven't decided yet."

"I've been talking to you for over an hour! Surely, you have an inkling! Do I need a lawyer?"

"The only thing I'm certain of this minute is that I need another coffee." She reclined in her chair again. "Want one?"

Mason sighed and nodded.

Louise turned to the officer beside her.

"Right away, ma'am." He stood and left.

"You enjoy having power," Mason said.

"Not really."

"You look as if you do."

"Means to an end. I get a lot done with it."

"I never had power. If I had any, I could have controlled my son. He might still be alive."

She considered telling him she was sorry for his loss. She decided against it. It may weaken her stance.

In a tiny room that would struggle as a broom closet, never mind an interview room, Louise had peppered him with questions. He'd mustered the most horrified expression imaginable when she'd asked about the extracted teeth, but she was far too experienced to give his reaction any credence.

"You were never questioned regarding the murders of Bobby White and Henry Clark, were you?"

"No."

"Yet, you were close friends?"

"Not really. We were only friends for a month."

"Mrs. White said you were in her son's room."

"It was a long time ago."

"Doesn't seem like something you'd forget in a hurry. Weren't they kissing?"

"That's right, yes. But it was almost half a century ago."

"Why were they kissing?"

"We were playing truth or dare. Henry dared Bobby to kiss him when he wouldn't answer his question."

"What was the question?"

"I really can't remember."

"Did you know they were homosexual?"

"No. Is that for certain?"

"Mrs. White says they were."

"I wasn't sure. Like I said, it all seemed like a game to me."

"Did you have sexual relations with either of them?"

"No."

"Are you homosexual, Mr. Rogers?"

"No."

"You said you had only been friends for a month?"

"That's right."

"How did that come about?"

"Well, a month before, I didn't have any friends. Then I had two."

"Why didn't you have any friends?"

"I was introverted. I didn't like to socialize all that much."

"So, why did you start socializing with Bobby and Henry?"

"They were similar, I guess. They had each other, but that was it. I guess they took pity on the quiet boy in the corner, and we started to hang around a bit together."

"Did you kill them?"

"No, ma'am, I did not."

"When was the last time you saw them?"

"I'm not sure. I remember the announcement at school that there'd been an accident, that they were dead.

Obviously, the nature of their deaths weren't revealed to us, but we all found out soon enough."

"How did you feel?"

"Sick ... devastated ... disturbed. How do you think I felt? I was fifteen, and they'd been nice to me."

An hour of questioning had left Louise fatigued, and she drank the coffee quickly despite the heat. She noticed Mason doing the same.

"You know, I've nothing to hide. If that knuckle dragger hadn't come over to throttle me, and then threaten to gun me down, I would have happily answered his questions."

"He's had a shock, and it's left him rather unstable. He shouldn't have been working."

"That's alright then. Maybe I shouldn't have defended myself?"

"You had a shotgun to the back of his head, Mr. Rogers. That didn't look like self-defense."

"I feared for my life."

"You seemed to have it under control."

"Go after me for it then, ma'am. Then believe me when I say I'll go after his badge."

"And what makes you think I care about his badge, Mr. Rogers?"

"I don't, just giving you a statement of fact."

Louise made some notes while Mason fidgeted in his chair. "How did you feel when you heard the body of Collette Jewell had been recovered from the Skweda?"

"Unsurprised, actually."

"Really? Why's that?"

"Because the disappearance of that poor girl was the worst thing that ever happened to me. You never expect trauma like that to go away. So, when it returns, you're unsurprised."

"Describe that ordeal to me."

Mason led Louise through the investigation, including, in detail, his ill-treatment by Earl Jewell and his persecution from the Davis brothers and other like-minded individuals. "A very different version of events from the one left to you by Earl, I imagine."

"I'll be honest," Louise said. "I haven't had time to read the investigation yet. Listen, with me here, the investigation will run properly, Mr. Rogers, you can be sure of that, and I firmly believe in innocence until it is proven otherwise. That said, I assume you'll be staying in town for the foreseeable future?"

"I haven't been anywhere since my wife died over ten years back. I wouldn't know how to leave anymore."

"Okay. I'd appreciate it if you put a pin in your complaint against Chief Jewell, at least for the time being. He's on leave, and if you drag him through the mud, he's going to expect me to do the same to you. I think it is a messy situation all would prefer to park until after we get to the bottom of all of this."

Mason nodded. "Can I go? My dog will be hungry."

"Yes. Go and feed him."

The X-rays showed no damage to Peter's skull, but the doctors opted to keep him for observation anyway, leaving Jake alone on the return journey. On route, he contacted Lillian and briefed her on his discussion regarding Mason's background.

"The Davis family are a bad lot. Those brothers have spent more time in our cells than the cleaners."

"I'd like to get a look at them."

"I can describe them to you. It's safer that way."

"It's not enough. I've got a feeling there's something in this feud. Despite only being one surviving Rogers left, it rumbles on. We need some clarity on how it all began."

"And what happens when the Davis brothers realize Mason is the prime suspect again? I don't think you appreciate what they're like!"

"I probably do. You know, back home, we have our own version of rednecks."

"Well, you should know that stoking the fire is not a good idea then. Drawing them out could put Mason in grave danger. And we still don't know if he's guilty of anything! We could be putting an innocent man through more trauma!"

"I have an idea. A card we can play. It'll keep them quiet, at least for the moment."

"Go on."

Jake told her.

"Yes, it would ring true, but I'm still not convinced it'll work. You're not dealing with rational and intelligent people here."

"I'll meet you on the road into Forest End."

Lillian sighed. "And if it doesn't work and they hit Mason again, like they did in the past, you won't feel bad?"

"It'll work, Lillian."

Mason declined Louise's offer of a lift from the police station and headed off on foot instead. He'd kept himself in shape over the years and so moved at a fair pace anyway. Along the way, he passed many people he knew by name.

Some nodded a greeting; others kept their head down. No one stopped to talk.

It's happening again.

On Main Street, he passed Lynn, his most regular customer, carrying a brown paper bag. She must have been shopping elsewhere. With a twinge of disappointment, he felt obliged to stop and accepted that it was because his store had been closed. "Did your husband enjoy his paper today, Mrs. Hindley?"

She avoided eye contact. "He hasn't woken yet."

"Ah ... okay. Sorry, I've been out. Did you stop by the store?"

"No," she said, still looking down.

He nodded at her paper bag. "You went to Davis Conveniences?"

"Yes. I was over on the other block. Thought I'd take a look."

"Worth trying the competition, I guess." He smiled.

She didn't return the smile, because she still wasn't looking at him. "I've got to hurry back, before Paul wakes."

"No bother. I'll see you tomorrow."

She nodded and turned away.

It's happening again.

As he neared his store, he saw that his door was open and increased his speed, then he ran his fingers over the broken frame. Someone had jimmied it open.

He turned around. In broad daylight? With people about?

It's happening again.

He pushed open the door and entered his empty, silent shop. He listened for Kyle's scratching and yapping at his apartment door. Nothing.

"Kyle?" he called as he headed down the aisle, where

hours earlier he'd been facing off against Gabriel. His hand settled on the handle of his apartment. He heard a whimper, and his breath caught in his throat. Turning, he saw the small black bundle twitching several feet away in a pool of vomit. He ran, slid to his knees, and cradled his boy's head. "Kyle?"

His poisoned dog convulsed and died in his arms.

10

FOREST EDGE REMINDED Jake of home.

The trees ended by a beautiful creek which had broken loose from the Skweda some distance away. The steep gradient sent the water rushing forcefully over rocks. Closing his eyes, Jake welcomed the soothing sounds as he waited.

When Lillian arrived, Jake left his car by the wild, fast-moving brook and jumped into her vehicle. As they drove away, he watched this glory of nature shrink in the sideview mirror, then he focused on the dirt track that Lillian was veering onto and was stunned by how everything could so quickly turn to shit. The color and freshness was soon gone, while the shrubbery became tangled and unwelcoming, and the light struggled more and more to find its way through the matted canopy.

Then, as they turned into the farmyard, Jake couldn't hold back any longer. "Jesus!"

"I tried to warn you," Lillian said.

Rotting fences were strewn all over the property, and any attempts to surmise how the place was once organized would be doomed to failure. Large swathes of the patchy grass were singed brown. The smell in the air indicated that burning here was regular. Countless rusted vehicles peppered the ruined farmyard. Many had missing wheels, while others were missing doors and, in some cases, even roofs.

"A fucking junkyard," Jake said.

"It's how they made ends meet. Weighing in scrap, repairing and selling vehicles."

"Is that profitable? How did they get enough together to own a thriving convenience store?"

"The brothers used to do odd jobs for Jotham MacLeoid."

"Odd jobs? Is that your euphemism for violence and drug dealing now? For pity's sake, was there anyone not on that psychopath's payroll?"

Lillian wound her vehicle around the scattered wrecks, aiming for a decrepit, yellowing farmhouse.

"You'd think with a bit of money in the bank they'd have cleaned up the place," Jake said.

"When you've lived in squalor for as long as the Davis family have, I guess you just accept it as normal."

"Maybe we should talk to them about aspiring to something better before they destroy any more of the environment. I can't believe how beautiful it was back there and how fucked up it is here."

Lillian stopped beside a line of noisy coops. "The chickens sound unsettled."

"Locked in there, are you surprised? Anybody buying eggs at their convenience store could do with stopping by and seeing where they're sourced."

"Maybe they're allowed to graze in the junkyard?"

Jake smiled and opened the door. His hand flew to his nose. "Fuck. Do you smell that?"

Lillian put her hand to her nose too.

They exited the vehicle, and Jake pointed at the coops. "It's coming from there."

Keeping their hands firmly to their noses, they rounded the first coop and looked in.

"Disgusting," Lillian said.

Most of the chickens were at the back of the coop, clucking and wallowing in their own filth. At the front of the coop were three chicken corpses. At first, Jake thought the nearest one was still moving, but it was merely the ravenous maggots writhing in the rotting flesh.

"Who are you?"

Jake and Lillian turned.

A squat, older man wearing a sweat-stained vest limped in their direction. His pudgy, hairy arms were covered in old tattoos, that had faded and blurred to the point that they resembled some unfortunate skin disease.

"I'm Officer Lillian Sanborn."

"I know who *you* are. I was asking about the reverse Oompa Loompa next to you."

Jake frowned. The insult was so obscure, it took him a moment to figure it out. "I'm new. The name's Officer Reynolds."

The man laughed. His teeth were blackened and crooked. "Rookie Reynolds, eh?" He eyed Lillian. "You training him, doll?" He winked, and his tongue darted over his top lip. "I bet you begged for that job. Can't let anyone else get hold of his white hammer—"

Jake stepped toward him.

He raised his hands. "Calm it, skyscraper. Just messing."

"You mess with the customers in your store too, Mr. Davis?" Lillian said.

He laughed again. "Call me Dom, ma'am. And look at me, you think my brother lets me anywhere near the store? Cam's the polished one. He can also hold his tongue. I struggle with that."

Jake narrowed his eyes. "We hadn't noticed."

"You a Brit? Shit. Can't remember last time one came into town. And I never had one on our land before."

"You could have tidied up for me."

"Why? Cam says there's no point in having land you don't use."

Wreck, you mean. "Where's your brother, anyway?"

"Well, he's ... how do they say it around your parts? He's off to see a man about a dog." He put on a dire, fake British accent.

"Can you be more specific?" Lillian said.

"Why? What you here for anyway?"

Jake got a nauseating whiff of the rotting chicken again and thumbed over his shoulder. "What happened in there?"

"What always happens ... Brady!"

"Brady?" Lillian said. "He's a child! What could he have to do with what happened to those chickens?"

"He got a new air pistol." Cam smiled. "And he's been out practicing as usual."

Jake grunted. "And you allow that?"

Dom shrugged.

It was Lillian's turn to step toward him. "You heard of the Preventing Animal Cruelty and Torture Act, Mr. Davis? It carries seven years in prison."

He held up his hairy hands. "Hey, don't shoot the messenger, Officer. His mother's in the house. She's the one who has lost control."

Jake heard the front door of the decrepit farmhouse ahead of them open. A Native American woman in a flowery dress walked to the porch's edge.

"Speak of the devil," Dom said. "And a devil she is." He winked and flashed his tongue again. "Never mind how quiet and timid she looks."

"You're starting to make me feel sick," Lillian said.

"Me too," Jake said.

Dom shrugged. "It's my land. Figure I can say what I want."

A slight breeze intensified the stench. Both Jake and Lillian covered their noses.

"The least you can do," Lillian said, "is clean that out. It stinks."

Dom shrugged again. "Why should I? Didn't you hear what I just said? It wasn't me. Never had children. Prefer my life to be my own. Like I said, it's up to the mother, and Carson, I guess—although mainly the mother, in my opinion. Carson has big responsibilities these days." Dom nodded, appearing contented over what he considered a profound opinion.

"And his son is not a big responsibility?" Jake said.

"It doesn't pay the bills."

"So, what is Carson's big responsibility?" Lillian asked.

"Well, he's at the shop."

"Because your brother doesn't trust you?" Jake said.

Dom smiled his blackened smile. "Something like that." He thumbed back at Felicity on the porch. "Doesn't trust her either. She's only good for three things: cooking, cleaning, and ..." He tapped his nose, and his smile grew an inch.

Jake spied Lillian's reddening face. He coughed to

distract her from her anger and nodded at her to indicate it was time to play their card.

Before Lillian could do that, the front door opened again, and a young male teenager peered out. He stared at the visitors for a moment and went to his mother, who looped her arm around him and pulled him in tightly.

Jake nodded toward Felicity and her son. "Is that Brady?"

Dom turned to look. "No. That's the eldest. Owen. He's mute."

"I heard the diagnosis was non-verbal autistic," Lillian said.

"Yeah, so his mother keeps telling me, but it's a mouthful. Mute does the job."

Jake felt his blood boil.

"Hey, why you here again?" Dom asked.

"We haven't told you yet." Jake played the card. "It's regarding Brady, and, as you have happily admitted to washing your hands of the boy, I think it's best if we just go right up and talk to Felicity."

Dom contemplated this. He looked back at mother and son on the porch. "Can't see a problem. Best if I come along though."

"We'd prefer you didn't," Lillian said.

Dom shook his head. "Nah. Cam won't like that."

"Just us, Mr. Davis," Jake said. "That's the deal."

"No deal." He narrowed his eyes, and his arms stiffened at his side.

It was the first display of anger he'd seen from Dom, which was rather surprising, considering his reputation.

"The other deal," Lillian said, "involves taking him into custody. Then his mother will have to accompany him."

Dom took a deep breath and thought for a moment. He

curled his top lip. "I'll stay right here where I can see you then. And I don't want you in the house."

"Why?" Jake asked.

"It's a mess," Dom said.

Jake looked around. "After seeing this, I'm sure that won't bother us."

Dom narrowed his eyes again and took two steps backward. "Stay outside."

Jake smirked at Dom, and then, with Lillian, approached Felicity and Owen on the covered front porch.

As they neared, Owen turned toward his mother and pressed his face against her chest.

She wrapped her arms around him.

Jake let Lillian ascend the steps first, so as not to worry Owen further. Not because she was female, but because most human beings looked far less threatening than he did. Rotten floorboards creaked as they approached them.

When they were several feet away, Felicity said, "Please don't come any farther. He won't like it."

Lillian stopped and turned toward Jake with a guilty look which demonstrated that she was having second thoughts about unnecessarily worrying this timid part of the Davis family.

Jake nodded for her to continue. He'd already pondered it long and hard. It seemed the speediest way to the information they needed.

"Mrs. Davis. I'm Lillian Sanborn from the Blue Falls PD. Would you prefer to send Owen somewhere so we can talk?"

"He stays with me. He wouldn't have it any other way. Besides, I prefer to keep him away from his granduncle." She nodded in Dom's direction.

Jake looked back. The pig stared at them while he scratched his armpit but remained out of earshot.

"Why?" Lillian asked.

Felicity opened her mouth to speak, but then thought better of what she was going to say. She thought for another moment and said, "My son has needs. Dom isn't patient with them." She stroked Owen's hair while his face remained buried in her chest.

"Are you sure it's okay to talk in front of him?"

"He's tougher than he looks."

"It's about his brother, Brady," Lillian said.

"Figures. What's he done now?"

"Shoplifting. We have several unhappy shop owners in Sharon's Edge."

There was some truth in this. Brady had recently been caught shoplifting in two stores. Both store owners had contacted the police. However, when the store owner found out that the boy was a Davis, they'd opted not to file a report, claiming they preferred their stores standing and not burned to the ground. Technically, there was no reason for Lillian to be here, but she wasn't lying; the boy had been filling his pockets at someone else's expense.

Felicity nodded. "It happened before, but it didn't come to anything. The store owners let it go because he's only young."

Do you really believe that? Jake thought.

"It can't go on," Lillian said. "We've decided to take this to the next step."

Felicity's face flushed. "Which is?"

Jake stepped forward. "Is Brady here?"

Felicity pointed out a window on the second floor where a small, pudgy face was pressed against it. "He's locked in his room today."

Lillian and Jake exchanged a look.

"Why?"

She nodded toward Dom again. "Shot him in the ass with his air pistol."

Jake forced back a smile.

"Is Brady safe here, Mrs. Davis?" Lillian asked.

"Of course! Why do you ask that?"

"Locked in his room? The chickens in the coop? The violence against his uncle?"

"I also know Peter Sheenan," Jake said.

She flinched. "So?"

"He's worried about you, and he's worried about your children."

"We're fine. There's nothing to worry about!"

"To be honest, Mrs. Davis," Lillian said, "I think it's time we all got together in the station—us, you, Brady, and his father, Carson. Hash this out."

"No," Felicity said, chewing on her lip. "That's not a good idea."

"It is," Jake said. "We can nip this in the bud before it gets any worse."

"*No!* You don't understand."

"What don't we understand, Mrs. Davis?" Lillian asked.

"Have you really spoken to Peter?" She looked up at Jake.

He nodded.

"Peter should have told you that this isn't a good idea," she said.

"How so?" Jake asked.

"Because Cam, Brady's grandfather, wouldn't like us going with you. He'd get angry. And when he's angry, he's ... he's ..."

"He's?" Lillian prompted.

"He's unpleasant. Is there some other way we could clear this up?"

Lillian and Jake eyed each other again. Jake said, "Maybe, yes."

The young boy turned. He leaned back into his mother while she kept her arms looped over his chest. His hair was neatly cropped and waxed back. He was also neatly dressed in a shirt with the buttons done to the collar. He stared off into the distance with tired eyes.

"Hello, Owen," Jake said. He waited for their eyes to lock onto each other, but they didn't. He looked back up at his mother. "Did you hear about the body recovered from the Skweda?"

Felicity frowned. "Yes, but what does that have to do with us? You can't think—"

"Calm down, Felicity. It's not what we think at all. I'm just going to ask a few questions, and if you help me, we'll help you and see what we can do about moving on from this situation with Brady."

She nodded.

"Has any of the men you live with mentioned the recovery of this body?"

"Carson hasn't, but Dom and Cam have."

"What have they said?"

"They said it's the body of a young girl who went missing in the nineties."

"Well, that isn't confirmed yet, Mrs. Davis," Lillian said.

"How did they seem when they were discussing it?" Jake asked.

A look of nausea swept over her face, and she looked away. "Not how people should seem."

"Sorry, Mrs. Davis?" Lillian said.

"They seemed happy about it."

"Happy about a dead child?" Jake asked, inching forward, sensing the information he'd come here to find.

"Yes, because they believed that Mason Rogers would finally get what's coming to him."

Jake nodded. "Okay, so their hatred of the Rogers family is still very much alive?"

"Yes."

"We were worried about coming here and asking you questions," Lillian said, "in case it put Mason back on their radar."

"He was never off their radar."

"Still, if you mention our visit, it is best to keep it to Brady, and the fact that he's on a warning. We don't want them to think the link between Mason and the deceased girl is under investigation again," Jake said.

"So, he's suspected again?"

"Your discretion in this matter will be repaid. Brady will have nothing to worry about regarding this current crop of charges."

She nodded. "I won't say anything."

"Can you tell us what is driving this hatred, Mrs. Rogers? Why are Cam and Dom Davis so desperate to see the end of Mason Rogers?"

She waved her hand over the dishevelled farmland. "Because the Rogers family caused this."

"How?"

"The way Cam tells the story is that back when they were children, Silas Rogers' evil shit of a son came by one night and poisoned all their cattle. Mad as they come, apparently. When they woke the next morning, their farming business was ruined. They've been on a downward spiral ever since. Carson isn't that interested, to be honest. He had a few run-ins with Anthony Rogers before, you know, but nothing too bad. Cam and Dom won't ever let it go though. They seem to think they'd be millionaires living on their own island by now if the Rogers kid hadn't done what he did."

"So, what happened to Mason after he poisoned the cattle?"

She looked confused. "Sorry. Did I not make myself clear? It wasn't Mason."

Jake felt his heart rate accelerate. "Sorry, I don't understand. Who was it then?"

1975

THE HEAT PRESSED down on Mason Rogers.

It had been Bobby's idea to go to the patch by Waterford's. "Mom and Dad love it out here. They said I was, you know, made here."

Henry laughed. "That's a lot of information!"

"I just wanted you to know how quiet it is."

"And that we won't be disturbed?"

Mason had stayed quiet regarding the plan because nothing had occurred to him. In conversations, things rarely occurred to him. That was the reason he had so few friends, and probably the reason Henry and Bobby had taken pity on him.

Despite being close to the crumbling, yellowing mill, the patch was quiet, because the sloping fields had broken up into woodland.

They stopped when they came across a small ditch which, during rainfall, would be waterlogged and potentially dangerous but was, today, dusty and dry.

Bobby laid out some rugs and sat down. He handed out

three cans of Coke, which were still reasonably cold despite the hot weather.

"How long has the Waterford Mill been out of action anyway?" Henry asked, sitting down.

"How am I supposed to know?" Bobby laid back on the rug with his hands behind his head. "I'm surprised someone hasn't bought the land though. Mason, have you ever been up here before?"

"No."

"You can sit down," Bobby said to Mason, patting the rug beside him.

"I'm okay. My legs are stiff," he lied. "Last weekend ploughing with Dad has left them worse for wear."

The truth was that he was uncomfortable.

Last night had been traumatic. Watching Bobby and Henry—the only two boys at school who had ever really shown him any kindness—kissing each other had been devastating. All because of a stupid game ...

Yet, the noises? And the way their hands had moved over one another?

No, it hadn't been a game. It had been real. Too real.

Thankfully, Bobby's mother had been there to put a stop to it, but then, all night, Mason had lain awake, staring at the ceiling, sweating. What had that been? What had he witnessed? Was that who they were, *really*?

And now, he'd chosen to stand here, alone with them again. What did that mean? *Was he just like them?*

He shrugged off his backpack and leaned against the edge of the ditch, which drew level with his shoulders. The conversation between Bobby and Henry, with Mason on the fringes, continued for quite some time. On occasion, his friends worked really hard to get him to contribute. This saddened him. Even now, when his discomfort around them was clearer than ever, they persevered. It seemed like a determined display by two altruistic boys. Or was it something else?

It didn't bear thinking about. Although not thinking about it just made it more potent.

Eventually, the conversation turned, inevitably, to last night's game of truth and dare.

"Let's play again," Bobby said.

Henry nodded.

And there it was. It wasn't altruism, after all. They had sinister motivations.

"Do you want to play too, Mason?" Henry asked.

"No."

Henry smiled and winked. "We'll go easy on you."

The disgusting innuendo. Their grotesque efforts to flirt with him. He didn't know whether to scream at his betrayers or burst into tears. In the end, he didn't opt for either. He just remained there at the edge of the ditch—numb, frozen, and pathetic.

The game went in the same direction as it'd done the previous evening, and despite Mason's very best efforts to shut out the trauma, he just couldn't. Tears streaked his face. This was a sin. What would his mother and father say? They were god-fearing, and they would feel compelled to act on this situation. They would beat him, lock him up for days on end, and all because he'd tried, for the first time in his lonely and pathetic life, to build a friendship.

As they rolled on the rug, they became hungry animals, panting and consuming. He tried to keep his eyes closed but couldn't. He saw their hands sliding into each other's clothing.

A boot landed on the ground near his head. He looked up at Liam standing at the edge of the ditch. His elder brother wore his favorite khaki army pants and jacket, like the soldiers he'd revered since an early age but would never emulate because of his medical condition. Liam smiled, exposing swollen, toothless gums.

Mason said, "You followed—"

Liam silenced him with a finger to his mouth and pointed at the two boys.

Mason spied his friends, completely lost in each other.

They'd managed to pull off each other's shirts and were ravenously kissing. It was starting to look aggressive.

Mason glanced at Liam and recognized their father's claw hammer in his hand.

Liam shushed him again and lowered himself into a seating position on the edge. He slid off so he was standing beside Mason.

Mason grabbed his arm. "Please ... don't."

Liam shook him off, grinned, turned forward, and took a deep breath.

Bobby, who was currently lying on Harry, had his head turned in Mason's direction as his lover probed his ear with his tongue. His eyes snapped open the moment Liam pounced with the hammer held high.

"*Stop!*" Bobby managed to roll free as he shouted.

Harry stared up, his eyes widening as the hammer came toward him.

Mason managed to close his eyes, but he was too late to close off his ears to the thudding sound. He could now hear Bobby scurrying away.

"Please, please ... I don't want—"

Even with his hands over his ears this time, Mason heard the thud of Liam striking Bobby. Mason allowed himself to slip down the side of the ditch, pulled his knees to his chest, and crossed his arms around them.

"Please ..." Bobby said.

Another thud.

Bobby gurgled.

"Jesus. You're *fucking* stubborn, not like your boyfriend." Liam said. "Turn so I can get to the back of your head."

Thud.

Mason kept his eyes closed and shook. He had very few happy memories to retreat to but opted for the first time his father had allowed him to drive a tractor, and then commented on how he was a natural. The retreat was short lived. Liam's hands were on his shoulders. He opened his eyes to see specks of blood dotting his brother's cheek.

"All done," Liam said.

Tears streaked Mason's face. "How could you?"

"No, Mason, how could you? They're faggots. Why are you here?"

"I ... I ..."

"It's okay, brother. That's why I followed. To look after you."

"They were my friends."

"They were sick, and they'd have made you sick too."

"This is wrong."

"It's not about what you wanted. It's about what could've happened, and I prevented it. Now, get up. We've got a long day ahead of us. We must get started. I've had an idea, but we need Dad's pickup."

"You can't bring a pickup here!"

"No, but we can bring it up to the old mill. Then, if we can find some kind of trolley, it would really help us get them—"

"You're insane!"

"I'll accept that from you," Liam said and kissed

Mason's forehead. "Because for you, I'd do anything. We've got each other, and it's all we've ever really had."

"Please, we can't ... We just can't."

"We can. And we will." He stood back. "Now stand, soldier! *Now!*"

Mason rose to his feet and noticed his brother looked so proud of what he'd done.

"But before we go"—Liam reached into his pocket for a pair of pliers—"I'm going to take what I don't have and what they don't deserve."

11

MASON SAT IN the corner of his lounge while the daylight died. With one hand, he clutched Kyle's flank, and with the other, he stroked the angular, bony head. Mason had already cleaned the feces and vomit off the dead animal, so it looked almost content, as if were merely sleeping. "Cruel bastards. Cruel, cruel bastards."

Mason stroked until the darkness settled completely on the lounge and the poor animal was cold. Despite his overwhelming sadness, he didn't cry. He was a man calloused by great tragedy in his life and had learned to control outward displays of emotion. Even when he'd found out that Anthony was in Jotham MacLeoid's killing pit, he'd wept only briefly.

He heard the back door open, then slam shut. He remained seated.

"It's all right, Kyle," he said. "You aren't missing much in this world anyway. You're better off wherever you are."

The kitchen door opened, and light flooded his lounge. Mason shielded his eyes while they adjusted, then looked up at his older brother.

"I've seen it all now," Liam said. "Sitting in the dark. I thought your self-pity was the thing of the past." He switched on the light. "I thought we'd seen the back of it when you found your new friend." He nodded at the dog in Mason's lap.

"Kyle's dead."

"Come again?"

"Dead. Poisoned. I found him in a puddle of shit and vomit."

Liam sighed. "The Davis brothers." He closed the kitchen door behind him.

"It's happening again."

Liam approached the sofa. "Life is an echo."

"I'd prefer it not to be." Mason stroked Kyle's head again. "I can't survive it again."

"Why not? You have something very different this time." Liam sat on the sofa and interlaced his fingers behind his head. "You have me by your side."

Mason shook his head. "I don't want that to be the answer."

"Why?"

"I'm too old to go to war. I'm tired."

"Then let me look out for you." Liam smiled, exposing his toothless gums. "You know I live for it. What're big brothers for?"

"Where've you been anyway?"

"Out walking off the disappointment of earlier."

"And what if someone saw you?"

"They didn't, and even if they did, so what? They'd just think I was a tourist."

"This place hardly gets any tourists anymore. They'll notice. Be careful."

"Jesus, Mason! Tiptoe here, tiptoe there. You're a

Rogers! Be proud. How did you ever cope while I was away?"

"Just fine."

"Now we know that isn't true—"

"*Listen!* I had to knock Peter unconscious because of you! He's a good man. He's never done anyone any harm."

"You saved his life, brother. Imagine if he'd seen me." He smiled again.

"You'd have enjoyed that, wouldn't you, you twisted prick?"

"I enjoy what is necessary. I don't understand what's so wrong with that."

"Lots ... *Jesus* ... If you weren't so fucking noisy back here, all these things wouldn't be necessary."

"Being noisy almost eradicated one of your problems. *Gabriel Jewell*. And let's be honest, that's one massive problem."

"Christ, that's why you're in this mood? Because you didn't get your sick hands on him?"

"Say all you want, Mason, but you resist the inevitable. These things are—to use the word again—*necessary*."

"The teeth? Are they *necessary*?"

Liam looked away. "Asking me that! You of all people!"

Mason laid Kyle's stiffening corpse beside him and stood. "I had to dispose of those teeth for you. I ground them to dust. You talk about what you do for me, big brother, but what do I have to do for you?"

"The longer we wait, the more our problems mount—Jake Pettman, Gabriel Jewell, and now the Davis brothers again."

"I will handle all of them."

"How? By pleading? By crawling on your fucking knees?"

"How incompetent do you think I am?"

Liam raised his eyebrows. "Look at Kyle."

"Fuck you. That isn't my fault."

Mason turned for the door to the shop.

"Remember what Dad used to say," Liam said. "Don't leave a problem for tomorrow that you can solve today."

"Dad is long gone, and I've seen how you solve problems. There has to be another way."

"Let me know when you find out what it is. I'm all ears, but don't take too long. Who knows, next time, it might not be a dog. Next time, you might come back to find me dead."

Mason reached for the handle. "I think you can take care of yourself, Liam."

STUNNED by the sudden heavy snoring, Kayla stopped stroking Gabriel's hair and held her breath. *Is this my moment?*

Earlier, after he'd raged at her to speak, she'd caved.

"Thank you, thank you," he'd said over and over, slipping to his knees and placing his head in her lap. "When I was a young boy, I used to stroke my sister's hair, and sometimes she would do the same for me. Will you stroke my hair, Kayla?"

She'd been in no position to refuse. She'd never seen Gabriel so volatile, and having seen her brother's throat cut in front of her, she knew what this man was capable of. So, she'd stroked his hair.

After her captor had fallen silent, she realized she'd never seen him in such a vulnerable position before. However, what opportunity was there, really? She was sitting at the end of her bed and had no access to weapons.

All she had were her hands, and how could these frail, small things be a weapon against this giant of a man?

So, as she'd stroked and he'd moaned, looking more content than she'd ever seen him, she'd felt overwhelming despair, because she'd not heard him close the door at the top of the stairs, yet, here now, with only one chance, she was clueless. Until the unbelievable happened, and sleep took him.

Stroking his thinning hair with one hand, she reached for the pillow on the bed with the other, then drew it toward them. She let it hover over his head. *It would be easy to press it over his ugly face ... But then to hold it there? Impossible. He would wake and break me in two.*

She held her breath, ceased stroking, reached underneath his head, and lifted it slightly. She paused. Her heart pulsed in her temples.

The snoring continued.

She slid the pillow down so it was sandwiched between her legs and his head. Again holding her breath, she eased herself to the right, sliding her legs free of the cushion so it lowered itself to the ground and took his head with it. She panned from legs to the opened door of her prison. *Was this really happening?*

She raised her knees and started to stand—

The snoring stopped.

She froze half with the palm of her hand pressed to the wall to steady herself and watched him. Her lungs were close to bursting from the air she held inside them.

He reached up and rubbed at his nose.

Was he going to wake? She stared at the door. So close. Biting her bottom lip, she tasted blood. *Run?* Close to tears, yet desperate for freedom, she stood upright. It was now or never.

The snoring started again.

She released the air in her lungs and breathed. When she looked down at him, she was relieved to see that he remained undisturbed by her sudden gulp of air. Then, without looking back, she moved for the door.

The adrenaline of leaving that place for the first time in over a month flooded her. The urge to scream for help was overwhelming, but she was uncertain if anyone outside the house would hear her. When she beheld the stairs she had to climb, nausea swept over her. So many times, she'd listened to that hulking man ascend and descend them. The steps were loud, creaky, and they would wake her even from the deepest of sleeps.

She looked back at the snoring bastard and realized her best bet was to lock him in. Her gaze fell to the staple mounted on the cell door. An open rusted padlock hung from it with the key protruding.

The snoring stopped again.

She lunged forward and shoved the door. It was badly fitted, and the floor caused some resistance. She thrust harder.

"Kayla?"

The door was stubborn; it was not going to close.

"No!" The hasp that crossed the door to lock it was not pushed back far enough on the vertical trim and was wedging the door open.

"What's happening, Kayla?"

She could hear him scrambling to his feet. She lashed out at the hasp, and it thumped against the frame. With the obstacle clear, she managed to slam the door.

"Get back here!"

She snatched out the padlock, threw the hasp over the staple, then realigned the padlock to slip through. The door shook. The padlock didn't connect with the staple and, instead, hit the floor.

He came again, and this time she heard the wood splintering. "After everything I've done for you!"

Spinning, she dove for the steps. If she hadn't met the wall with the palms of her hands, she would have hit the floor, and then it'd be over. She heard the door crash open behind her. As she charged up the old steps, she kept her focus on the open door on the first floor.

"You can't get away!" His voice echoed around her head. He was so close. Within touching distance.

She was only a couple steps from the summit, trying to ignore the expectation that his hand would land on her leg at any moment. After bursting onto the first floor, she thrust the door backward. There was no resistance this time, and it swung ... before bouncing open again.

Gabriel screamed.

She noticed his outstretched hand.

"My fucking fingers!"

Kayla thrust the door again, but he was wise to it now and recoiled his hand in time. The door slammed shut. She reached for the deadbolt, but it was stiff and refused to move. She got both hands on it and thrust with everything she had. "Close ... please close!" It didn't. Remembering the rifle Gabriel kept with his jackets at the front door, she sprinted down the hallway. She heard the door burst open behind her.

"I think you've broken one of my fingers!"

"Shit!" The rifle wasn't there. She felt tears in her eyes. *Now what? Upstairs? No time* ... She could hear him breathing behind her. She was out of ideas. Her hand instinctively flailed for the front door handle. She knew it was useless, but what the hell. She tugged, and the door opened.

Fresh air raced in and over her. *"Help me!"*

A hand closed over her face.

She bit hard.

The bastard yelped and snapped his hand back.

She flung herself outside. *"Help me!"* She ran over the driveway toward the streetlights.

MASON COULDN'T BELIEVE what he was seeing.

He'd been standing over the road from Gabriel's house for almost twenty minutes, summoning the courage to knock on the bastard's door. His plan had been to reason with Gabriel, talk to him in the same way he'd spoken to that female lieutenant, make him see sense—try to make him believe the lies.

Yes, this route had been a long shot, but anything was preferable to Liam's plan—if it could be called a plan. Most would see it as an all-out war, not that Mason's existing plan amounted to much now anyway.

A girl, early teens at the most, was sprinting from Gabriel's house, screaming for help

What the hell is going on?

"Help me!"

For a moment, Mason thought the fleeing girl might actually make it. She was halfway up the drive, and Gabriel was only just emerging from his house, but then, as is so often the case—and Mason was very experienced with this himself—shit happens.

The young girl clipped the sideview mirror of Gabriel's

car and went into a spin she couldn't recover from and hit the deck.

Instinctively, Mason looked both ways, preparing to cross the road to assist, but checked himself. This, here, could be an opportunity. For so much of his life, the Jewell family had been second only to the Davis family in poisoning his existence. Now he was witnessing something that might offer him a way out with the Jewells, a way out that didn't involve Liam and his baser methods.

He stepped backward to watch.

Gabriel knelt beside the girl and took a handful of her hair.

She writhed in his grip. *"Help me!"*

The chief of police pulled her head back and slammed it into the concrete.

She continued to struggle. *"Help—"*

He slammed her head again, and she went still.

Gabriel scanned the area.

Mason eased himself into the shadows, optimistic he wouldn't be seen.

The bastard slipped his hands under the girl and lifted her.

She flopped in his arms, and her limbs dangled.

He carried her into his house and closed the door behind him.

"Gotcha," Mason said.

When Cam and Carson Davis arrived home from closing the store, they found Felicity pinned to the wall by her throat.

"Hands off, Dom," Cam said.

Dom looked at his older brother, then back at Felicity. "You don't understand, Cam."

"Are you going to make me repeat myself, brother?"

Dom released her.

Gasping for air, Felicity reached for her throat.

Dom eyed his brother. "Please listen to me, Cam—"

Cam rose a finger to silence him.

"Dad," Carson said. "This can't go on—"

Cam turned the finger toward his son, and it had the same effect. "Go and see your children, Carson, upstairs."

"Yes, Dad."

Cam waited until he could hear the thumping of his son's shoes on the stairs. He peeled off his jacket, threw it over a kitchen chair, and undid the top three buttons of his shirt. He watched Felicity stare at the floor, clutching her neck, still catching her breath. Then he looked at his fat brother leaning against the kitchen sink.

"I was just trying to get the truth out of her," Dom said.

"With that?" Cam pointed at the lump in his brother's pants.

Dom glowed red and moved his hands to conceal his erection.

"Get me a glass of water." Cam nodded to Felicity.

Felicity didn't move; Dom, her assailant, was still blocking the sink.

"Out of her fucking way, brother."

"Yes ... sorry ..." Dom moved to the side.

Felicity filled a glass from the tap. She turned, strode over, and handed it to Cam. She then sat at the kitchen table.

Cam drank the water in one mouthful, then fingered the rim of the glass. "I've not had a good day."

Neither Felicity nor Dom responded.

"I had to poison a dog, and I quite like dogs." He dropped the glass on the tiled floor, and it shattered. "So, to come back to a happy home is not too much to ask for."

Dom nodded. "But if you let me explain—"

Cam silenced him with his finger again and retrieved a roll of dollars from his jeans' pocket. He threw them onto the kitchen table in front of Felicity. "And we had such a good day at the shop too. Bastard Rogers was in the clink all day, so we doubled our takings. I was going to suggest a celebration to raise my spirits." He looked at Felicity. "All of us together, you know, like the good old days, before everything got so serious with the new business." He observed the smashed glass on the floor. "Dom, any problems in this house are dealt with by me, and me alone. You both know that already."

"Sorry, Cam," Dom said.

Cam pointed at his head. "Our family has only been blessed with one thinker. It's not a problem, unless you make it so.

Dom apologized again.

"So, take off your shoes."

Dom paled. "Cam, I understand. I do. There is no need—"

"Take off your shoes." He looked from Dom to Felicity. "Both of you."

Felicity didn't argue. She just kicked off her shoes under the kitchen table and glared at him.

"Dom?" Cam said.

Dom kicked off his shoes.

Cam adjusted his position so he was standing directly behind the shattered glass. He opened his arms. "Now, who's going to welcome me home with a hug?"

Dom looked at Felicity, but she was still too busy glaring at Cam.

"Felicity?" Dom said with a quiver in his voice.

Cam smiled. "Now, really, Dom ... I'm your big brother. You should be first over. Come on. Get over here, you big lug." He widened his arms.

Dom eased his way forward. "Please, Cam."

"Come to me, brother."

Dom stopped at the edge of the smashed glass and looked at his bare feet. He opened his arms to try to hug Cam without stepping into it.

Cam stepped backward.

Dom lifted a foot, looking down. "I don't—"

"Come."

Dom eased down his foot but avoided putting any pressure on it. "Is that enough?"

Cam shook his head. "The other foot."

When Dom lifted the other foot and his weight went into the other, there was a crunch.

Cam smiled as his brother winced and groaned. When tears of pain streaked Dom's face, Cam pushed his brother away from him. "Enough! You stink. I've changed my mind. We'll hug when you've showered."

Dom hopped backward and sat on the floor beside the sink, picking glass from his foot.

"Felicity?" He turned in her direction.

She stood at the table, then marched toward him.

"Wow, you do look angry," Cam said.

"I've done nothing wrong."

"She's lying," Dom said.

Cam glared at his brother. "Aren't you busy putting your foot back together?" He turned back to Felicity. "Tell me what my brother is so concerned about and we'll save our hugging until later after a few drinks."

Felicity shrugged. "I told him already. When the police came—"

"The police?" Cam raised an eyebrow.

Dom said, "I tried to tell you! Why do you think I was so wound up! They came about Brady."

"Brady? Why?"

Felicity explained.

"And that's it?" Cam said.

"That's not it," Dom said, wincing as he plucked out the glass. "That bitch was talking to them for a while."

Cam lifted a finger again. "Watch your mouth, Dom. What else, Felicity?"

"Nothing."

Cam sighed. "Look down, Felicity."

She surveyed the blood-stained glass.

"You can either stand in it or sweep it up. What else?"

She shrugged again. "I don't suppose it matters anyway. You already know about the dead girl. They wanted information about your rivalry with Mason."

"Why?"

"I don't know."

"What time was this?"

After Felicity told him, Cam thought about it. It couldn't be about the poisoned dog. The timeframe didn't fit. The police were here because they suspected Mason over that dead girl—Collette Jewell. It was happening again. He smiled. "What did you tell them?"

"Not much," she sneered.

He smiled and widened his eyes. "I love this new feisty you, Felicity, so I'll give you another chance. What ... did ... you ... tell ... them?"

"I told them how the rivalry started."

"Why?"

"Because they threatened to take Brady to the station. I thought giving them information they could probably get elsewhere was the safer of the two options."

Cam nodded. "So, you told them about Liam poisoning our father's cattle?"

She nodded.

"Good decision, Felicity." He watched his brother, who looked shellshocked. "Did you hear that, Dom? She made the right decision."

Dom nodded and muttered under his breath.

Cam paced around the kitchen, thinking. "They could have got that information anyway, and you know what this means, don't you?"

Dom sucked in air through gritted teeth as he cleared debris from his wound.

"It means Liam will be on the cops' radar too. And maybe, *just* maybe, they'll finally find him. They could even drag this bastard back to town! Imagine that!"

Dom looked up at him. "Really?"

Cam nodded.

"Both of them? Both of those fucking brothers in Blue Falls?" Dom smiled.

Cam smiled too. "Maybe, I was wrong. Maybe, there is still cause for celebration after all."

12

JAKE'S DREAMS WERE full of dead children. After waking, he reached to the other side of the bed and let his hand settle on Piper's back. He closed his eyes and tried to push the dead children from his thoughts, so he could rest.

In Jake's arms lay Paul Conway, or at least what was left of him. Paul had been caught in the blast zone of a car bomb set for Paul's neighbor, an aging KGB defector. "I'm sorry," Jake said, because although he hadn't planted the bomb, he'd been working for the monsters who had.

The boy with the broken face stared up at Jake.

"I truly am," Jake said.

Paul opened his mouth to speak, but blood swelled up and out of his mouth and gushed down the sides of his burnt face.

Jake clutched the dead boy to his chest and wept. He could sense the people crowded around him, close to him, taunting him, and heard them whisper his name over and over. Jake realized the person in his arms was no longer Paul

Conway. He now cradled the head of Madelyn Thompson, the girl recovered from the killing pit.

Her lips and sides of her mouth were cracked and blistered from the disinfectant she'd been forced to drink. "You came too late for me."

"I know. I'm sorry."

"But you put a stop to it."

"I tried to." Jake was now standing at Lookout Corner by the Skweda River.

Two men were laying two small bodies in the undergrowth—the Bickfords.

"Stop!" Jake said.

After laying down the bodies, the two men towered over them and spent some time staring down, considering their handiwork.

Jake turned and looked across the river. The water flowed fast and smashed into the rock jutting out.

He heard Madelyn Thompson's voice again. "You tried to stop it."

"You can never stop it," Jake said.

"Jake?"

"It goes on and on—"

"*Jake?*"

Jake opened his eyes.

Piper was leaning over him. "Are you okay?"

"Yes."

"You're sweating, and you were calling out."

"Yes, it wasn't the most pleasant dream. I've had it twice tonight."

"Want to talk about it?"

"Not, really. Not now." His cell vibrated. "What time is it?"

"About three in the morning."

Which meant it was probably a call from the UK. He scrambled for the phone. "Hello?"

"It's me," Sheila said.

"Is everything okay?"

"I don't know."

Jake sat upright in bed. This wasn't like his ex-wife. She'd not phoned him since he'd left, and when he would phone her, she would sound far more caustic and dismissive than this. "What's happened?"

"I think someone's watching the house."

Jake clutched his chest. It felt as if someone had just reached into his ribcage and taken hold of his heart. "How do you know?"

"Two nights ago, I saw a car on the street I didn't recognise—a black BMW. I noticed it from my bedroom window. Last night, it was back again."

Jake swung his legs out of bed. He wanted to feel his feet on the ground. He wanted to feel *steadier*. "Is someone sitting in it?"

"I can't tell."

"Someone may have a new car, or a late-night visitor. Go and knock on some—"

"I've done that already. I wanted to see if there was a problem before phoning you."

Desperate to avoid calling me at all costs. Is that really what it has come to? "You should phone me whenever there is a problem. This is more important than your feelings towards me."

"Well, we have a problem."

Jake felt Piper's hand on his back. He stood up and let it fall away and paced around the room. "Is the car there now?"

"No. It's always gone by morning."

"Do you have a registration."

"Yes." She read it to him.

"Okay, let me think."

"Is this because of the people you were mixed up with?"

"I don't know." And he genuinely didn't. He knew he was a wanted man, that giving SEROCU the slip had put a target on his head. But would they really move against a civilian family out of revenge or to draw him out? Surely, he wasn't worth that amount of heat. Yet, here was his worst fear in danger of being realized. There was, of course, only one option. "I'll have to call you back. You're not going anywhere, are you?"

"No."

"Good." As soon as he'd finished the call, he dialled the UK international code and punched in a number he'd dialled thousands of times in the past but not for a long while.

"DCI Michael Yorke, can I help you?"

"Mike, it's me."

Silence.

"It's me. Jake."

"I know who it is."

"I guess it must be a shock, but—"

"Let me pull over. You're on speaker, but I'm struggling to keep the car straight right now."

"Sorry, Mike."

"Jake, where are you?"

"I'm far away."

"Yes, I'm aware. You sent a postcard from New England."

"I wanted to let you know I was okay; you deserved that."

"I deserved that." Yorke grunted.

"Sorry, yes ... that I was alive, that I was safe. You're my best friend."

"Am I?"

"Of course."

"So why don't you tell me why you left?"

Jake sighed. He paced around the motel room. "I can't do that Mike."

"Shouldn't best friends be open and honest?"

"Not if it puts them in danger, no."

"It's SEROCU, isn't it? You got mixed up in something."

Jake didn't reply.

"I'm assuming then that this isn't a social call?"

Jake sighed again. "I wish that it was. I'm sorry, Mike, but I need you right now. I really do."

"Need me?"

"Yes."

Yorke sighed. "You know I would never refuse you, don't you?"

"I do."

"Yet, you refuse me the truth?"

Jake felt a tear in the corner of his eye. "Don't Mike. Not now."

"When then?"

"It's not safe for me to ... Look, I love you like a brother."

Silence.

"Mike?"

"Jake, come home. Do you want me to beg you?"

"There's nothing I want more, Mike, but it can never happen."

"This is all my bloody fault."

"I'm a big boy. The choices I made were mine, not yours."

"I took my eye off the ball. I always had your back, but I got distracted."

"Well, if you hadn't been distracted, you probably wouldn't still be here, buddy. The lives you saved. You're the best man I've ever known, Mike ..." He took a deep breath. "I need you to check on Sheila and Frank for me."

A pause. "I do, Jake ... *regularly*. I want whoever you've had dealings with to know that moving on your family would be costly to them, that they are heavily monitored."

"I know, and I'm so grateful, but Sheila is convinced someone is watching the house." Jake recounted the details of his phone call with Sheila. He also gave him the vehicle's registration number.

"I'll phone back on this number when I know something," Yorke said.

"Thanks, Mike. You can't let anything happen to my family."

"I won't, Jake."

After the phone call, Jake sat back on the bed.

Piper attempted to stroke his back. This time, he let her. "What's happened?"

He told about Sheila's concern.

"Then who did you call?"

"The best man I know."

She stroked his back. "Well, then you must hold him in high regard, because you're the best man *I* know."

Jake started to cry. "You couldn't be any more wrong, Piper."

They fucked, as they so often did, long into the night.

Then Louise left her two exhausted subordinates and

returned to her room. They were staying in the Shephard's Hotel in New Lincoln, the wealthier of the three towns pinned to the Skweda, so she had a television and minibar. She indulged in both as she lay back on the double bed. When she realized CNN had dragged nothing meaningful from the world this evening, she killed the television and reviewed her interview with Mason.

There was no need for recordings or transcripts, because she wasn't interested in the words. She'd scrutinized his story to death already. She was interested in his face, his eye movements, his twitching, and his posture. With her eyes closed, she observed him in memory.

He was innocent. He hadn't killed the little girl or those two young men in 1975. But there *was* something; he *knew* something. And that *something* may just unravel this whole web.

She texted her husband, Robert. *Been a heavy night, but it did the trick. Will get some sleep now. Missing you x*

Then she scrolled through snaps of her three young girls on her cell and waited for the vodka and her sexual exertions to work their magic and put her to sleep.

FOUR IN THE morning and Liam Rogers couldn't sleep. With dangers coming in from so many different angles, his brother was responding too slowly for his liking.

"*It's in hand,*" Mason had said before retiring.

In hand.

Liam snorted. Had Gabriel Jewell, Jake Pettman, or the Davis brothers ever been in anyone's *hand*? And were they really about to settle into one now?

Liam left his brother's sofa. He equipped himself with

the hammer he'd killed Bobby and Henry with and the pliers with which he had taken the mementos. Then he pulled on a ski mask. He also slipped Mason's cellphone, which he'd left charging in the lounge, into his pocket. It wouldn't be cold, so he didn't bother changing out of his pajamas, but he did slip on a dark gray raincoat and zipped it up.

He was careful exiting through the kitchen door, so as not to wake his brother, who would attempt, and potentially succeed, in talking him out of this. With the kitchen door closed behind him, he embraced the darkness and the emptiness of Main Street. *So, where to first then? The Davis farm? Jewell's home? The Blue Falls Motel?* So much choice. He relished this freedom.

He watched the neon sign of the Blue Falls Motel flickering over the rooftops of Main Street. Might as well begin with the closest option. Enjoying the reassuring weight of his toolkit in his backpack, he broke into a jog, as he always did when he went hunting.

Jake tried to lie still to allow Piper some sleep, but she must have sensed his anxiety, because she was restless. Occasionally, she reached to stroke his back and ask if he was okay, but he refused to divert his attention from his cellphone, which he stared at. Eventually, the pain of lying still got too much for Jake, so he grabbed his phone and stood. "Please get some rest, Piper."

He went into the bathroom and, in the darkness, sat on the toilet seat. He pressed the button on his cell to light the screen to double check he hadn't missed a call or a text.

Nothing.

He sat there, continually checking, only stopping when he realized he was draining the battery.

Liam slowed down before reaching the Blue Falls Motel, then steadied himself against a lamppost to catch his breath.

Many years earlier, before killing Henry and Bobby, Liam had been on a ten-mile run with the hammer, the pliers, and some rocks in his backpack. He recalled his desperation to be a soldier; fuck his pre-existing conditions. He'd kept himself as fit as he possibly could just in case the army ever became so desperate for recruits that they'd take on the sickly boy with no teeth.

On the day of the murders, he'd eaten a large breakfast. He always did this before heavy exertions; during wartime, one had to be prepared to do whatever, no matter how full a stomach. That memorable day, he'd vomited on route to meet Mason and his two faggot friends.

How fit he'd been! Even after a ten-mile run, with puke on his chin, he'd killed those two boys without needing to lean against a lamppost and catch his breath. Now look at him—a puffing and panting old man stalking into the Blue Falls Motel parking lot.

He straightened his back and puffed out his chest. He may not be as fit as he once was, but he'd give anyone else within ten, or even twenty years of his age a good run for their money.

He stopped by a solitary car in the lot.

And one thing was for certain. Despite his grand age, he'd not forgotten how to kill.

He ran his gloved hand down the deep scratch on the side of the Ford rental. *How did you do that, Jake?* He surveyed the motel room; both him and Mason had observed Jake entering a couple days back. He reached into his backpack for the hammer that had ended Bobby and Henry. He smiled at the camera mounted high on the motel walls.

Probably not in use, but if it was, no matter. He doubted anyone would be monitoring it at four in the morning, and even if Liam hadn't been wearing a ski mask, he doubted anyone would recognize a man who had departed Blue Falls half a century ago.

He approached the door, readied the hammer in one hand, and, with the other, prepared to knock.

When the cellphone rang, Jake shook so hard he almost dropped it. "Mike?"

"Jake, it's fine. Take a deep breath."

Jake did. It was no help. He stood and paced in the darkness instead. "Talk to me, Mike. Please."

"The car belongs to someone having a relationship with the young lady living opposite."

"But Sheila told me she went door to door to try to find out who owned the BMW."

"The man is married with kids. It took my badge to dislodge the truth from the young lady in question."

"Thank god. Are you sure?"

"As sure as I can be without going around to this fella's house and ruining his marriage."

"No. Jesus, I don't know what to say."

"You can tell me where you are."

Jake placed his forehead against the bathroom mirror. "I

just can't, Mike. We've been through this. I will not put you in that position."

"And how do you know I won't just attempt to trace this number after this phone call?"

"I know you won't, because if you do and they find me, you'll blame yourself for what comes next."

"It seems you know me a lot better than I know you."

Jake rolled his head on the mirror. "You know me, Mike. You know me better than anyone. But I made a mistake, and I must pay for that—for the rest of my life if need be."

"*Nonsense*. This must end, Jake. You know that as well as I do."

"Maybe, but until it does, this is how it's got to be." He lifted his head from the mirror. "I have to go and phone Sheila."

"First, promise me something."

"If I can, yes."

"If you get into any trouble, call me. *Any trouble*. Day or night. You *call* me."

"I will," Jake lied. "I will." After hanging up, he dialled Sheila's number.

LIAM DIDN'T KNOCK and dropped his fist to his side. Knowing Jake Pettman was a dangerous man would steady most hands in this situation, but it wasn't the reason for steadying his. He steadied his hand because he understood the importance of reconnaissance. He shuffled to the side and placed his face against the glass. The blinds were down, but they trembled, and Liam reasoned a fan was set on full throttle in there. Sure enough, the blinds slightly lifted at the corner when the air stream drew near, and Liam saw inside.

A naked woman lay face down on the bed.

No sign of Jake. *I wonder what you're up to at this ungodly hour, Pettman?* Staring at the naked woman, Liam licked his hollow gums. He spied the hammer in his hand, and several possibilities flickered in his mind. *While the cat's away, the mice will play.*

He sidestepped backward to the front door. Yes, this was not to plan, but didn't he deserve some fun? He'd spent his entire life worrying about his brother. How nice it would be just to consider number one for a short time? *Especially with so fine a woman lying on the other side of the door ...*

Mason's cellphone buzzed. He reached into his pocket. The message on the screen was from an unknown number: *We left your dog suffering and that is your fault. Do everyone a favor, put one of your guns in your mouth and pull the fucking trigger or we will come and do it.*

The Davis brothers, Liam thought. *They always were so eloquent.*

Liam smiled and stepped back from the door. This message may just be what he needed to rile Mason into some serious action. He sighed when he considered the beautiful creature behind the door. Unfortunately, now was not the time to play. There were too many fish to fry, and drawing heat upon himself this early was not the strategic action of a good soldier.

He replaced the cell in his pocket and put the hammer in the backpack. *Temper your impulses, soldier.*

He jogged back to Main street. When he reached the front of his brother's general store, he saw that the text wasn't the only message the Davis brothers had delivered this evening. The front window had been smashed. Liam wasn't surprised, but he was disappointed he'd missed it.

Mason felt the sofa move as Liam sat beside him, but he didn't look. Instead, he stared at the brick in his hand.

"I saw the mess, brother," Liam said. "We could take the brick back round to them if you want. I can think of more creative ways to put it to use."

Mason felt a tear run down his face.

"They also sent you this," Liam said.

Mason listened to him read the threatening text message. "One thing they never had was a way with words." From the corner of his eye, Mason watched Liam lean over and place his cell on the coffee table.

The bastard pinched the sleeve of Mason's striped pajama top. "Get out of these and let's go put an end to this."

Mason swung the brick. The crunch of his brother's cheek was sickening but, at the same time, quite satisfying.

Liam slipped from the sofa, clutching his cheek. "Fuck ... fuck." He slumped onto the floor. "Fuck!"

"I told you not to go out," Mason said, rising.

Liam bashed his feet on the floor. "I'm your fucking brother. Everything I do, I do for you."

"*Bullshit*. You're in it for yourself, always have been."

Liam removed his hand. Blood spewed from a rip in his cheek. "Good job I don't have any teeth."

Mason raised the brick above his head.

"Fine. Whatever makes you happy, brother." He smiled, but then winced.

"You've never brought me anything but more pain." Mason gritted his teeth, preparing to bring down the brick.

"That's gratitude for you. You forget, little brother. Where would you be if it wasn't for me? In jail. For the murder of a little girl."

Mason squeezed the brick so hard he thought it may just turn to dust. "I didn't kill her."

"It matters not. I solved the problem. I always solve your problems. Henry and Bobby?"

"They were my friends. My *only* friends."

"They were faggots. They just wanted to use you."

"You don't know that."

"I know. You had happiness for a bit. You had Lorraine, and you had your son."

"They're both gone."

"And was that my fault?"

The brick suddenly felt heavier in Mason's hands. He lowered it to his chest. "I want you to leave."

"If I leave, brother, you'll be dead within the week."

"I have my own plan." He threw the brick on the sofa and turned his back on his brother. "I want you gone. *Now*."

"Whatever you wish. I'll leave you to your shit show. But, once I'm gone, I'm not coming back, no matter how hard you beg me."

"Don't worry, I'd rather die."

Liam winced and sighed again. "Carry on like this, Mason, and it may just have to be that way."

13

"COME IN, OFFICER Sanborn."

Lillian opened the office door. "Good morning, ma'am. Could I have a quick word?"

Louise was sitting beneath a portrait of a serious-looking Earl Jewell and behind Gabriel's desk. Gabriel was an immaculate man who demanded order around him. His desk rarely had more than a neat pile of files and a single cup of fresh coffee on it. If he could see the three empty coffee cups and paperwork strewn all over it right now, he'd have been a candidate for a heart attack. "Of course, take a seat."

Lillian sat.

"You want to talk alone?" Louise looked from side to side at her two officers. Ewan, the tallest of the two, was leaning against the glass window that looked out on the department, thumbing through a file. The other one, Gordon, was grinning inanely at Lillian. She scowled in his direction, and he looked down at the file in his hand.

"No, it's nothing personal," Lillian said. "I just think I may've discovered something of interest."

Louise leaned forward and put her hands on the table, accidently knocking over a framed picture, which Lillian couldn't recall ever seeing on Gabriel's desk before now.

Lillian reached to pick it up, but Louise was quicker. Lillian caught a glimpse of three young black girls, dressed in matching blue dresses, before Louise stood it back up, facing her.

"What have you found out?" Louise asked.

The male officers maneuvered to the sides of the desk, laid down their files and stared at Lillian, making her squirm as she recounted her discovery of the rivalry between the Rogers and Davis families, her visit to the Davis farm, and the revelation that Mason had an older brother named Liam.

She was careful to leave Jake out of the recount. The last thing she wanted was to be side-lined by these superior officers due to her involvement of a civilian in the investigation. The fact she had no reliable colleagues within her department and that Jake was one of the most capable detectives she'd ever met would surely fall on deaf ears.

Afterward, Louise smiled and reclined in her chair. "You've been busy, Officer Sanborn, but I'm not surprised." She nodded at the window that looked out on the other officers in the department. "I suspected right away that you were the only person who could get anything done around here."

Lillian felt her cheeks flush. "So, what do you think, ma'am?"

"I think that until we have some DNA results, we are floundering around for leads of any kind. However, you have just floundered onto a good one, and I think we should take a look. Well done, Officer."

"Thank you, ma'am," Lillian said, but she wasn't proud of herself, not at all. She remained interested in only one thing: finding the truth. "How did the interview with Mason Rogers go, ma'am?"

Louise smiled again. "Okay. But there's one thing I need to make clear to you, Officer Sanborn."

"Of course, ma'am."

"There's us and"—she pointed to the window again—"and them. I will bring you into the loop, but you must remain loyal to us. I know you're desperate for the truth and that a wise officer such as yourself knows the best chance lies with us, but I still want to hear you say it. Are you batting for the right side here, Officer Sanborn?"

"Yes, ma'am, of course."

"Good. Listen, I think Mason Rogers is innocent. I don't think he killed Collette Jewell or those boys in seventy-five."

Lillian nodded, trying desperately to conceal the feelings of doubt that overwhelmed her.

Louise smiled. "You're wondering how I could possibly know that, aren't you? Well, extensive training in interviewing, experience, good old-fashioned women's intuition—take your pick. Look, I know I could be wrong, and I'm keeping our options open, believe me, but these are my initial impressions."

"And Lieutenant Price is never wrong," Gordon said.

"Well," Louise said, looking up at Gordon, "at least not as long as you've known me—which isn't long, to be fair. Anyway, despite his innocence, I'm still certain he's concealing something. He was close with the two boys who died in seventy-five, potentially sexually, and Collette Jewell was last seen heading to his store. Throw in the extracted teeth and you've got a lot of coincidences." Louise stood. "But thanks to you, we've now got another piece of the jigsaw. A rivalry, a brother, Liam Rogers—the story grows." She paused to think. "So, Officer Sanborn, I'm impressed by your resourcefulness, so I'm interested to hear what you think our next move should be."

Before she could worry about making a ridiculous suggestion, Lillian followed her instincts. "I would ask Mason where his brother is."

Lillian nodded. "Great call. Can you and officer Taylor head down there now?"

Fortunately, Louise was referring to Ewan and not Gordon, the slimeball who'd given Lillian the inane grin when she'd first entered the room.

"And good luck," Louise said, straightening her picture on the table.

"They're beautiful, ma'am," Lillian said.

Louise looked confused. "Sorry?"

Lillian nodded at the frame. "Your children. They're beautiful."

She looked down at them, smiling. "Yes, indeed. Beautiful."

"You just couldn't help yourself, could you?" Priscilla said.

Gabriel surveyed the emaciated Charles Stone. An oxygen mask clung to his ashen-gray face while the machines beside him hummed. "How long has he got left?"

Priscilla shrugged. "Two weeks ago, they said a week."

"He always was a stubborn bastard."

She nodded and sighed. "You know, he liked you, Gabriel."

Gabriel eyed Priscilla at the other side of the bed and smiled. "As opposed to yourself?"

"It's not important. It's not about liking or disliking. Nothing is that simple."

"Everything can be made simple. You want your husband to die so you can be the chief selectwoman. And I want Mason to die because he killed my sister."

"Without even knowing if he really did it?"

He refocused on Charles. "He did."

"Even if that were the case, can you imagine the damage caused by the chief of police murdering a suspect in a crime?"

"The same damage caused by the chief selectman and his wife murdering their son's killer?"

"But the MSP weren't involved in that, Gabriel. If you hadn't pulled that stunt and stopped me, no one would have been accountable. What do you think happens if you execute someone under the nose of these people?"

"Frankly, I really don't care."

"Well, I'm going to have to care for both of us then! I'm not about to let everything myself and my husband built here go up in flames. The bastards will investigate everything. It won't just be you who burns, Gabriel."

"So, why am I still standing? I saw the firepower coming into your house. Two armed bodyguards. Really? Who do you think you are? The Queen of England?"

"You're still standing, Gabriel, for the same reason that Mason needs to stay standing."

"Because sweet Louise and her two bagboys will be suspicious?"

Priscilla looked down at her husband. "You know, he was always the one with the people skills; he could also beat around the bush for god knows how long and still get his own way. I just don't have the patience."

"Don't beat around the bush then, Priscilla. Call it."

"If you wait until their investigation is concluded and they leave, I'll serve Mason Rogers up to you, and you can do with him as you wish."

"How can you serve him up to me if he's in custody?"

"He won't be. They won't find any evidence on him this time, in the same way they didn't find anything on him last time."

"How can you be so sure?"

"If they had anything, don't you think he'd be in custody by now?"

"There's still forensics."

"Don't be ridiculous. The body has rotted under water. There are no fingernails to dig out DNA from! So, when they give up and leave, I'll afford you the luxury you never afforded me; you can kill the person who murdered someone you loved."

"It's a nice offer, but I'm not prepared—"

"And I'll give you half a million dollars to quit your job and walk away from Blue Falls."

Gabriel widened his eyes. Unexpected. He snorted. "And then I'll be looking over my shoulder for the rest of my life!"

"You'll be doing that anyway. You might as well hope I'm telling you the truth."

Charles coughed, and Priscilla ran her fingers through her husband's thinning hair.

"Why don't you just put a pillow over his head?"

She glared at Gabriel. "Because that's not who I am."

"It's exactly who you are."

"You think you have the measure of me, Gabriel, and I

believe I have the measure of you. So, my offer should interest you. Go away and think about it; accept it as soon as you can, because if, and when, things get worse, you may not find me in such an accommodating mood."

THE EXISTENCE of Davis Conveniences repulsed Mason, and he'd never even driven past for a sly peek. He looked at the store front, licked by a light green paint, for the first time. The displays, most notably one of a well-known brand of dogfood, were meticulously organized. The sign above the shop was written in a fashionable font, using an array of colors, and even came with an eye-catching logo: *Davis Conveniences* wrapped around a heart. It was a warm and welcoming store, *certainly* not befitting of its cold and unapproachable owner, Cam Davis.

Despite being on the verge of losing everything, potentially even his freedom, Mason felt strangely elated as he strode through the shop door to confront the spectacled Cam Davis, who was preoccupied by his cash register at the counter. *My last stand,* he thought. There was something romantic in that.

"As I live and breathe, Mason Rogers!" Cam looked up from his cash register and plucked off his spectacles.

Mason nodded. "Cam."

Cam looked him up and down and smiled. "Wow! Now this is something I never thought I would see."

"We need to talk."

Cam nodded and studied his cash register. "Maybe you could help me out first. New technology, eh? Driving me nuts. They said it would make things easier." He chuckled and eyed Mason. "Ah shit. Hang on, sorry, I'm forgetting.

They cost a *fucking* fortune; you probably don't have one at the moment. I heard business was bad."

Mason smiled. "You heard, did you? Did you not just assume it from the fact that most of my customers are now coming to your shop?"

Cam shrugged. "All's fair in love, war, and business. You left the market wide open, Mason. People were desperate for quality and hurting over the high prices you were charging."

Mason cracked his knuckles.

Cam grinned. "Aren't we a little old for a tumble in the aisles? I have a reputation to maintain."

"Ha! And what reputation is that, Cam? Local bad boy turned good?"

Cam nodded. "Sounds about right."

"I think you're underestimating the memories of the folks around here."

"They're coming in droves, Mason."

"Times are tough, and people are desperate."

"Maybe," Cam said, rolling his shoulders and loudly cracking his back. "Or maybe those memories you speak of take them back to a time when the Davis family were upstanding members of society until their livelihood was cruelly snatched away from them?"

"After everything you and your family have done, do you really think people will accept your family into their world again?"

Cam opened his hands to gesture the shop around him. "The proof of the pudding is in the eating! I don't know, maybe they're happy to see balance restored? After all, it was your family who wronged mine, not the other way around."

"It was my brother. It wasn't my family."

"Same difference."

"Not really."

"Okay, so tell me where the disappearing Rogers boy is then?"

"I don't know. We never heard from him."

"Bullshit. Are you telling me Ma and Pa Rogers never spoke to him again?"

"I don't know, but I'm certain I didn't."

"Liars make my skin crawl, especially when they're on my property. The fact is that you and your family protected him. Rather than have him face up to what he'd done, you hid him away."

"What was the alternative? What would you have done to him if he'd stayed?"

"How little you think of us."

Carson Davis came out through a door behind the counter. In contrast to his burly father, Carson was a wiry man. He had a moustache so thin it looked like it'd been pencilled on. He nodded a greeting at Mason; there was no malice in the nod. Mason didn't know Carson, but, unlike his father, he possessed a reputation of being introverted and well-mannered. He was probably a large part of the reason that locals had become more trusting of the Davis clan and had frequented their new store.

"Is it tidy back there, son?" Cam asked.

"Yes, Dad."

Cam smiled at Mason. "At the moment, we're having to bring in so much stock things get messy quick."

Mason narrowed his eyes.

"Which reminds me, Carson," Cam said, "can you head over to the Stevenson farm?"

"Yes, Dad."

Cam was still smiling at Mason. "You could stick

around if you want. The quality of the vegetables is superb. I could fix you a box."

Mason gritted his teeth. His deliveries from Stevenson had dwindled recently—not only because the demand in his shop had deteriorated, but because Stevenson was sending most of his produce here.

"So, what brought you in here today, Mason?"

"I got your messages."

"Messages? What messages?" Cam looked at Carson. "Did you send any, son?"

Carson shook his head.

Cam refocused on Mason. "Sorry, you must have made a mistake."

"Kyle. You're a cruel man, Cam Davis."

Cam shrugged. "Kyle? Sorry, I really don't know what you're talking about—"

Mason slammed his palm on the counter. "He was a pup, you sick bastard."

Cam shook his head. "Still not following."

"I got your threats on my cell too."

Cam looked at his son, and then back at Mason, his eyes wide to demonstrate his disbelief. "Listen, I know you lost your boy recently, Mason, but you can't just come in here—"

Mason pointed at Cam. "Don't you *dare*! You don't get to mention my boy."

Carson flinched while Cam raised his hands in surrender. "Fair enough. I respect that. Like I said, I don't want any trouble in my store—"

"And you raped my wife!"

Cam scrunched his face in disgust. "Really? You honestly believe that?"

"Believe?" Mason sneered. "I know."

Cam touched his chest. "Do you think I need to rape anyone?"

Mason was breathing quicker now. He was struggling to keep himself calm but knew he had to. Fighting was not the purpose of this visit.

"Why am I still a free man then?" Cam asked.

"Because you wore a mask. You wore protection. You were careful."

"You're delusional, Mason. *Absolutely* delusional. According to your family, your brother was a schizo. Ever wondered if you are too?"

"So, did I imagine what you did to me outside my shop that day?"

Cam lifted his eyebrows. "No. That definitely happened. But what do you expect? You were a suspected child killer. *Actually*, maybe I should change that *were* to *are*."

Mason looked at Carson. His head was lowered. "I'll head off now, Dad."

"You do that, son."

After he'd left, Mason said, "He's different to you."

"Soft, you mean?"

"No, just not a prick."

Cam smiled. "Time you got to the point. As fun as it is being stuck on this record with you, I've got shit to do."

"I didn't come here to fight; I came to make you an offer."

Cam snorted. "You want to make me an offer! What could you possibly offer me? Your business is on the verge of collapse—"

"You can have my shop."

"*What?*"

"I don't want it anymore. I have enough money saved.

I'll sign my shop over to you so you can expand the delightful Davis Conveniences onto Main Street."

Cam snorted again as he regarded Mason. Then he shook his finger at him. "Nice try. Why the hell would you do that?"

"Because I've had enough. There's nothing for me in Blue Falls. I'm leaving. Let's just say I owe you for the damage my family caused you. Let's bury the hatchet."

"Bullshit. You think I raped your wife and killed your dog!"

"Enough is enough. Take the store."

"I could just buy another property on Main Street if I wanted to expand. What makes you think—"

"There is no better property for a shop than mine. You'll save a fortune in renovations too. Look, I'm going, one way or another, just take the fucking shop. I'm repairing the damage my brother did."

Cam considered and shook his head. "No. I'll decide when it ends. And it ends when I see your brother."

"My brother could be dead for all we know," Mason lied. "You going to let your pride fuck up this lottery win for you? No bullshit. Take the property. We owe you. I can make peace with that."

Cam chewed his bottom lip. He rubbed his tattooed knuckles against his chin. "Interesting idea. How does it work?"

"I'll sign it over tomorrow."

"That easy?"

"That easy."

"And then what? You leave Blue Falls?"

"If they don't succeed in putting me in jail."

"Did you kill that young girl?"

"Would you believe me if I said no? Do you even care? Really?"

Cam smiled. He wrote a number on an old receipt by his till. "Put your lawyer in touch with mine by tomorrow, and you have a deal."

Mason said. "Fuck you, Cam. I will."

14

"DO YOU WANT to talk about it?" Peter asked.

Jake glanced at the Vietnam Vet riding shotgun in his rental car. "What makes you think I've anything to talk about?"

"Your eyes are like two piss holes in the snow. Something kept you up last night."

"Observant."

"I was a soldier. It paid to be vigilant. So, do you want to talk?"

"Like a hole in the head, old man. Cheers for asking."

"No worries. Was worth it to be so politely declined."

Jake entered the Davis farmyard and weaved around the battered, old vehicles. He wondered how many years they'd get away with leaving these old metals to rust before the environmentalists descended.

"Dirty bastards." Peter was a descendant of the region's natives, so he took wanton destruction of his ancestor's lands very personally indeed. "Jesus ... I hope she's okay."

Jake pulled up alongside the chicken coop that had repulsed both him and Lillian the previous day.

"I don't want any trouble. Do you think they'll still buy that you're a cop?" Peter asked.

"He didn't seem suspicious of me yesterday. My name's Officer Reynolds, by the way."

A loud clunk on the windshield made Jake flinch. "What the fuck?" A small dint had appeared on the outside of the windshield exactly in front of Jake's head. Tiny cracks were already emerging from it. He'd seen this happen before, of course, when, on a motorway, a pebble had hit his windshield—never when he was stationary though. Jake leaned forward and touched the glass. Smooth. The crack had not come through.

"Someone taking pot shots at you?" Peter asked.

"I think I know who." Jake pointed ahead at the porch where a young, round boy cradled an air pistol. "Damien over there."

"That's Felicity's boy, Brady. Where did you get Damien from?"

"Have you not seen *The Omen*?"

"What's that?"

"Google it. Anyway, that's one little shit who doesn't care if I'm a cop. Sure you still want to check in?"

"Desperately, but I don't want to lose an eye. I brought you for protection not to incite them!"

"He's a good shot too. You should look in that chicken coop on the way past."

Felicity stepped onto the porch and shouted her son's name.

He then relinquished his air pistol.

"A firm hand. I like it," Peter said and stepped out the car.

As they approached the house, Jake asked, "Can I bill them for the dint in the windscreen?"

"Just let me do the talking. I'm here to see that everything is in order, not instigate a war."

"At least that smell has died down. They must finally have gotten rid of the dead chickens."

Felicity finished admonishing her son with a swift hand to the back of his head, and he stormed into the house. She approached the steps, wearing a much darker dress than the previous day, although it was still flowery.

When she reached the top of the steps, Jake noticed the black eye, and he gritted his teeth.

"It's good to see you, Felicity," Peter said. "Is now a good time?"

"I guess. Why are you here, Peter?"

Peter turned to Jake. "Officer Reynolds is a good friend of mine. He told me about yesterday. I wanted to check that you were okay."

"I'm fine."

"Your eye," Jake said. "It wasn't like that yesterday."

Felicity shrugged. "I'm clumsy."

Peter held up a plastic bag. "I've got some treats for the children. Is it okay if we come inside?"

"Other than me and the boys, there's no one else here, so it shouldn't do any harm."

"Where are they all, Mrs. Davis?" Jake asked.

"Carson and Cam are at the shop. I don't know where Dom is. He sometimes starts early at the Taps."

Felicity turned and walked through the entrance.

Jake and Peter eyed each other and followed her in.

In the kitchen, Brady sat at the table with another air pistol dismantled in front of him. He was cleaning the parts with a damp cloth.

His brother, Owen, sat beside him with a pack of

playing cards. He was organizing them into piles according to their suits.

"How many guns have you got, Brady?" Jake asked.

Brady glanced up at him. "Five."

"A small armory then."

Brady looked confused. "Sorry about your car. I wasn't aiming for you."

"And here's me thinking that was a bloody good shot. What were you aiming for?"

"The old cars."

"I can see how that would be fun." *Better than those poor chickens, at any rate.*

After he'd finished organizing the cards into piles, Owen gathered them altogether and turned to his mom, holding them out.

"Of course, darling," Felicity said. She took the cards from him and shuffled them. "He loves cards. Wants to be a magician. You're good, aren't you, honey?"

Owen just stared his mom. He was yet to acknowledge the presence of Jake and Peter.

"He can't talk, you know," Brady said. "Mute."

"Non-verbal autistic," Felicity said, glaring at Brady as she shuffled.

Peter turned his bag upside down over the table. Lots of packets of Haribo tumbled out. "Used to drive my own mother mad with these, boys. She used to say they'd make my teeth fall out." He turned, smiled at Jake, showing his new teeth, and whispered, "It seems it wasn't the sweets that got them in the end." He turned to Felicity, who was in the process of handing the shuffled cards to Owen. "Can we talk without the children?"

"Brady, take your brother and the sweets up to your room."

"Shit. Do I have to?" Brady asked.

"Yes, you do, and watch your mouth."

Brady muttered another obscenity under his breath, and they abandoned his gun to move around the table to gather the Haribo. "Come on then, O."

Owen touched his waxy quiff, checking it was solid and sharp, and with his cards, followed Brady.

"Brady," Felicity said. "Are you forgetting your manners?"

Brady sighed and turned. "Thank you for the sweets."

"You're welcome, young man."

Jake watched the boys leave, his heart full of sympathy over their miserable lives.

Peter turned to Felicity. "Did Carson hit you?"

Felicity baulked. "Carson? He wouldn't hurt a fly."

"Who did?"

Felicity shrugged and smiled. "You didn't buy the fact that I'm clumsy then?"

"Let us help you," Jake said.

"And how do you propose doing that? Peter has been trying for years to help, haven't you?"

"This is the worst I've seen," Peter said. "Enough is enough. Who hit you?"

"Cam. Dom. Cam or Dom? Does it matter? They're both pricks."

"Last time I came here, you said they didn't hit you," Peter said.

"They didn't ... then. Well, times change, you know?"

"How have they changed?" Jake asked.

She stared at Jake. "I used to let them fuck me, and now I don't."

Jake flinched.

"They don't take kindly to rejection." She pointed at

her eye. "They think they can change my mind, but I'm stubborn, you know. You just have to look at the state of my arms and back to see how stubborn I can be."

Jake reached down and squeezed the top of a chair at the kitchen table. He was trying to keep the anger out of his face but, in doing so, risked destroying their furniture.

"Does Carson know about any of this?" Peter asked.

She laughed. "Of course he does."

"And he doesn't do anything?"

"Like I said before, he wouldn't hurt a fly."

"But you're his wife," Jake said.

She shrugged. "I'm his wife, and Cam's his father. There's a pecking order. In his way, he's actually kind of sweet to me."

"Anybody who lets this happen is not sweet," Jake said.

"He doesn't know any different. He grew up watching it happen to his own mother."

Jake took his hand off the chair. "And now your children are growing up and watching it too—"

"*No!*" Felicity pointed at Jake. "No, they are *not*. Those bastards wouldn't dare. Not in front of my children. I told Carson I would suffer anything to keep my children safe, but if they ever hurt me in front of them, I will kill the old rats while they sleep, and if they take my children from me, then at least they'd be away from this hellhole. My children will never know what I've suffered. *Never.*"

"The truth can't stay hidden forever. They've raped you."

"I consented every single time. *Every time.* I kept life quiet. My misery was a small price to keep my boys safe."

"It's still rape," Jake said. "They've intimidated and coerced you."

"Yes," Felicity said. "They *did*."

"What's changed?" Peter asked.

"I've stopped kidding myself. My boys aren't safe. Look at Brady. He's shoplifting, and he's obsessed with guns. How long before he shoots someone?"

Jake thought about the dint in his windscreen. *Not long.*

"There is nothing to be gained from my silence and submission any longer. Look at Owen. Look at the pain on his face." Her eyes filled with tears. "It has to end. In fact, it *has* ended. I'm taking my life back."

"Not like this," Peter said. "Not by angering them, by frustrating them. You're going to get yourself killed."

Tears streaked her face. She wiped them away, shook her head, and smiled. "How are they going to kill me if I'm not here?"

Jake watched Peter's eyes widen. This was clearly something Peter had been so desperate for, for so long.

Peter said, "Where are you going? Do you need somewhere to stay?"

She shook her head. "I have somewhere to go."

"Fantastic," Peter said. "This is the right move."

"Yes. For so long, I loved Carson, and I loved how much he adored Owen and Brady, and I was willing, in my naivety, in my *fucking* stupidity, to do anything to keep us together. But I've met someone else, and they've made me realize it doesn't have to be like this. I want Brady to go to school. I want Owen to be a magician. I want to be with someone who doesn't pimp me out to their redneck relatives."

Peter took one of Felicity's hands.

She looked up at him. The tears were still flowing.

"Who is it?" Peter said.

"You know him, Peter. He's one of us. He understands

me. But you can't say anything, Peter. He's coming for us tomorrow."

"Of course, I won't. So, he's Abenaki?"

She nodded. "He's done some questionable things himself, but he's changed. He worked as a driver for Jotham Macleoid for a time, but he was doing it to support his mother."

Jake saw the color drain from his friend's face.

"And who didn't work for that animal?" Felicity continued. "Anyway, his heart is in the right place; he did it for his family."

Peter's hand dropped from Felicity's.

"Who is it, Felicity?" Jake asked.

"Oliver Sholes."

Peter turned away.

Jake knew the story well. Oliver Sholes had promised to help get Peter into Jotham's property so he could free his dogs, but he'd betrayed him. The little shit had left him to the mercy of Jotham and was the reason that all his teeth had been knocked out.

Jake sighed and refrained from stating the obvious on Felicity's decision. *Out of the frying pan and into the fire.*

LILLIAN AND THE MSP OFFICER, Ewan Taylor, had been sitting outside Rogers general store for the best part of an hour. The Closed sign hanging in the front window was a peculiarity for 10 a.m. on a weekday, so they'd both ventured around the back to knock on his apartment door, but there'd been no answer.

As they waited for Mason's return in Ewan's sporty Audi, the two officers chatted at length. Lillian realized quickly that Ewan, like her, was a conscientious individual, chiefly motivated by justice.

"I have to admit that when I saw the car, I thought otherwise," Lillian said.

"I said I've always wanted to do the right thing; I never said I wanted to go without."

She laughed, then realized she could really grow to like the tall officer who, like his superior, Louise, also wore a tailored suit and took pride in his appearance. Lillian noticed that Ewan was regularly steering the conversation back to Louise. He was either in complete admiration of her, professionally, or harbored a massive crush on her.

Surely, he wasn't silly enough to think it could go anywhere. She had three kids! She decided to remind him of this. His reaction may enlighten her to his agenda.

"Lieutenant Price seems so capable," Lillian said.

"She's solid as a rock. I've never seen her lose control. Not once. You couldn't ask for a better boss."

"Well, with three children, I guess she has a lot of practice."

Ewan looked at her. There was the reaction, although the reaction was different to what she'd anticipated. It was one of dismay, as if Lillian had said something totally crazy.

"Are you all right?"

He looked away. "Yes, of course. Fine."

"You don't look it."

"Just not had breakfast yet, and it was a long night."

"We're batting on the same side, remember?"

He grinned at her. "Do you know how many small towns Louise has asked that question in?"

Lillian shook her head.

"In the same number of towns we've been stabbed in

the back! That verbal contract means nothing. It's always us, and it's always you."

"You're wrong this time."

"I've heard it before."

"I'm more like you than them."

"I know you believe that," Ewan said.

"I fucking despise everyone I work with."

"Again, I've heard it before. Next, you'll be telling me it's about being the only woman in a patriarchal department."

"Well, I won't tell you the obvious, but I will tell you that there are times when I sit at home, staring into space, nauseated over the incessant misogyny I face on a day-to-day basis."

Ewan took a deep breath and nodded. "You do handle yourself better than most, I'll give you that."

"Listen. I operate in the twenty-first century, unlike my colleagues, and unlike those who've stabbed you in the back."

"This isn't a job interview."

"I wish it was."

Ewan laughed. "I'm the wrong man for that; although I'm sure if you help us, the lieutenant's word will go far and wide."

"Seriously, Ewan, believe that you can trust me."

"Alright, already! I do!"

"So, tell me then. Why the reaction when I mentioned the lieutenant's three children? I will be open and transparent with you about everything." *Apart from about Jake Pettman*, she promised herself, *because I owe him more than you ever know*. "You have my word."

"The story is sad, and it has no relevance to what is happening."

"This doesn't sound like transparency to me."

"If you let it slip that you know, I could lose her trust."

"I won't."

He stared at Lillian and took another deep breath. "What the hell. I hope I'm right about you."

"You are."

"One evening, six years ago, Louise came home from work, and her husband and three daughters were gone."

"Gone?"

Ewan nodded.

"Where?"

Ewan shrugged. "Just gone. Disappeared. They haven't been seen since."

"Six years ago?"

"Just over." He sighed. "I told you the story was sad."

"There must be more to it than that."

"There isn't. No evidence of forced entry, no traces of intruders. Their vehicle was still in the driveway."

"People don't just vanish."

"Well, they do—all the time, actually."

"Yes, but not whole families! Not without a trace."

Ewan shrugged again. "Without a trace. The case has long grown cold."

"That's awful."

"I know."

"Could they have just left Louise? Hidden away from her?"

"But why? By all accounts, her husband adored her, and I know she adored him."

"Wait." Lillian shook her head. "She was texting her husband when I drove her to the station last night. She *told me* she was texting him!"

"Yes. The story doesn't get any brighter, I'm afraid. It's

her defense mechanism. While she works, she tries to think of them as alive. It keeps her going. She is forever texting and looking at photographs of them. It seems to work too. She's never anything but professional."

"I'm not an expert, but that doesn't sound like the best way to handle grief."

"Like I said, it seems to work for her."

"And then what? When she's not working and when she's at home, does she not have to confront the reality of what's happened all over again?"

"She's not one to sit and dwell. When she's not working, she's trying to find them. Everyone else has given up, but she won't. Not ever."

"Can't say I blame her."

Ewan nodded. "She's the best I've ever met. I wouldn't be surprised if she unearths the truth."

"That is one of the most horrendous stories I've ever heard," Lillian said.

"Well, you wanted to know. But whatever you do, don't show her any sympathy. She'll see it as condescending. It's safer to wave a red flag at a bull."

"I won't. I'm not supposed to know, remember?"

He nodded. "That's right."

"How long have you known her?"

"My entire career. Ten years. If it wasn't for her, I wouldn't be where I am now. She taught me everything I know."

"You have a lot of respect for her."

"Yes."

You're also in love with her, aren't you?

Ewan stared out the windshield onto Main Street with a sad expression.

15

GABRIEL RECOGNIZED Officer Taylor's Audi outside Mason's shop on Main Street. He leaned against Lance's Laundrette, which had been boarded-up over four years ago. "Fuck!"

Having heard his expletive, the Baileys, an elderly couple, nodded a greeting as they walked by but passed on the opportunity to stop and chat.

"Sorry," Gabriel said, annoyed with himself for swearing out loud. It seemed his last handful of Adderall was starting to kick in, and he was becoming twitchy again.

When he was sure the Baileys were out of earshot, he kicked the boards behind him with his heel. Everything had been so much simpler *until* Priscilla Stone had made her offer. His plan had been to kill Mason for murdering his sister and plant one of his own guns on him. Self-defense—an easy sell after what had happened yesterday in the store. But that offer from Priscilla ... well, it was lifechanging. If he waited out the investigation and the MSP did not find the evidence needed to incarcerate Mason, Gabriel would *still* be able to kill him, and ... half a million! He'd be rich!

He could leave Blue Falls with Kayla, and they could start a new life together. She would soon change her mind about him when she realized how wealthy they now were. She would grow to love him as he loved her.

But, despite having made up his mind, he still wanted to look that bastard Mason in the eyes and tell him his days were numbered, that murdering his sister was a death sentence, and that it would, most definitely, come to pass.

However, that couldn't be now. The MSP were at his store.

He kicked the boards again and walked back around the corner to where he'd parked.

Gabriel considered Priscilla's offer all the way home, but it was only when he was unlocking his front door that he decided to tell Kayla what was happening. She'd be still sore at him for his heavy-handed approach the previous evening, but money—or, at least, the promise of money—had a way of changing perceptions. In this instance, he hoped that would be very much the case. He opened the front door, and his guts froze. The door under the stairs was wide open, just like last time when that worm Ayden MacLeoid had slid in through his kitchen window.

And those very same brutal questions from last time assaulted him: *Was she gone? Kayla? Beautiful Kayla? His Kayla?*

He reached for his rifle beneath the jackets, only remembering when his hand closed on empty air that he'd relocated the rifle to the lounge after Kayla had discovered its location. He reached for the hunting knife he had sheathed on his leg, the one he'd slit Kayla's brother's throat with.

He moved quietly down his hallway. Last time, the element of surprise had worked; if this intruder was still here and not driving Kayla to the police station, then it would work again. He peered into the kitchen. No smashed window this time but an open back door. The frame was cracked. *What bold bastard jimmied open the chief of police's door?*

Gabriel moved the knife from one hand to the other. If they were still here, he would enjoy gutting them. As he descended the steps, he kept to the edges by pressing himself against the wall. The creaking was far less pronounced if he did this. He recalled the relief he'd felt last time when he'd heard Kayla talking to Ayden. This time, he heard nothing, and it was hard to keep his heart from sinking.

When he reached the final steps, he saw the open door. He was too late. His legs quivered under the force of despair. If he hadn't still been pressed against the wall, he may just have fallen. He sucked in a lungful of air and forced himself to retain some semblance of control. Now, in a truly dire situation, he needed it more than ever.

Keeping the knife raised, he took the remaining steps quickly and turned into the room.

Ashen-faced, Kayla stared up at him with a gun pointed at her, but he couldn't see the wielder.

Riding the adrenaline, he stepped farther into the room and saw the intruder.

Mason.

"I should have shot you dead yesterday," Gabriel said.

"You should have, but you didn't."

Gabriel nodded at the gun. "Is that mistake going to cost me my life?"

"I only brought this to keep Kayla silent."

"First name terms?"

"How would I not know who she is? She's the daughter of the man who controlled the town. I can see why you waited until after her father was dead."

I didn't, Gabriel thought. *But you don't need to know that.*

Mason lowered the weapon. "Unfortunately for the world, you'll live to fight another day."

"Unfortunate for you, perhaps." Gabriel raised his knife and inched forward.

"That's a chance I'm willing to take. Killing me serves no purpose, Gabriel. I told your daddy all those years ago that I didn't kill her. And nothing has changed."

"Forgive me, but I'm struggling to believe that."

Mason slid his gun into a holster under his jacket.

"Foolish," Gabriel said, taking another step.

"You may want to hear what I say before you kill me."

"Unless it's a confession, I'm not interested."

"Everyone has secrets buried, Gabriel. *Everyone*. But this?" He opened his hand toward Kayla, whose eyes darted between them. "This is something truly unexpected."

Mason took a few steps backward, and Gabriel considered attacking but checked himself when he realized he'd be leaving the door unblocked for Kayla to have another shot at escape. "This conversation would already be over if I had my gun."

"This conversation would never have happened if I'd sent the photographs I took last night to Lieutenant Louise Price."

His guts froze again. *Of course. The bastard wouldn't be here without leverage.*

"Out front, Chief. I watched you bounce this poor girl's head off the floor."

Gabriel's eyes darted to Kayla and the plaster on her forehead. He took a deep breath, but it felt labored, as if a noose had found its way around his neck and started to tighten. *Clever boy.* "Give me your cell."

Mason shrugged.

"I'll take it from your corpse." Gabriel knew as soon as he finished his threat that Mason wouldn't have been stupid enough to bring along the only thing keeping him alive. His airway continued to constrict. "I'm going to enjoy gutting you."

"And then my brother will do what I should really have done last night and send those photographs to the real police officers."

"Brother? Who? You don't have a brother."

"Liam."

Gabriel remembered the story. "The one that killed the Davis' cattle?"

Mason nodded.

"I don't believe you. Your parents sent him away when he was a kid."

"Doesn't mean he didn't come back."

Gabriel snorted. "Came back? I'm not sure the Davis family would have allowed that."

"Trust your instincts then, Chief." He opened his arms as if he was receiving an embrace. "And gut me."

Gabriel pointed the knife at Mason. "After I skin you."

Mason closed his eyes. "Kayla told me what you did to her brother ... in front of her."

"That's nothing compared to what I'll do to you in front of her."

"So, what're you waiting for?"

Gabriel pointed the knife at Kayla. "Stay there." He stepped toward Mason and gritted his teeth. He thought of Louise opening the message on her phone. He lifted the knife. He imagined the lieutenant's eyes widening. "Fuck!" Gabriel let the weapon fall to his side. "Why are you even here? Why did you not send the photographs already?"

Mason opened his eyes, looked back at Kayla, and sighed. "I'll burn in Hell for not sending them, but I need you."

"You *need* me?"

Mason eyed Gabriel and nodded. "Apart from Lorraine, Blue Falls never gave me anything. I'm done with the place."

"So, fuck off already! Why are you still here? You could be long gone."

"And you'd have let me go, would you? You could have joined the Davis brothers in waving me off and wishing me well."

"You could have slipped away."

"And be looking over my shoulder for the rest of my life?"

"So, what's the alternative? Taking us on?"

"No. I want to do this right. If my brother had his way, then believe me, this would be all over by now. But no, not after what he did last time."

"Last time?"

"Don't be dumb, Chief. Who do you think killed Henry and Bobby in seventy-five. He bashed their brains out with a hammer right in front of me!"

Gabriel's eyes widened. "And their teeth, he took them, didn't he?"

Mason nodded.

"So, he killed my sister too."

"No."

"But her teeth were gone!"

"It wasn't him. I'm telling you the truth. I'm laying everything out on the table for you. The missing teeth must be a coincidence."

"*Bullshit!* You know who killed Collette."

"I don't."

"You're lying!" He lifted the knife again. "You're fucking lying!"

Mason looked back, narrowing his eyes, and raised his voice for the first time. "Listen. I'm the one holding the cards here, not you. I have solved my problem with the Davis family, and now, I have solved my problem with you, because as much as it disgusts me to my very soul, I will keep your secret safe."

"But why? You'd solve your problem by sending those images to the MSP."

"Because you're going to help me with my third and final problem."

"Which is?"

Mason took a deep breath. "Jotham MacLeoid fell when Jake Pettman came to town, didn't he?"

Gabriel shrugged.

"I think he killed Jotham, and I think he killed Anthony, my son."

Gabriel shrugged. "I wouldn't know."

Mason smiled. "But you do, don't you, Gabriel? You know."

"What makes you say that?"

"Because if you didn't know it was Jake Pettman, you would've already had him under investigation."

"How do you know I didn't?"

"Who was it then, Gabriel? This happened on your patch, and you know nothing? Suspect no one?"

Gabriel chewed his lip.

"And please show me more respect than the long-gone out-of-towner excuse. Blue Falls has spun that yarn far too many times. Tell me the truth, Gabriel. Was it Jake Pettman?"

No, Gabriel thought, *because it was me. I shot your son in the head after he threatened Jake. The vile little prick had it coming too.* Gabriel took another deep breath. Sharing the truth with Mason was appealing, but it probably wouldn't be wise. He nodded instead. Better he thinks it was Jake at this stage. He opened his mouth to give him more detail—

"No," Mason said. "My dreams are tortured enough as it is."

"So, is that it? Is that all you wanted? The truth?"

"No, of course not. He still remains my third and final problem. I can't walk away with him living and breathing after what he did to my flesh and blood."

"So, kill the bastard then. God knows, not many people would miss him!"

"Are you not listening? I want to leave. *Start again.* Murder won't help me with that."

"I still don't understand what you're saying here!"

"I'm saying I won't get away with killing Jake Pettman, but I bet the chief of police can."

JAKE'S VEHICLE juddered on the dirt track leading from the Davis property.

"Of all the people," Peter said, "it had to be that little shit."

"I guess I don't need to ask where we're going." Jake said.

"I'll go alone if you'd prefer."

"I'd prefer not to be visiting you in a cell. Best if I come."

"What do you think I'm going to do? Rip out his throat?"

"I remember the day you woke up in hospital and said that was exactly what you were going to do."

"I was angry."

"Uh-huh."

"He fed me to the lions. Promised to get me on the property, then watched as I was shot in the guts and handed over to that maniac."

"I know the story, Peter. You bring it up ... often."

"Jesus, his poor mother! If she ever found out what her beloved boy did to me, she'd never forgive him."

"You've got a big heart. Lesser men would have told her."

Peter rustled in his jacket pocket. "Can I smoke?"

"No."

Peter removed a cigarette, lowered the window, and lit it with an engraved Zippo.

"Nice lighter. Never seen it before."

"From my army days. Got it out last night."

"Who had it engraved?"

"Someone special. Her name was Tong. Vietnamese."

Jake smiled. "What happened there then?"

"I came home."

"Did you not try to stay in touch?"

"This isn't helping, Jake."

"Yep, fair enough."

Irene Sholes let them into an orderly home with a mantlepiece laced with Abenaki trinkets and weaved throw pillows on the sofa—a complete contrast from the chaos the Davis family operated in. No wonder Felicity fancied a change.

"Sorry to disturb you, Irene, but I was hoping to speak to Oliver."

"Of course," Irene said, placing a hand on Peter's arm.

She wasn't being flirtatious, Jake observed. Peter had led the Abenaki Council in a time when she'd been financially supported. Her affection was born from gratitude.

Jake could see now how devastating to her the truth about Oliver would be.

When the police had tried to get the truth from Peter as to what had happened the night on Jotham's property, he'd pleaded amnesia. He'd lost a lot of blood from the bullet in his stomach and had sustained head wounds after having his teeth smashed in. It was hard to argue against this claim. Consequently, Oliver never saw justice for his treatment of Peter.

Before Peter had even broached the subject, Irene said, "I know about Felicity Davis."

Peter nodded. "I suspected. You okay with her coming here?"

Irene nodded.

"The Davis brothers are dangerous individuals."

"I know, but I've never seen my Oliver so happy."

Peter eyed Jake.

Jake detected the grimace he was hiding behind his stony expression.

Oliver walked in and noticed Peter. His face went grey. "Peter?"

"Long time, no see."

Oliver's eyes darted left and right. "You look well."

"New teeth." Peter smiled, displaying them.

Oliver nodded and smiled.

Peter regarded Irene. "Can we speak to your son alone? We won't be getting in the way of your plans. You have my word."

"Of course, Peter. You don't need an excuse. You always have our best interests at heart."

Peter smiled at Oliver. "Yes, Irene. I do."

After Irene left the room, Peter moved for Oliver.

Fortunately, Jake managed to grab his friend's shoulder before he could launch the young man through the closed door after his mother.

Peter took a deep breath through his nose and looked at Jake.

"That's why I came," Jake said.

"That's why I brought you," Peter said.

Oliver, pale and shaking, cowered against the door. "Peter, I'm sorry. I had no choice, the situation I was—"

"Save it, you little shit. You led me to my death. That dear woman behind that door is the only reason you're still standing. That, and the large man behind me holding my shoulder."

"And I could easily lose my grip," Jake said. "Especially when traitorous scumbags are involved."

"I worked for Jotham MacLeoid! Do you think I had any choice?"

"You should choose better employers," Peter said.

"Or join a union," Jake said.

"Why did you come here, Peter? Why? We could have had this out away from Mom."

"I'm not here about you and me, idiot; although that situation is far from resolved." He paused to look back at Jake. "I'm calm, now. You can let go."

Jake nodded and released his shoulder.

Relief settled over Oliver's face. "Why are you here then?"

"Oh, let me see," Peter said. "Having been set free from one set of murderous bastards, you saw fit to get involved with another set?"

"I don't know what you—"

"Felicity Davis."

"Oh."

"Yes, oh."

Oliver shrugged. "I love her."

"Spare me," Peter said. "I doubt you've ever loved anyone other than yourself."

"I do. We hit it off at last year's Abenaki heritage weekend."

"Surprised she was allowed to go," Peter said.

"She was, because she's allowed to see her mother. Her children weren't. I don't think Cam Davis wants to accept that his grandchildren are Abenaki."

"And, what? You've been sneaking around together ever since?"

Oliver nodded. "About the size of it."

"And now you intend to bring her here. How do you think that will play out?"

"I don't know. But I love her, and she can't be there anymore. The things they do to her—"

Peter held up his hand. "Enough. I know. Me and you are on the same page with that one. I just didn't expect the solution to come in the form of a spineless cretin." He sighed. "However, that's the way it has panned out, so I guess we have to make the best of a bad situation."

"We?"

"Yes, we," Peter said. "Imagine if I let you do this alone?"

"It's all planned. I really—"

"Well, let's consider the last time you planned something. Oh, yes, it didn't work. I'm still here, and your employer is dead."

"Listen. You have to trust me this time."

"No, Oliver, not only did you kill the trust between us, but you buried it in an unmarked grave in the middle of nowhere. You tell me your plan, and then I'll tell you how it's going to go."

Oliver shook his head.

"Chin up, son. You just got yourself a partner."

GABRIEL CURSED the existence of Mason Rogers. He also cursed the existence of Adderall. The combination of both sent him into a frenzy. When he felt this way, he had to move quick. His desire to take Kayla would become overwhelming within minutes. Soiling her was not an option.

So, after opening a video on his laptop that would help him relieve some of the tension, he fixed himself to a radiator pipe with a special set of handcuffs that operated on a timer.

Thirty minutes.

He was trapped. Kayla was safe.

He started to pleasure himself over a video of a man

babysitting two girls. Both girls were in their mid-teens and oblivious to their guardian's intentions. As usual, the acting couldn't have been any more wooden. So, as he always did, Gabriel tried to block out the fact that it wasn't real. But this time was different. The amphetamine was bringing a clarity to the proceedings he wasn't used to, and he couldn't ignore the falsity of what he watched.

Nineteen minutes.

He was no nearer to finding an end to his frenzy.

He gritted his teeth and masturbated more aggressively in the hope he could *force* himself to a conclusion. He understood that sexual pleasure came predominately from the mind, but with the Adderall adding a rigidity to his thought processes he wasn't used to, he would have to try for matter over mind rather than the other way round.

Once the wooden conversation had ended and the man had started to force himself onto the two girls, Gabriel hoped it would be enough to steer him towards climax. Except, it wasn't. *Because* it was there again. The great lie. The man wasn't taking advantage of the girls. *Not really.* The chemical in his blood gave him razor-sharp focus like never before. He sensed their willingness behind their false, bewildered expressions. They were actresses, and they were performing for a paycheck.

The frenzy and frustration caused tears to roll down his face.

He thought of Kayla.

No ... no ...

He increased his hand's speed, desperate to find an end that seemed nowhere in sight. He surveyed the handcuffs.

Eight minutes.

It should be enough time.

It wasn't.

Kayla hadn't moved from the bed since Gabriel and Mason had left the basement. Over the past hour, she'd curled up and tried desperately to sleep. She was unlikely to be treated to a pleasant dream—most had been horrendous of late—but anything was preferable to the cold harshness of reality that her problems had doubled and that two evil people were now holding her captive.

Additionally, Mason had just put further pressure on Gabriel—a man losing more of a grip on reality by the day. What would this mean now? For her?

As if he'd heard her question and was now here to answer it, he pounded down the stairs. "Kayla?"

She remained curled up, pretending to be asleep.

"Kayla?" He sounded desperate.

She listened to the padlock rattle as he impatiently attacked it. She tasted sick in her mouth but kept her eyes squeezed shut.

The door opened. "Kayla, please, I need you now! More than ever! I'm losing control! Turn, look at me!"

She kept her eyes closed, but she knew it was pointless.

"Please. I'm begging you!"

She opened her eyes. It was more dangerous to ignore him.

"Turn!"

She turned over.

He'd changed into a dressing gown. It hung open. He was holding his erection. His face and body were shiny with sweat. His face twitched, and his eyes rolled back and forth. "I tried, Kayla, I tried. I really did, but the videos won't work anymore. And I need a release. I need you. You must understand!" His hand flicked back and forth over his erection.

Kayla covered her face. "No ... please ... no." She tried desperately to block out everything with thoughts of the kind women who used to work in her father's lab. They used to talk to her on their breaks and bring little gifts with them to work. But the grunting and moaning from Gabriel cut through the memories, and then she felt the noises growing louder as he drew nearer. She rolled farther toward the edge of the bed.

He grabbed her leg. "Kayla, please, you have to look at me. You have to."

She tried to shake off his hand, but his grip was too tight. "No, no—"

"Look at me!"

She opened her eyes, expecting to see him standing over her, but he was kneeling now, which was welcome, because she could no longer see what he was doing with the other hand. His breathing had accelerated, and the sweat was building on his face. She felt his hand moving up her leg and over her thigh. "Please."

"I can't help it—"

"*Please.*" She felt his hand loosen, and, for a second, she hoped he would withdraw, but then she felt his fingers exploring the area around her crotch. She drew back her legs and kicked out. She managed to put one of her bare feet in his face.

He slumped backward.

She went to kick him again, but this time missed completely. She scurried backward until she was at the end of the bed and drew her knees to her chest.

He lay back on the floor, his dressing gown spread out

around him, groaning as fluid bubbled out and over his slowing hand.

She gritted her teeth and tried to force back the vomit she could still taste in her mouth.

After his breathing steadied, he rose and fastened his dressing gown. He didn't look at Kayla. Instead, he turned his back and left the room. He stopped just outside and slowly turned to face her. "I'm sorry."

She shook her head. Her tears were coming now.

He closed the door.

AFTER DRESSING, Gabriel sat in his lounge. He spied the laptop and the handcuffs lying by the radiator and sighed. He was so glad Kayla had eventually fought him off. If she hadn't, then what? Would he have soiled her? And if he soiled her, would he still love her? And if he didn't love her anymore, then what? It didn't bear thinking about.

Now he had to focus on other matters. Mason wanted an end to Jake Pettman to keep his secret about Kayla. Gabriel believed he knew how to make this happen without getting his own hands dirty.

Back when Jake had first arrived in town, Gabriel had made inquiries in the UK. It seemed Jake hadn't quit his job and was running from something. When Gabriel had confronted him about this, Jake had become very hostile. Having learned much about Jake Pettman's character in recent months, as well as watching him execute Jotham MacLeoid with no compassion, Gabriel suspected Jake had gotten himself into a serious situation in the UK—a situation that had caused him to hide in the middle of nowhere.

"If I make this phone call," Gabriel had said to Mason, *"one way or another, his whole world will come crashing down."*

Mason had contemplated it for a moment. He'd clearly had a more black and white solution in mind—a bullet to the head perhaps. Despite this, he'd nodded in agreement. It did, after all, have an element of intrigue about it; how far could the man who murdered his son fall?

Gabriel scooped the notebook from his coffee table and punched the number into his cell.

As the phone rang, he remembered Jake's threat to expose Gabriel's interest in the younger generation if he ever pursued this angle. He sighed. What choice did he have? Hopefully, the departure of Jake Pettman—either in a body bag or in handcuffs—would come sooner rather than later, and if his accusations did ever come to light, it would just be his word against Jake's.

"Wiltshire Police, how can I help you?"

"Superintendent Joan Madden, please?"

"Can I ask who is calling?"

Gabriel went through the formalities.

"What's it regarding, sir? I'll see if anyone else can help."

"I have information regarding the whereabouts of DS Jake Pettman. And no one but your superintendent will do, I'm afraid. I know she wants to find Jake. I know she wants to find him very badly indeed."

16

MASON WAS lost in his own world as he unlocked his store door and didn't even glance at Ewan's Audi.

"Is he ignoring us?" Ewan asked.

"I don't know. He doesn't look with it to me," Lillian said.

"You want to lead?"

"Really?"

"I'm not precious. Besides, you probably have an existing relationship with him. Might be best to go in gentle first."

"Are you saying I'm gentle?"

"No, I'm just saying—"

"Relax, I know what you mean."

Lillian went in first.

"Lillian," Mason said from behind his counter, "what can I do you for?"

"I'm here on police business, Mason."

"Now, why doesn't that surprise me?"

Ewan entered and Mason sighed. "I guess I was a fool to think we'd put all of this to bed yesterday?"

Lillian smiled. "Why were you out, Mason? I've never known you to close the store during the day."

"Policing my opening hours now?"

"No, just curious."

"The stress of all this is getting to me. I have to go for more walks to clear my head these days. Besides, it's not like I'm doing much business anyhow."

Lillian nodded. "We all want this to be cleared up as soon as possible."

"You know this has plagued me most of my life?" He drummed his fingers on the counter and regarded Ewan with a narrow-eyed stare. "Was I not thorough enough yesterday, young man?"

"No, you were thorough, Mr. Rogers," Ewan said, "but new information has come to light."

"Unless my DNA is on the girl's body—which it won't be, as I never *ever* touched her—it'll be pretty irrelevant, but do fire away, son."

Lillian raised her hand toward Ewan to suggest she wanted to keep leading. "Mason, we know you have an older brother."

Mason focused on the counter, drummed his fingers on the surface again, and looked up with a wry smile. "Good for you. I've known that my whole life. What's the relevance?"

"The relevance is, Mr. Rogers"—Ewan stepped forward so he was now closer to Mason than Lillian—"we didn't know."

"But what's to know, young man? It's not a secret. You didn't ask."

Lillian closed the gap with Ewan. "It wasn't mentioned in the last investigation Earl Jewell ran."

"Because it wasn't important."

"I imagined he looked into it though?"

Ewan shrugged. "Maybe he did. I can't remember. Maybe his paperwork was just shoddy. Who knows?"

"In fact, the only people who have mentioned an older brother to us are the Davis brothers."

"Sounds about right. They have reason to never forget him."

"The poisoning of their parents' livestock?"

Mason nodded.

"That makes him a person of interest," Ewan said.

"Why?" Mason asked. "He left when I was fifteen, so he wasn't here when Collette disappeared. My parents sent him away before the Davis family could get their dirty hands on him. He's had the good sense never to return, if he's even alive."

"What makes you say that?" Ewan said.

"Liam wasn't a well young man. Wanted to be in the army, but his health issues prevented that."

"The Davis brothers seemed to think he was mentally ill, and that could go some way to explaining what he did to the cattle," Lillian said.

"Physical issues kept him from the army. Mental issues! Those two are a fine pair to talk!"

"If he's alive, we need to find him, Mason," Lillian said. "Earl Jewell may not have considered it relevant, but we want to be thorough."

"If I knew where he was, and if I thought he was involved, I'd happily tell you. I don't like being your only suspect. It's starting to play havoc with my digestion."

"You must know where he went."

"He was seventeen when he was sent away from Blue Falls to live with family."

"Okay, where's that then?"

"Not sure. We have a big family. My father had eight brothers. One of them, I suspect."

Lillian and Ewan exchanged a glance.

"Do you have any names or addresses?" Lillian asked.

"I've never had much to do with any of my family. And after what happened with my brother and that cattle, no one ever seemed to make much of an effort again. A shame really. Especially when you consider the only family I ever had after my parents were Lorraine and Anthony, and now they're gone too."

"I'm truly sorry for that," Lillian said.

Mason sighed. "If I could be of more help, Lillian, I would."

AFTER THE OFFICERS LEFT, Mason locked the front door for the final time. Selling groceries had been top of his priority list for so many years, and now, it no longer even figured. It was a strange turn of events, but he'd be glad of the change of scenery. Tonight, he'd leave Blue Falls and not look back.

He went through to his apartment and saw his brother sitting on the sofa and holding a blood-stained tissue to his cheek.

"You gave me quite a whack there, brother."

Mason turned as he closed the door and placed his own forehead against the wood. "Jesus. I thought you'd finally gone."

"Even though you almost killed me, I just couldn't leave you. Blood is thicker and all that."

"Why ... why ... why won't you leave!"

"Because you're facing great peril, brother, and the only way out of this situation is to match fire with fire."

"We're not at war, Liam!" He turned around. "And you're not a soldier!"

Liam looked away and shook his head, licking his toothless gums.

"Anyway, it's irrelevant. I've already solved the problems," Mason said. "Without your help, I might add."

Liam narrowed his eyes. "How?"

Mason explained his agreements with Cam and Gabriel.

"And you trust them?"

"Yes."

"They're the enemy."

"Not anymore."

Liam stood. "Bullshit! Anyway, I don't need your permission. If you're lost to delusion, I'll do whatever is necessary to protect you, brother. Just like last time."

"If you go near any of them, I'll call the police, and I'll tell them what you did to Henry and Bobby."

"And implicate yourself as an accessory?"

"It'll be far worse for me if we play your game. How will it end then? In blood and fury." Mason reached for his sidearm.

Liam smiled. "Really?"

He pointed the Springfield in his direction. "I'm afraid so, Liam. I've locked my doors for the final time. Tonight, I'm gone. I can't allow your methods to bring everything crashing down."

Liam continued to smile. "So, what now, brother? Kill the only person who ever gave a goddamn about you?"

Keeping the gun trained on his brother, he walked to the corner of the room and retrieved some old twine from a drawer. "Sit on the floor, Liam, and put your arms behind your back. This will be finished tonight. The shop will be signed over to the Davis brothers, and then you can just come with me. We will start a new life together. And, in years to come, you will thank me for it."

Despite being desperate to update Jake on today's discoveries, Lillian was even more desperate to locate the relative who Liam Rogers was sent to live with, so both she and Ewan shut themselves away in a back office with a lot of determination. And hunting down a string of relatives in Maine, most of them old and a few of them dead, really did take a motherlode of it.

After three coffees and many dead ends, an exasperated Lillian contacted Silas Rogers' youngest brother, Nile, who was nursing a hangover from celebrating his ninetieth birthday the previous day.

"Sorry, dear, repeat that name to me again. I still possess most of my faculties, but hearing is my Achilles heel now."

"Liam Rogers," Lillian repeated.

There was a pause. "Liam? Silas's son?"

Lillian stood up with the phone in her hand. "Yes."

"A good man was Silas. Aye, a very good man. He made more of an effort to stay in touch than most of us boys. Of course, it was different back then, you know. We didn't have email and the like. Pen and paper were the order of the day."

Lillian drummed her fingers on the table, feeling her impatience grow, while holding onto the resolve to remain polite. "So, the son, Liam?"

"Always a sickly boy. I seem to remember a lot of anxiety in Silas's letters regarding his boy. It was almost as if they believed he would never really live that long. Proved them wrong. Much to the dissatisfaction of Paddy, no doubt."

"Paddy?"

"Another of my brothers. The poor fool who took the lad Liam in. I can't remember the particulars; mind you, I can't be sure if I was ever told, but I think the boy got in some kind of trouble with the law and had to make haste. I couldn't tell you what happened between them then, because me and Paddy haven't been in touch since we were in our twenties."

"Why?"

"Something and nothing. Bad words over a few beers. Been that long I can't even remember what they were. Such a waste, eh?"

"Yes. Do you know how I can get in touch with Paddy?"

"You got a phone line to Heaven?"

"I'm sorry."

"Don't be. If you die old, you die right. There is something you should know though."

"We'd appreciate anything you can tell us, sir."

"His daughter. A pleasant lady, her name escapes me now, called a couple of years back. She was the one who let us know he'd passed."

"Do you have contact details?"

"As a matter of fact, she left them. She said I was welcome to the funeral and that I should contact her." He sighed. "To my shame, I didn't go. I was bedridden with an ailment that is best not discussed with a young lady like yourself."

Lillian rolled her eyes. "Do you think you could find me those contact details?"

"Give me a minute."

While she waited, Ewan entered the room, holding her fourth cup of coffee. He mouthed, *Anything?*

"I hope so."

She took the cup and was taking a mouthful of coffee when Nile said, "You there, dear?"

She pulled the cup away and spilled some coffee down her chin. It burned. "Yes ... yes, I'm here."

"You got a pen?"

Her heart rate surged. She slammed down the cup and grabbed a pen.

While at Peter's property, collecting both the pickup and the rifle contained within, Jake spoke to his friend away from Oliver. "I really don't like this."

"I wasn't seeking your approval," Peter said, checking that his rifle was loaded. "Besides, it will go just fine."

"Were you on that same train of thought when you broke into Jotham's property?"

Peter smiled. His gleaming white teeth really did look out of place in his weathered face. "Fair point. But the odds are stacked better in our favor this time. Late afternoon, so Cam and his son will be at the store. Dom, as well you know, is stupid. Felicity will drug him, then walk her boys to the creek. We'll get them back to Oliver's mom's house quickly, then they can all lay low for a week or two until we can move them out of town."

"Yes, but this all depends on the bastards having no idea about Oliver's involvement with Felicity."

"Well, obviously they don't, or he'd have been dismembered already."

"I get that, but someone else could know; someone could have seen them together at the festival, for example. Someone could have spoken to the brothers; they could be anticipating tonight."

"Not many people speak to the Davis brothers. Not willingly. Anyway, to get Felicity and her children away from that poisonous life, we'll have to take some risk."

Jake nodded and sighed. "I guess, but I still don't like it."

"I understand, and you don't have to come if you don't want."

"Well, that's certainly not an option. Last time I let you out on your own, you came back with no teeth. I don't want you losing anything else important. You drive alone, and I'll take Oliver. You going at each other behind the wheel of a car sounds more dangerous than the Davis brothers."

"Okay, I'm just going in to change." Peter threw his rifle into the pickup. "Give me five minutes."

Lillian hadn't seen Louise since hearing the tragic tale about her missing family, and so when she entered her office with Ewan, she looked away. It was all she could do to prevent herself bursting into tears.

"Everything okay?" Louise said.

Lillian forced her gaze onto the lieutenant and forced the sympathy from her mind by quickly getting to the point. "Liam was sent to live with Silas's brother, Paddy Rogers, in Portland."

"Silas's plan was to keep his boy alive," Ewan said. "Liam had a rather large target on his back for killing the Davis livestock."

"But he was just a child. Would the Davis family really have targeted him?" Louise asked.

"Liam would have already turned seventeen. He'd be fair game," Lillian said. "Unfortunately, the brother, Paddy, died a couple of years back, but I just got off the phone with his daughter, Olivia Rogers."

"Good work! Does the daughter know where Liam is?" Louise laid her tense hands flat on the table.

Lillian shook her head. "She was born after Liam left Paddy's residence, so she never met him."

"Shit." Louise lifted her hands. "So, no idea where he went?"

"No. But Olivia talks about Liam's stuff being in their attic. Books about the war and clothing. Fatigues, mainly. Camouflage jackets and trousers. It seems he was fascinated with the army. Everything is still there. He never returned for them."

"Do you think he's dead then?"

"I don't know, but what Olivia said next was really interesting, ma'am." Lillian exchanged a glance with Ewan to check if her bizarre revelation deserved a place in this room.

He nodded.

"Olivia's mother died a couple months after her father, Paddy. Just before she died, Olivia tried her luck at asking about her mysterious uncle one last time and the stuff in the attic. She was used to being told to mind her own business, so she was stunned by the response. Just give them away to charity, she was told. Olivia asked her mother if Liam, the uncle she'd never met, would want them if he ever returned.

She was met with an unexpected answer." Lillian took a deep breath. "'How can he return to a place he's never been?'"

"But his stuff was there," Louise said.

"Yes," Lillian said. "Olivia was confused, so she pressed her mother on that. It turns out that Silas Rogers had simply sent his son's belongings to Paddy's home."

"But I don't understand," Louise said, snorting, "Why was Liam not with his belongings?"

Lillian felt herself growing pale. What she was about to say turned the investigation on its head.

"Lillian?" Louise said, standing up.

"Olivia's mother said Liam had never actually left Blue Falls."

AFTER HIS STUPID brother Mason had left to discuss the ridiculous sale of his property to the Davis brothers over coffee with his lawyer, Liam had twisted free of the rope he'd been bound with.

"How will you silence your critics when you can't even tie a knot properly, brother?"

Truth be told, wriggling free of bondage had not been the easiest task. He was drenched in sweat. He took a long hot shower while he formulated his plan. Despite the itch to get going, he slowly dried himself. From this point until he'd delivered the last blow, he had to be meticulous—like the soldier he was born to be.

Afterward, he examined the wound on his cheek. It wasn't as bad as he'd first suspected, and he protected it with a Band Aid. Then he shaved and used Mason's clippers to give himself a buzz cut. Yes, it was an induction cut, and today wasn't his first initiation into the military world, but God, it felt like it! It had been so long since he'd executed those faggots.

He slipped in his false teeth and smiled at his aging, handsome face. *Never too old, Liam, never too old.*

Patiently, he ironed every crease from his green camouflage military uniform. He slipped it on and tightly laced his black army boots. He armed himself with Mason's Springfield, which was quite small for his liking but would do the job. He didn't wish to rifle through Mason's gun store in case anyone spotted him through the window. He also sheathed a knife on his leg, then hoisted on his backpack, that contained the hammer which had ended those two queers all those decades ago.

He secured a camouflage army cover and headed into the kitchen. He took the keys for Mason's pickup from the hook over the sink and placed his hand on the kitchen door. He turned back to look at his brother's apartment. "This is for you, dear brother." He opened the door. "Always for you."

Liam headed off to war.

17

LILLIAN AND EWAN drove to the Woodhouse farmland which, over thirty years ago, had been owned by Mason's father, Silas Rogers.

As they exited the Audi, Ewan asked, "What do you hope to find here, Lil?"

"I don't know, but we just found out that Liam never left."

While approaching the farmhouse, Lillian looked around at the orderly and trim fields. Having seen the state of the Davis farmyard, she appreciated the pristine acreage more than ever.

They tried the bell, and when there was no answer, they knocked too. Still no answer.

"Shit," Lillian said.

"Exactly," Andy Woodhouse said, coming around the side of his house in dirty fisherman waders. He stopped just short of the officers, looked at his gloves, and smiled. "Won't offer to shake your hands. Been cleaning out the pigs. How are you, Ms. Sanborn?"

"Fine, Mr. Woodhouse, sorry to disturb you. I'm here on police business."

"Unless I'm in trouble for how badly it smells in the pen round there, I couldn't imagine what for."

"It's about the Rogers family."

"Is family the right word?" Andy asked. "Last time I checked, there was only one of them left."

Well, two potentially, Lillian thought. "Did you know Mason had a brother?"

"Yes, of course. Liam. Been a long, long time since someone mentioned that name though. Why do you ask?"

"We're trying to track him down. We thought we'd come to where he started out."

Andy nodded. "Well, you thought correctly."

Lillian felt a rush of blood. "What do you mean, Mr. Woodhouse?"

"Follow me and I'll show you."

THE THREE MEN waited beside the rapid, tumultuous creek at Forest Edge. They were almost half an hour early for the rendezvous with Felicity and her two sons. Such was the nature of the three men, combined with the fact the relationship between two of them was at a breaking point, conversation was at a premium.

Jake surveyed the area. As far as he knew, this was the only way in and out of the Davis property. If Camden and Carson returned earlier than anticipated from the store, they were in serious trouble. Jake stared at the entrance to the dirt track. There'd also be similar problems if cast-off Dom decided to venture out of the farmhouse before Felicity.

"You better have the time right, Oliver," Peter said, gripping the rifle slung over his shoulder.

"I do. It's all I've thought about for days."

Peter looked up from the brook and sideways at Oliver. "You *also* better take good care of her."

"I've never been more serious about anything in my life."

"I hope so. Don't make me regret not killing you after you put me in the hospital, or the Davis brothers will be the least of your worries."

Jake's cellphone rang. He saw that it was Lillian. "Listen, you two, I have to take this. If you end up wrestling in that creek, I'm not coming in to separate you."

Liam couldn't believe it. He blinked and looked through his binoculars again. Yes! He was here for the Davis family, and here was Jake Pettman on a platter. Talk about killing two birds. He moved the binoculars from Jake, who was on his cellphone, to the other two men, who were deep in conversation by the creek. He recognized his brother's best friend, Peter Sheenan, but he couldn't recall meeting the second man. Peter was armed with a rifle. He couldn't tell if Jake or the second man was armed, but it was best to assume they were.

He lowered the binoculars and leaned against his brother's pickup. He'd managed to bring it off the road among a small patch of trees. Unless someone went out their way looking, they wouldn't see him if they drove past.

He formulated his plan of action.

After approaching quietly through the trees, he would break out several yards behind the group. Not only did he have the element of surprise, but he was also a good shot, so it wouldn't be too problematic. He would plug Peter first, then put one in Jake and the other man before they could unholster any concealed weapons.

His heartrate increased; he couldn't wait. He took a deep breath.

Be calm, soldier. Be meticulous, be methodical.

He set off through the forest.

Be effective.

"Liam's gravestone!" Jake said into his cell.

"Yes. Andy led us right into the Rogers' family graveyard," Lillian said. "About three generations worth of them here. Very old school."

"Bloody hell! On his property? How does this Andy feel about that?"

"It's a bit of a trek from the farmhouse, so it's not so much of an eyesore for him and his family. They'd agreed to preserve it when they bought the property. Andy said it was a no-brainer, really. He was in no mind to disturb the dead."

"So, I guess Liam is no longer a suspect."

"He died in seventy-three."

"The year the Davis livestock was poisoned."

"May of seventy-three, Jake. He died a month before the poisoning."

"Wait. That doesn't make sense."

"Tell me about it."

"So, the Rogers family faked his death?"

"It doesn't ring true. If they faked Liam's death to spare him the Davis family retribution, wouldn't they have at least gotten the month right? Unless they were going to argue that it couldn't be him because he'd already passed? But then the Davis clan might have turned their vicious eyes on the younger brother, Mason, which could have been devastating."

"So, not a fake death?"

"Well, a fake death also needs an audience. As far as I know, no one knew he'd died. And the audience it would be meant for, the Davis brothers, still believe he hopped town."

"Which means Liam could actually be right there in the ground?"

"Without digging it up, we can't be a hundred percent, but it seems the most likely of the two options."

"So, if he was already dead when the livestock was poisoned, and the Rogers family lied and said he'd fled, then it kept him as the prime suspect—one who could never be found because he was *actually* dead—then they were obviously desperate to protect someone else."

Jake waited for Lillian's response. It didn't come. His blood ran cold; she was clearly thinking the same thing as him.

Mason.

They'd come full circle.

"You need to contact medical professionals from around that time, Lillian. Someone must know if it's really Liam who is dead and how he died. I'm assuming there was no death certificate?"

"No, there isn't. I've checked. I also discovered that a Dr. Wilbur Hampshire serviced this area in seventy-three. We are on our way to see him."

"Okay."

"Jake."

"Yes?"

"I've just been to Mason's store. He's not there. If it's him, he'll know we're drawing close."

"Making him dangerous."

"Yes."

"I'll look for him. You just get to the truth."

"Be careful."

"You too."

He hung up and marched over to Peter and Oliver.

Peter eyed him. "You have to go, don't you?"

"Yes."

"We got this covered. Our relationship has been blossoming."

Jake nodded. "Are you sure?"

"Positive. You want to tell me what the call was about??"

That the net is closing on your best friend? No. Not really. "Later, Peter." Jake jogged to his vehicle.

WHEN LIAM REACHED the edge of the woodland, he heard the roar of an engine and saw the glint of the departing vehicle through the tree leaves. He peered out the woodland and saw that Jake had left. Wallowing in disappointment was not the place of the motivated and vigilant soldier, so he shrugged it off and stepped from the woodland with Mason's Springfield raised.

Both Peter and his companion faced away from him. He hated to shoot someone in the back, but where the enemy was concerned, principles were best sacrificed.

He shot Peter's companion in the back of the neck.

The young man jolted forward, spun, displaying wide, confused and *dying* eyes, and disappeared into the creek.

"Put down the rifle, Peter," Liam said.

Peter continued to face away and didn't move. "Mason?"

"Last warning, Peter."

"Mason, is that you?"

Liam shot into the air.

Peter flinched. "Okay, okay." He knelt, laid the rifle on the ground, and stood.

"Now turn and look at me."

Peter turned slowly with his hands in the air. He looked completely baffled. He had blood dripping down his face where it had surely sprung free from the young man's wound. "Mason, what are you doing? What are you *wearing?*"

"I'm not Mason," Liam said.

"I don't understand."

"I'm not Mason; I'm Liam!" He raised the gun and aimed it at Peter's heart.

"Okay, okay. I understand. But tell me, please, why're you doing this?"

"Because you're in the way. I'm here to put an end to the Davis family, and you made the mistake of crossing my path."

"No, I—"

Liam shot Peter three times in the chest.

The old man tumbled backward into the creek, and Liam was filled with mixed emotions.

He was anxious about telling his brother he'd had to kill his best friend but, at the same time, was ecstatic over the accuracy of his shooting.

Dr. Wilbur Hampshire was out back, tending to his butterfly garden, when Lillian and Ewan arrived. The doctor's wife took the visitors to him.

He closed the gate behind him to stop his precious specimens from escaping and joined the two officers on his back porch. He spoke as he climbed the steps. "One of my favorite poets, Maya Angelou, wrote: *'We delight in the beauty of the butterfly, but rarely admit the changes it has gone through to achieve that beauty.'* Throughout my career, I saw many people heal but only after they went through dark trials of solitude and pain. The butterflies remind me of what is possible."

"Why did you ask us here?" Lillian started. "Why couldn't you just speak to us on the phone?"

"Because sometimes beauty is not achieved, and, in those instances, a phone call will not do justice to those concerned. Would you like a drink?"

"No, sir," Ewan said. "We just want to know about Liam Rogers."

Wilbur removed his hat and sat on a chair. He fanned himself with the hat, and beads of sweat ran down his forehead. "I remember seeing Liam Rogers on the day his first tooth fell out. Poor boy. He was in his back garden, playing with his toy soldiers. Such an excitable and happy young man, full of vigor. He had leukaemia, and we first spotted it through a bad case of gingivitis. The gums swell and bleed, and patients can lose teeth. This poor boy lost quite a few before it was through with him." He sighed and fanned himself again. "And I never saw another person so affected by the deterioration of another than his younger brother, Mason Rogers."

Lillian sat on the chair beside him and sighed. "It was Mason who poisoned the Davis livestock, wasn't it?"

Still fanning himself, Wilbur said, "You have to understand that Mason was not a well boy to begin with. He suffered from schizophrenia. We treated him as best we could, but his case was very severe. A few days after Liam's death, Mason did what you just described. I remember asking him why. He told me it was because the Davis brothers, Cam and Dom, had been bullying his dying brother at school, and *voices* had instructed him to take revenge this way. It sounded reasonable and in line with his condition, but it was only after the bullying was queried at school that it turned out that it wasn't Liam who was bullied after all. It was Mason." Wilbur sounded hoarse. He coughed and paused for a drink.

Lillian grew impatient. "So, Mason took revenge on behalf of himself rather than Liam?"

Wilbur shook his head. "No. It would be reasonable to assume that, but the more I spoke to Mason over the next couple days, the more I realized this wasn't the case."

"I don't understand."

"Mason had *fractured*, Lillian." He stared hard at her. "I recognized Liam while I was talking to Mason. Mason's defense mechanism to his brother's death was dissociative identity disorder."

"Multiple personalities," Ewan said.

Wilbur nodded. "Mason was one very traumatized boy. After I'd worked out that he'd split in two, I questioned him on it. Mason responded as Liam. He admitted to poisoning the livestock. I remember Mason staring into my eyes and saying, as if he were actually Liam, 'I protect my brother, whatever the cost.'"

"So, you supported Silas Rogers in his lie that Liam was responsible for the poisoning and that he'd been sent away into hiding?" Lillian asked.

Wilbur nodded. "I did. And I'd do it again. Mason was a good boy. He was suffering enough. Would we really want to add the Davis family to his troubles? Tragically, Liam was gone. The Davis brothers couldn't harm him, so to pretend it was him seemed like the most sensible option."

"But he was dead!" Lillian said. "Where was the death certificate?"

Wilbur looked down. "I never submitted one."

"Why not just say Liam died just after the poisoning?" Ewan asked. "Change the date on his gravestone. Same thing, surely?"

Wilbur shook his head. "We considered it, but it just felt too risky. Liam wouldn't have had the energy to do what he did to the Davis animals in the final stages of his illness. And someone would question it. And, if we said he'd died in another way—an accident, for example—that would have just brought unwelcome attention from others. Even an autopsy, perhaps? It just seemed tidier at the time."

"You didn't think of coming forward with any of this when Collette Jewell vanished?" Ewan asked.

"Why?"

"Because Mason Rogers is a dangerous individual, and you *knew* that."

"I never said he was dangerous."

"How can he not be?" Ewan asked.

"Up until I retired, I treated Mason Rogers for both schizophrenia and dissociative identity disorder. Mason would go through periods of seeing and interacting with Liam, which was a result of the schizophrenia. Then, when the stress became too much, he would switch personalities and become him. But I know Mason, and I know Mason's version of Liam. I know them both very well. Mason wouldn't hurt a fly. Liam is edgier. Yeah, sure, he can be hot-headed, but he adores Mason, and unless his brother is under threat, I doubt he would lift a finger. The murder of a fourteen-year-old girl is not something that would have my alarm bells ringing. Why would I subject my patient to unnecessary stress? I only have to report him if they admit to planning or committing a crime."

"How about the murder of Bobby White and Henry Clark in seventy-five?"

"Again, they were his friends. Mason was distraught, and he never suggested that he, acting as his brother, had anything to do with it."

Ewan stepped forward. "So, when you talked about butterflies, Doctor, you said this was one instance in which beauty was never realized. What did you mean?"

"Exactly what I said, really. I could never really guide Mason to the respite he so deserved. He grew more bitter as he aged, and him and his version of Liam would argue even more. When I retired, I know he stopped seeking medical help. It pains me that he never became that butterfly I so desperately wanted him to become."

"What did they argue about?"

"The Davis family. Liam became more frustrated with Mason over his inability to stand up to them. Camden's and Dominic's treatment of Mason during the first Collette Jewell investigation was atrocious. Mason even told me that one of the two men had raped his wife. She refused to go to the police, so neither of the brothers faced justice. Liam—or, at least, Mason's version of Liam—became more exasperated."

"So, do you think Liam ... sorry, Mason would ever move on the Davis brothers?"

Wilbur shrugged. "I always doubted it. You'd have to be suicidal, wouldn't you?"

"And what if you did become suicidal? What if you'd had enough and decided to close up shop? What then?"

Wilbur looked away. "I don't know. I haven't spoken to Mason in a long, long time."

Ewan took another step forward and stood over Wilbur. "Did Mason, or Liam, ever threaten to hurt the Davis brothers?"

Wilbur looked away.

"That would count as planning a crime, making it your duty," Ewan said.

"I never believed he would actually do anything."

"I hope you're right, Doctor," Lillian said. "I sincerely hope you are."

18

CAM AND HIS lawyer stood outside Mason's store, staring at the Closed sign on the door.

Cam checked his watch. "Well, this is the only meeting I've ever been on time for."

The lawyer, Bryce Middleton, smirked. "The least you can do when someone is giving you their livelihood."

Cam pulled a packet of cigarettes from his pocket. "So, where the fuck is he?" He took out a cigarette and offered one to Bryce, who tore off the filter and put it in his mouth.

After Cam had lit both the cigarettes, he tried the handle. The door glided open. "Guess he wants us to come in." He took a puff on his cigarette, threw it on the ground, and stamped on it. He winked at the lawyer. "No smoking in my shop."

The lawyer took a long, greedy drag on his filter-less cigarette, threw it down, and followed Cam into the shop.

At the end of the aisle, they banged on the apartment door and waited. "For fuck's sake," Cam said. He tried this handle too and also found it unlocked.

They walked through into the lounge. The air smelled

of sweat. Cam scanned the room at the piles of dirty clothing and old magazines. "Going to have to tidy up this place before I move in."

"Tidy like your home?" Bryce said.

Cam laughed. "No. This little place here will be mine. Time for a change." He straightened his back and listened to it crack. "Blue Falls number one businessman has a reputation to uphold." He wandered around the room and knelt to grab a long rope by the television. It had a knot in one end. He let it dangle to the floor. "Maybe the bastard was finally planning to hang himself." He snorted. "Well, he can sign the fucking documents first." He threw the rope on the floor.

"One problem," Bryce said.

"Oh, and what's that?"

"He's not fucking here."

Cam sat on the sofa. "He will be."

AFTER FINISHING his phone call to Lillian, Jake exited the car, marched up the driveway, and pounded on the door.

Gabriel looked edgy when he answered. His top lip was trembling, and his eyes were darting back and forth too quickly. Jake was yet to see the chief of police display any fear, so he doubted it was that.

"What's wrong with you?" Jake asked.

"Drank a bottle of whisky last night."

"That'll do it."

"Why are you on my fucking doorstep?"

"Pains me to say it, but I want your help."

"Want or need?"

"Let's keep it at *want* for the moment. I don't want you having delusions of grandeur."

"What's it to do with?"

"Mason Rogers."

Gabriel took a sharp intake of breath through his nose. "Well, you've come to the wrong place. I'm off that case."

"That's precisely why I came to you. Not sure those who have commandeered your department want an outsider poking around."

"Funny that. Neither do I, really."

"Guess I'll go elsewhere," Jake said, turning.

"Okay. What do you know?"

Jake turned back. "Listen, I don't want you flying off the handle. I just need your help to find him. You've spent a huge chunk of your life obsessing over him, so I guess it won't take long."

"So, tell me what you know!"

"Once you assure me that we are simply finding him and handing him into the station before any damage is done."

"Jesus! I assure you! Don't you think I want this done with too?"

Jake told him what he knew about Mason and his condition. He watched the information sink into Gabriel. He pressed his fist to his mouth, and his eyes darted back and forth.

"So, we're simply finding him and getting him off the street."

"Off the street like we got Jotham off the street?" Gabriel asked.

Jake wasn't sure if he was being sarcastic or serious. "Nothing like that. The man is ill. We deliver him, and the truth will quickly follow. You must remember, Gabriel, that we still don't know if he's responsible, and if we take the law into our hands, it won't wash this time—not with the state police on your doorstep."

"I understand. Let me get my rifle."

"Jesus. I knew this was a fucking mistake."

Gabriel stepped out and closed the door behind him. "Pipe down. I was joking. Shall I follow you?"

"No, we'll go in my car."

Gabriel turned to lock the door, accidentally dropping his keys. "Shit," he said, swooping for them.

"Are you sure you're all right?"

"Never been better."

Owen shuffled the cards.

"Much better, honey," Felicity said.

Owen offered his mother a card.

She chose a jack of diamonds, stole a quick look, then placed it at the bottom of the pack.

Owen cut the cards, looked through them, then removed the jack of diamonds.

Felicity resisted the urge to stroke his waxed hair and disrupt his immaculate quiff and clapped instead. "Bravo."

"So fucking lame," Brady said.

Felicity glared at him.

"He knows the card you put it next to," Brady said.

"Go to your room and get your bag," Felicity said.

Brady shrugged and disappeared upstairs.

She watched Owen shuffle again; if his brother's comment had hurt his feelings, it wasn't clear in his expression. Still, no emotion was ever clear in her son's expression.

She listened to Dom's loud snoring. There was no danger of him waking. She spied his coffee cup on the table. An elephant would struggle to move after the dose she had administered. She eyed the bags by the front door and checked her watch.

Ten minutes until their life would change forever.

LIAM LEFT his car at the entrance to the Davis land and, buoyed and energized over his first two kills of the day, moved far quicker than any old man had business doing through the junkyard. He weaved skilfully past the old vehicles, occasionally ducking and surveying the farmhouse to ensure his approach was going undetected.

Dominic Davis was a stupid man, but stupid men were often more dangerous than intelligent ones, and being a soldier, Liam was not about to underestimate any enemy.

When he reached the bottom of the porch steps, his heart thumped. Going undetected had left him ecstatic.

Steady yourself, soldier.

He closed his eyes and recalled the moment he had beaten those two faggots to death with a hammer. He'd been calm and ruthless in the execution. There was nothing wrong with enjoying it, but too much emotion can unsteady even the strongest soldier.

He opened his eyes, took the hammer from his backpack, and climbed the steps to the porch.

BRADY CAME DOWNSTAIRS with a duffel bag. He put it on the floor with the others and regarded Felicity with tears in his eyes. He turned to Owen and put his arms around him. "I'm sorry, O. It was a great trick."

Felicity felt tears in her own eyes. She put her hands on Brady's shoulders. "I'm proud of you both, I really am, and I'm so sorry for everything I've put you through."

A knock sounded at the door.

Her blood ran cold.

"Upstairs!" She pushed her children toward them.

Another knock. More insistent this time.

She waited until her children were on the first step before turning to face the front door. She looked through the spyhole.

An empty porch.

She secured the chain across the door, then partially opened it. "Hello?"

No answer.

Who the hell was it? Cam and Carson back early? No. They wouldn't play games.

It must be Oliver. He must have gotten spooked, waiting at the creek, and had just come all the way in to get them. She slid back the security chain and opened the door. "Oliver?"

She felt a hand on her back. It almost made her jump out of her skin. She looked back and saw Owen. "I said *upstairs*, honey."

Owen didn't move.

She sighed and stepped onto the porch.

An older, wiry man stood to her left in an army uniform. He was wearing a cover, so it took a moment to recognize him.

"Mr. Rogers?" When she glimpsed the hammer in his hand, it was already arcing through the air. Her collar bone cracked. She thought of the night before when Cam had dropped that glass. Wanting to cry out, her mouth fell open, but everything was too fast and painful.

The next blow hit her chest, and she felt a rib shatter. She dropped to her knees, screaming, and lifted her head in time to see Mason raising the hammer.

Owen stepped in front of her.

No! She reached for him.

Owen's head snapped to the side when the hammer hit him in the face.

She beheld the profile of her baby's beautiful face as he coughed and spat fragments of teeth. *NO!* She looped her arms around Owen's waist and tugged him backward from Mason.

The bastard managed to swing again.

Owen's head jolted down this time. The monster had caught him on the top of his head. He fell backward onto her.

She took his weight, then let him roll to the side. "Please ... Please, don't hurt my boy." Felicity lay on her back. She looked sideways at her coughing son, who was clutching his mouth and making a horrendous noise.

"Hurt. That's all you've ever done. Your family," Mason said, "Hurt, hurt, and hurt."

She looked back.

He was smiling. He wasn't going to stop. He was enjoying himself too much. He lifted his foot and stamped on Owen's stomach four times.

Her boy's hands fell away from his mouth. Blood and broken teeth speckled his cheeks.

She tried to lift her arm to grab at him, but a shattered collar bone and rib restricted her movement, and her hand flailed uselessly.

Mason knelt beside her son with the hammer raised

above his head. He brought it down with great force, and she heard his face being smashed.

She closed her eyes. *No, no, no ... This can't be real.* She heard the hammer come again and again and felt Owen's warm blood on his face. "Stop ..." She opened her eyes at the soldier.

He looked like a man possessed, swinging and swinging, most of his face and uniform red with blood.

She heard the crunching of tires. "Help ..." Her head fell to the side, and she saw her husband's car stopping beside the chicken coop. "Help ..."

Carson, the man she'd been planning to leave for a better life, was now her only hope of continuing one. He was out of the car, charging toward the house. "Felicity! Mason, *leave my family alone!*"

Her head burned as Mason's fingers tightened around her hair. She felt herself being dragged through the door. She caught a glimpse at the remains of her beautiful baby's face, and, as the bastard slammed the door after them, she wished for her own death.

CARSON LOOKED at Owen and howled. He tried to steady himself against the wall, but it did no good. He started slipping to his knees. *Felicity ... Brady ...*

They could still be alive. He straightened upright and reached for the doorhandle. Locked. His car keys and house keys hung from a chain on his belt. He thrust the key into the lock and burst through the front door. He saw the pile of bags. He had no time to consider the significance.

A blood trail stained the floor where Felicity had been dragged. It arched around to the kitchen sink. Here Mason stood, his face streaked with blood, presumably Carson's son's. His army uniform also glistened red.

On her knees, before him, Felicity, also covered in blood, trembled and wept.

Carson looked around, desperate for something to attack with. He remembered the knife rack which was nearer to where he stood than Mason. He darted toward it, slipped free a knife, and turned to face them.

"Beat you to it," Mason said, holding up a long kitchen knife and smirking. He pulled back hard on Felicity's hair.

"Please, no!"

Mason cut Felicity's throat. There was a hiss of arterial blood.

Carson charged with the knife raised. He didn't let the sight of Mason raising his gun slow him.

LIAM SHOT CARSON DEAD CENTER. It was comical to watch the worm claw at the hole in his chest as he leaned against the fridge. It was even more comical to watch him die on his feet, then fall face forward. Liam smiled. Carson had been a pleasant surprise. He'd assumed he'd still be manning the store at this time. Now he wouldn't need to take a short detour to kill him later, saving him time and providing him with some comic relief.

He noticed Felicity twitching. He kicked her out of his way, unconcerned about wetting his feet on the pool of blood growing around her. He was already covered in it from that little Davis bastard anyway.

Three down, three to go.

He checked his watch. Cam would already be at Mason's store, eager to get his grubby paws on everything his naïve brother had spent his life working toward, which left the fat child, Brady, and the even fatter old man, Dominic, primed for slaughter.

He paused and listened. He heard snoring from the other room. He noticed the bags at the door and recalled Peter and the young man at the creek. *My, oh, my!* He smiled at Felicity's body. "You were planning on leaving! In fairness, that does take some guts. In a way, that makes me kind of sorry I killed you. Saying that, I've probably saved you a whole heap of trouble. Your father-in-law, Cam, is a sonofabitch. He'd have hunted you down, and it would have got messy. Maybe not *this* messy, but messy all the same."

He left the kitchen for the living room. He strolled toward the sprawled-out fat man on the sofa. "Jesus. What did she drug you with? You're practically grey!" He smiled. "I could sit here and wait for you to wake, Dom. Explain to you what I'm doing, but then, is there any point? You were always thick as fuck, and it's your brother who really knew what was going on."

He shot Dom in the head, and the snoring stopped.

Now Brady.

He returned to the kitchen, spied the front door, and toyed with the idea of going back for his trusty hammer. Part of him had really enjoyed opening the mute boy's face like a melon. Yes, this sounded coarse, but he was a soldier! There was nothing wrong with taking pleasure in your work.

Deciding time was of the essence, he left the hammer and took the stairs two at a time. Again, not bad for an old man. In fact, he felt fitter than he'd been in years. God bless adrenaline.

It was a big house, and the hallway at the top was long.

Several closed doors ran down its side. He held his breath, which was a little tricky after his exertions, and listened.

Nothing.

He worked partway down the hallway, paused, and listened.

Still nothing.

He reached the door at the end, and, keeping hold of the patience that had served him well in his mission so far, he paused to listen again.

A shuffling sound came from within.

He reached for the handle.

Wincing and clutching a rib that was either broken or badly bruised, Peter eased himself into the driver's seat and propped his rifle against the passenger seat. He glanced at the creek, where the corpse of Oliver Sholes was floating. After closing the door, he squeezed his eyes shut and yelled with pain. Peeling off that bulletproof vest when he'd woken had taken every ounce of his willpower and strength, but now he had to find more.

Lives depended on it.

As he started the engine, he thanked his lucky stars. Yes, the pain was excruciating, but venturing into his house and slipping on his vest had been a masterstroke. If he hadn't, he'd be dancing off downstream with Oliver.

He sped down the dirt road at a speed his pickup had not seen in years, and, as he drove, tears streamed down his face. Not because of his rib but because the truth about his best friend was the greatest wound of them all.

FIRE IN BONE

Liam grinned when he saw the terror on Brady's face. He'd been crying hard, and his face was covered in snot and tears. Behind Brady, the bathroom window was tilted open. Liam laughed. The fat lump had clearly been trying to slide himself through the small gap the tilting window allowed.

Brady pointed an air pistol at Liam. "Stay back."

This made Liam laugh harder. "Really?"

"Yes, I'll shoot you."

"I can handle a pea-shooter. If you don't believe me, go downstairs and see what I've done to your family."

Brady flinched. "I'm a good shot. I'll take out your eye."

Like the rest of the house, the bathroom was large, and Liam doubted the plump little fucker was that good. Liam lifted his gun. "I don't need to aim for your eye."

Brady fired.

Liam listened to the pellet bury itself into the doorframe around him. "You said you were a good shot."

Brady cried. "Please."

"Tell you what." Liam lowered the gun. "To show you that I'm not all bad. I'll give you one more pop."

Brady took the cue to reload.

"But if you miss again, it really is game over. I've no more time left to play. By the way, game over is when I put one in your forehead. Deal?"

Brady didn't bother responding. He lifted the gun and, this time, didn't miss.

No time for stealth. Peter approached the farmhouse at such a velocity that he glanced a vehicle by the chicken coop. Then, he had to hit the brakes and turn the pickup sharply to stop himself from plowing into the farmhouse.

He felt his wheels leave the ground and, for one cold second, thought the whole vehicle might turn over. Instead, it juddered sideways for a moment before crashing into the side of the raised porch. He knocked his head against the glass and heard wood splinter, but the porch didn't crash down. It did seal off his exit though, and he'd have to go through the passenger side.

He stole a glance at the porch, and his breath caught in his throat. At the front door. Flesh and blood. He was too late.

There was an almighty crash, and the windshield exploded. Peter felt as if he'd just hit a brick wall at full speed. "Jesus ..."

Brady Davis was twisted up on the car's hood. His contorted face was turned toward Peter through the wreckage of the windshield. The poor boy wheezed, and blood oozed from the sides of his mouth.

Peter reached out and touched his cheek. "Just lie still."

Brady's wheezing became a gargle, which quickly faded to nothing, then his eyes rolled back.

Peter watched the boy's bloody twitching arm that hung in the vehicle. Peter leaned forward and looked upward to see the window Brady had been thrown through hung loose.

Mason stood there, looking down, holding his weapon.

Then the shooting began.

After Liam had unloaded his clip into Peter's pickup, he paused to look in the bathroom mirror and examine the pellet wound in the corner of his eye. *The boy hadn't been lying! He was a good shot.* A millimeter to the right and he could have lost an eye.

He headed down the hallway and the stairs, noticing a light spring in his step. *And why not?* This had been the first time he'd been at the center of a massacre after all! He stepped over the mute boy he'd smashed into pieces and walked to the porch so he could draw level with the driver's side of the vehicle. He raised his gun as he approached. He'd pumped it with a lot of lead, but it was better to be cautious.

He saw Brady's broken body on the hood of the pickup, but there was no sign of Peter in the driver's seat. Liam smiled. "How many lives do you have, little kitty?" He turned quickly with his gun at the high ready in case Peter had decided to creep up on him.

Nothing.

He laughed and called out over the farmyard, "Come on now, Peter! There can't be a great deal left of you. Step out from wherever you are and let me put you out of your misery." He scanned the chicken coops and the surrounding wrecked cars.

Nothing.

"Fuck it. You bleed out somewhere. I've got bigger fish to fry."

Liam eyed the pickup; it would be handy in getting him to his own vehicle by the forest. There he would disable this vehicle so Peter would have to go on foot. If, by some miracle, he hadn't already bled to death and could make it all the way to the creek! Stalling Peter would give him enough time to finish his plans.

He entered through the passenger side, brushing glass off the seat, and was happy to see the keys in the ignition. He was also happy to see Peter's cellphone on the seat. The dying man wouldn't be able to call for assistance. The opening in the windshield was big enough for Liam to see out of. He lifted Brady's arm out of the vehicle and tucked it around the remains of the windshield. "Sorry, son, but I've got enough blood on me."

And he really did; he was covered, but he kind of liked it. He really did feel as if he was in the heart of battle. And one that was still beating!

He moved the pickup forward, working it gradually from the porch, and then turned left. He accelerated before he reached Carson's car and smiled as he relived the moment he had opened a hole in that imbecile's chest.

The passenger seat window exploded. Liam swerved. The boy on his hood hit the ground with a thump. Liam blinked and smiled. "You missed!" He heard a thunk as the next bullet hit the side of the pickup. Liam punched the accelerator and kept his head low.

He heard the continuous popping of the rifle as he put distance between himself and that stubborn old bastard.

Part of Liam wanted to go back and teach him a lesson, use up the last of kitty's nine lives. But he'd spent more than enough time already, and he still had others to kill. Starting with the final Davis.

But that shouldn't take too long. All it needed was a phone call.

19

"LISTEN," JAKE SAID as he parked several doors back from the Rogers general store. "Lillian's been here already, but I want to double check he's not returned. This is to be *gentle*, Gabriel. If Mason is here, we shut him down and drop him at the station. They can take it from there."

Gabriel was chewing hard on gum. "I don't understand what's going on between you and Lillian. Never really have."

"It's a friendship. I know you're short on them, but they do exist."

"Still, why get yourself mixed up in all of this if you're supposed to be laying low?" Gabriel stared at Jake. "You know you're going to bring the wolves to your door, don't you?"

Jake sighed. "I respect her. She's good police, and she doesn't get a great deal of support from her own colleagues. I'm just helping her along. She reminds me of someone back home, someone who would never give up."

"You're bored. That's all this is. But know that your

boredom will get you killed. I'm assuming you ran with money in your pocket? I never understand why men such as yourself don't quit while the going's good."

The going hasn't been good for a very long time, Jake thought.

"Anyway, let's go," Gabriel said.

"No. That's not how it works. If he's there, I don't want him aware anything is going on. I'll talk to him about guns, like last time I was here, and then cuff him when he's unaware. You're only here in case something goes wrong."

Gabriel laughed. "So, I only go in if you don't come out?"

Jake nodded.

"With my rifle at home?"

Jake nodded again.

"Sounds like a suicide mission."

"Take it or leave it."

"Everyone this soft back in England?"

Jake smirked. *You wouldn't cope with the things I've seen, Gabriel.* "Anyway, I can handle it. I won't spook him."

"And if I do come in and have to save your ass? What then? You want me to throw rotten tomatoes at him?"

"You'll think of something," Jake said, opening the door. *Men like you always do.*

"You think you're better than me, but we're no different."

"The only thing we share," Jake said, stepping from the car, "is the air."

Cam's cellphone rang. He slipped it from his pocket and raised his eyebrows at his lawyer.

"Are we about to get stood up?" Bryce said.

"People, on the whole, don't stand me up." He answered his cell. "Yes?"

"A riddle. A place, once so alive, dead, awash with blood. Where am I?"

"Mason?"

"Close but no cigar. I'm Liam. So, the answer to my riddle?"

Cam stood from Mason's sofa. "Liam? I'm at your brother's shop. Where's Mason? In fact, where the fuck are you?"

"At your place, well, at least I was. Dead people aren't the best company, so I left."

Cam narrowed his eyes. "What're you talking about?"

"You're all alone in the world now, Cam. *All alone.* I wanted to give you a taste of how Mason has felt for so long."

Cam paced. "You're a lying, cowardly little shit."

"Cowardly?"

"You ran after what you did to my family. And you hid, like a rat in a sewer. And now you call me with this bullshit? When I see you, Liam, I'm going to pull your lying tongue from your head."

Bryce reached to the coffee table for a cigarette, ripped off the filter, and tucked it between his grinning lips.

"Really?" Liam asked. "Listen carefully. I smashed in your mute grandson's face with a hammer and shot your son in the chest. He died looking me in the eyes. It felt good. Before I shot your imbecile brother in the head, I did spare him the realization that it was over because your son's wife had drugged him. Yes, I know! She had the bags packed and was going to run on you. Wow, you really know how to keep house, Cam."

Cam swallowed. The story sounded elaborate. Too elaborate. In his experience, elaborate was often the hallmark of truth. His blood ran cold. "Where's Felicity?"

"I slit her throat."

"Bullshit."

"Then I threw your grandson out a window. He did manage to shoot me in the corner of the eye with a fucking air pistol though."

"No!" Cam kicked over the coffee table. "*No!*" Cam paced the room, rubbing his forehead. *Maybe the bastard had just seen Brady shooting his air pistol in the woods?*

Bryce was on his feet now, his hands in front of him.

Cam turned his back to him, ignoring his attempts to calm him.

"It sounds like you're starting to believe me now. So, shall we try the riddle again? A place, once so alive—"

"I'm going to flay the flesh from your fucking bones!"

"Dead, awash with blood. Where am I?"

Cam kicked the overturned coffee table again and again. A leg came loose and crashed into the television set. "Where *are* you? Where the *fuck* are you?"

"I'll give you a clue. Despite being dead and awash with blood, it's not your farmhouse. It's somewhere else entirely."

"If you've hurt my family, I will torture you. *Endlessly.* I will take pieces from you."

"The answer to my riddle is closer than you think. A cabinet sits above the television, Cam. Open it for the truth. Open it to discover the dead place awash with blood. I am close, and I will come closer if you do. This ends tonight, and you still have a part to play."

The cellphone went dead. Cam looked at his phone with the intention of calling back, but the prick had withheld his number. He looked at Bryce. "He says he's killed my family." His lips trembled.

"Yes, I could tell. You need to stay calm. It won't be true."

"It is. He knew about my grandson's air pistol. He *knew*."

"Still, that's not enough. He could have picked up that information anywhere. Besides, why would he do what he's saying?"

"Revenge. Revenge for the way we've treated his brother."

"It's too extreme. I don't believe it."

"That boy, Liam, he was insane. I wished him alive so I could kill him. Can you believe that? I wished him alive?" He noticed the cabinet above the television and stepped forward.

"What're you doing?"

"He said the answer was in that cabinet."

"Answer to what?"

"To his fucking riddle. Something about a dead place, awash with blood."

"Leave it closed, then."

"No. I have to know."

"Know what? It sounds threatening. Let's leave—"

Cam gripped the handle.

"I don't advise this," Bryce said, putting his hand on his shoulder.

"My family. He says he killed my family. I have to know." He opened the cabinet.

When Jake heard the explosion, he fell to his knees and relived that moment in Salisbury when he had seen fragments of metal and glass raining on the road beside an erupting car while a broken, *innocent* boy convulsed near the wreckage. *And it's my fault. I've been working for the bastards who did this, who took the life of a child.*

Snapping back to the present, Jake watched the plume of smoke rising from behind the general store. The glass on the front of the store had smashed, but the explosion hadn't completely decimated the shop. Ground zero had clearly been in the apartment bolted onto the rear.

Fortunately, Jake had only just exited his vehicle when the explosion occurred and was still a considerable distance from the shop. Apart from the ringing in his ears, he felt unscathed. He sprinted to the car from which Gabriel had already emerged and was staring wide-eyed at the growing smoke cloud.

"Is that it?" Gabriel asked. "After all this time, after everything he did to me and my family, he dies in a *fucking* gas explosion?"

"We don't know if he was in there, and we don't know if it was a gas explosion."

Gabriel shut the door. "So, we take a look?"

"If you do, it may be the last thing you do as an officer of the law. We leave. And we leave *now*. Emergency services will be here any second. We have no business being here right now."

"I'm the chief of fucking police!" He thumped his chest.

"You've been asked to step aside. Their next step will be suspension!"

"Is it not the same *fucking* thing?"

"Get in the car, Gabriel."

Gabriel bashed his fist off the car roof, climbed into the vehicle, and slammed the door shut. The Ford shook.

Jake sighed. Since renting this car, it'd been everyone's punching bag. He was dreading the day he had to return it.

MINUTES AFTER THE EXPLOSION, Liam drove into the Blue Falls Motel parking lot. He stopped the car and spent some time examining himself in the rear-view mirror. The blood of his victims had dried in the creases in his forehead and around his eyes. He wasn't about to wipe it off, for he had the look of someone who'd been in the heart of battle.

He reached to the passenger seat for his gun. Only two bullets left and *still* two birds were flying free—Jake and Gabriel. So he holstered the gun and reached for his bloody hammer. It would be best to try to conserve the bullets for Gabriel—a man who would be surely armed.

He stepped from the vehicle and moved quickly, unconcerned on this second visit about the camera mounted high on the motel walls; if it was in operation, what the hell did it matter? He was on the verge of ridding his brother of any worries, and there was no better swansong to aspire to. He would happily fall in the throes of victory. Nothing was more noble.

He pinned himself to the wall beside the motel door and spent a moment hypnotized by the smoke cloud rising over Main Street. He turned, knocked on the door, then turned back against the wall.

The door opened. "Hello?" *Not Jake.* A woman's voice.

He flipped around the open door and watched Piper's eyes widen, then he punched her hard in the mouth.

She stumbled backward, clutching her face, and fell onto the bed in the center of the room.

He entered, closed the door behind him, and locked it. He turned to see her scurrying backward on the bed with her hand still to her mouth. "Stop!" He pointed to the gun dangling from the holster on his belt.

She obeyed. She took her hands from her face. Blood ran from her lip. "Mr. Rogers? I don't understand."

"I'm not here for you, Ms. Goodwin. You yourself have never harmed my family. So, if you answer my question, I will leave you be. Some ice on that split lip will see you fine again in next to no time." He stepped forward, twirling the bloody hammer in his hand. "So, *just* one question, and then you live, Ms. Goodwin. Is that to your satisfaction?"

She nodded.

He took another step so his legs pinned hers to where they hung over the side of the bed. He switched his bloody weapon to the other hand. "But if you lie to me, I'll use this hammer to bash in your brains. Do you understand?"

She gagged and clutched her mouth again.

He transferred the hammer back to the other hand. "Do you understand, Ms. Goodwin?"

Clutching her mouth, she nodded hard. Tears streamed down the side of her face.

"Good. Now, where is Jake Pettman?"

Her knuckles glowed as she clutched tighter still to her mouth.

"I can't hear, Ms. Goodwin. Take your hands away."

She dropped her hands. Her words trembled and came out as little more than a whisper. "I don't know."

He took a sharp intake of breath, glanced to his side, and exhaled in a long sigh.

"I really don't!"

He looked at her, shook his head, and rose the hammer above his head.

Her eyes widened. "Please, I don't—"

He smashed her shoulder.

LILLIAN AND EWAN were on their way to the remains of Mason's store when her cellphone buzzed from an unknown number. "Officer Sanborn here."

"Hello, it's Wilbur here. I'm sorry to disturb you."

"No bother, Dr. Hampshire. How can I help?"

Ewan mouthed, *Who is it?*

She put her hand over the mouthpiece. "The butterfly doctor."

Ewan smiled.

"Something else came to mind after you left. It may be nothing, but I thought—"

"Go on."

"Well, it's something I shouldn't really be divulging, because it was told to me in confidence, but I feel it's the least I can do now. I feel I need to be making amends of some kind; besides, it probably won't be of use to you."

Lillian eyed Ewan, rolling her hand in the air to gesture how slow the man was in getting to the point.

"Well, it's just ... Mason Rogers had an affair. It was a long, long time ago now and so, like I said, probably isn't relevant, but there it is. Back in eighty-nine. Lasted a year or two I believe—"

Lillian lost patience. "Who, Doctor? Who did he have an affair with?"

After he said the name, she looked at Ewan with wide eyes. If Lillian had made a list of all the women in Blue

Falls that Mason could have had an affair with, this one would have featured very near the bottom.

Liam had expected Piper to scream. He'd not expected the fight back, however.

The bitch had got lucky, grabbed a plate resting on the bedside table, and struck him across the head.

He stumbled backward a step and freed her.

Seizing her opportunity, she yanked her legs backward and buried her feet into his stomach.

He slammed backward into the locked front door and doubled over. His vision blurred; she'd obviously opened the wound from the air pistol on his eye. He wiped his face with his sleeve; it stung to hell, but it helped clear his sight. "No way out for you now, Ms. Goodwin." He rose to his feet.

Piper rolled free of the bed, found her feet, and, clutching her shoulder while her other arm hung limply at her side, disappeared into the bathroom.

Liam heard the door slam, followed by the clunk of the bolt. He moved quickly; there might be a window in the bathroom big enough for her to climb through. When he kicked the door, his black army boots gave him a fair bit of force. However, the lock didn't burst, and the door remained firm, suggesting she was standing behind it, forcing it closed. "What now, Ms. Goodwin?"

"I call the police."

He glanced at her cellphone on the bedside table and smiled. "I think they'll be too busy for a while. I assume you heard the explosion? It'll take them a fair old while to piece Cam Davis back together again! Shall we try this again? Tell me where your boyfriend is, and I'll walk away."

"Fuck you."

"Ms. Goodwin." He slammed his fist into the door. "Or, Ms. MacLeoid, perhaps?" He paused for a response. He didn't get one. *Bullseye.* "A little birdie told me that you're Jotham MacLeoid's daughter, given away for adoption?"

Silence.

He smiled. "What Peter told my brother is true, then?"

"Police? Yes, there's an intruder in my motel room—"

Liam laughed. "Cut the bullshit, Ms. MacLeoid. Your cellphone is out here."

Silence again.

"You know I'm disappointed. I would have expected more from a MacLeoid. They had the whole town quaking in their fucking boots. Enough is enough. I'd move away from the door if I were you." He buried the claw of the hammer into the door and yanked a chunk of wood from it. He hit it again and again. After he'd opened a sizeable hole, he peered through.

Clutching her shoulder, Piper was on the floor with her back pressed against the sink and her outstretched feet pinned to the bottom of the door.

"Hello, down there." Catching his breath, Liam scanned the bathroom. A tiny window was situated above the toilet, small enough for a child perhaps but no more. "You know, Ms. MacLeoid, I came to you in a reasonable manner, but now, I'm tired and frustrated. And, when I really think about it, the way that your father led my nephew Anthony astray was very, very wrong. I've happily ended one bloodline tonight; I see no reason to keep yours going." He lowered himself to his knees and drove the claw of the hammer into the lower half of the door. He tore away more wood and drove the tool in again and again, clearing a larger hole than the one at the top of the door.

He paused to catch his breath, wiped the sweat and blood from his head, sighted one of her ankles just below the hole, and smiled. "What a situation we find ourselves in, Ms. MacLeoid. Anything you'd like to say before I break you into little pieces?"

"Fuck you, again."

Keeping hold of the hammer with one hand, he reached through the opening with the other, grabbed her ankle, and yanked it level with the hole.

She screamed and tried to wrestle free.

By pressing his feet against the bottom of the door for support, he could drag her foot and her leg through.

"Get off—"

He slammed the claw of the hammer into her calf.

She screamed again.

With one hand holding her leg and the other holding the hammer wedged into her, he panted through clenched teeth. He widened his eyes as he watched the blood bubble up. He was capable of such damage!

The blood ran over her leg and over his hand, so when she yanked her leg back again, it slipped through his fingers. The claw ripped through her flesh right down to her ankle where it hit bone and bounced loose. Her foot disappeared through the hole and into the bathroom.

Liam listened to the noises she was making; he'd never heard anything like it before. It sounded as if she was choking and gagging on her own screams. "Don't worry, Ms. MacLeoid. This won't go on much longer."

He felt his cellphone buzzing in his pocket. He hoisted it out, wiped his eyes with his sleeve again, and read the name on the phone. A trembling started in his knees, and, as he rose to his feet, he felt it spreading over his entire body. He steadied himself against the tattered door, but it didn't help, and the world pulsed around him. He could still hear the guttural screaming, but it sounded less overwhelming now, as if it was happening far away in another room perhaps. It no longer had any connection to him.

He read the name again. He gagged, and his mouth filled with bile. He leaned over the bed and let it dribble onto the sheets. Then he staggered toward the exit. He needed air.

He drew back the bolt while the phone buzzed hard in his hand. He looked at the screen again. He flinched. The name seemed to shout at him. He walked outside, took deep breaths of the air, and the world turned black.

MASON LOOKED at the bloody hammer in his hand, gagged, and let it slide from his fingers. He felt the impact on his foot, but it didn't hurt; he was wearing Liam's black army boots. Wincing, he touched the corner of his eye and noticed his bloody fingertips.

The cellphone in his other hand was ringing. He checked the screen. He couldn't believe it. As he answered, he steadied himself against the wall. "Hello?"

"Hello, Mason."

"I don't understand. I don't understand ..."

She gently shushed him. "Be calm, Mason."

He surveyed the army uniform. "I'm covered in blood."

"We knew this day would come, Mason."

He studied the glowing neon sign for the Blue Falls Motel. "I don't know what happened. I don't know what I've done."

"Let me help you."

"Yes, I love you."

"I know."

"But it's been so long."

"It had to be that way."

He saw his vehicle in the parking lot and started toward it. "I'm at the motel. I don't know how I got here."

"Meet me at the Skweda."

Mason cried. It burned the wound in his eye. "Why are you helping me?"

"Because of what you mean to me."

"But it was so long ago ..."

"Those feelings never go away. So, Mason, the Skweda?"

"Where at the Skweda?"

"Where we laid her to rest."

He opened his car door and climbed in. "Okay."

"But listen, Mason, go via Shawcross Lane. Avoid passing your store."

"Why?"

"Because they know now, Mason. That way is not safe for you."

He watched the cloud of smoke. *His store ... his life's work ...*

"Promise me that you'll go via Shawcross," she said.

"I promise." He paused, took a deep breath, and forced back more tears. "I think I've done some very bad things."

"We've all done bad things."

"I know ... I know, but not like this."

"Come now, then."

"I will, my love."

She hung up.

He closed the driver's door.

The passenger door opened. Liam climbed in and sat beside him. He was dressed in his army uniform and was covered in blood. He also had a military haircut. "You're not going, brother? Surely, you're not going to trust her."

"It's the end of the line, Liam," Mason said, touching his own head. He too had a military cut. He started the car and eyed Liam. "You should have stayed dead."

"You brought me back, brother."

"What have you done?"

"I came close to giving you the peace you so deserve."

"There is no peace for me, Liam. There never has been, and there never will be."

20

"NOW WHAT?" Gabriel asked.

Jake turned the vehicle into Gabriel's road. "We go home. We wait."

"Wait for what?"

"Wait to see if it's over."

"That's not my style."

"It wasn't an option."

A cat was walking across the road and stopped in the middle. Rather than carry on, it turned its green eyes on the car's occupants.

Jake brought the car to a halt.

"I'm glad we're not going to a casino," Gabriel said.

"Where I come from, if it crosses your path left to right, it's good luck," Jake said.

"My father was a gambler. He told me that if a black cat crosses your path in Vegas, it was an omen you were going to lose."

"I'm not superstitious."

"Me neither. I don't gamble either. I want to see the

body of the man who killed my sister before I believe it's really over."

Jake's cellphone rang, and he answered it as the cat continued on its journey. "Lillian?"

"Are you alone?"

"Yes," Jake lied.

"We're at the store now. The remains of two people have been spotted in the wreckage so far. It's too early to say who they are."

Jake started to drive, now the cat had cleared his path. He could feel Gabriel's eyes boring into him. "Okay, keep me updated."

"I will. That's not the whole reason I'm calling. I just heard something of interest from Mason's doctor. He called me back."

"Go on."

Lillian told him about the affair. "You think it's relevant?"

"I don't know, but eighty-nine is around the time Collette Jewell disappeared, so it's worth a look." He spied Gabriel, whose eyes could not be any wider.

"Ewan and I were going to check it out, but the lieutenant just told us to hang tight until we calm down this scene. We're stretched thin on the ground here, and the crowd is thickening. I wondered if you wanted to ask a few questions. She knows you're not police, so she'll knock you back, but I figured it was worth a shot."

Jake eyed Gabriel again. "Don't worry about that. I'm sure we'll get a response. I'll stop by. What harm can it do?"

After parking behind his ex-lover's vehicle, Mason exited the car and worked his way through the trees toward the Skweda. He could hear his brother crunching through the undergrowth behind him.

"You're making a mistake, brother."

"The only mistake I ever made, Liam, was listening to you."

"I'm only here *because* of you."

"No. You're only here because they never invented a medicine strong enough to keep you away."

"Up to you, brother. Go ahead and play the victim card, but I can tell you this; if you meet that woman at the water's edge, you'll end up the victim you so long to be."

"She isn't the problem." He hoisted himself over a fallen tree trunk. "The things you've done are the problem."

"Everything I did, you wanted, and you *enjoyed*."

"How could I? I was never aware."

Liam snorted. "Lie, then, brother. Lie to me, and to yourself. You lived through every moment. Every swing of that hammer. Every press of that trigger. Every *single* moment."

"It's you who lies!" He shook his head, gripped the sides of his face, and closed his eyes. "Just leave me alone!"

No reply.

Mason opened his eyes and turned. Liam had gone.

He turned back and meandered through the rest of the undergrowth. The sound of the Skweda grew louder. Occasionally, he steadied himself against a tree. His recent exertions—*Liam's* recent exertions—had been too much for an old man to bear. The pain in his eye really continued to bother him too, and he had to wipe at the blood regularly when it threatened to close off his vision.

He came through the trees onto the riverbank.

She stood with her back to him, looking across the river.

It flowed, as it so often did, quickly, and he was glad of this. The noise of the water on rocks and against the banks would surely have drowned out his conversation with his brother—a conversation which may have led to her being more guarded than she currently was.

She'd never known about his condition. And he'd certainly never spoken to her about his brother. Even on that awful night when Collette died and Liam had taken center stage to support with what needed to be done, she'd known nothing of his existence. Liam had listened to Mason more back then. Liam had promised not to betray the change of identity, and he'd come good on his vow.

Mason stood behind the woman he'd never stopped loving.

"That night we stood here, do you remember how calm the water was?"

"Yes," Mason lied. He couldn't remember, because it had been his brother standing here that night.

"Public perception of me is so skewed. They think I'm impenetrable, a woman made of iron."

"It doesn't matter what they think. I know the truth."

"Which is?"

"That you're just strong, and you love as well as the next person."

"You say I'm strong, but that night, I *needed* you. It was your strength that got us through it."

Not mine, Mason thought. *Liam's.*

"You waded out with that broken girl. You weighted her down. You laid her to rest. *You* saved us. Realizing how weak I truly was changed me. It is because of you, Mason, that I am what I am, and I thank you for it."

"I've missed you. Every day since that night, I've missed you. We can get away. We can still be together."

"But you're not listening. I'm not the woman I was back then." Priscilla Stone turned and raised her eyebrows. "Blood ... so much blood. What have you done?"

"It's complicated. It wasn't me. At least, it isn't the me that you know."

"So, we've both changed since that night. Maybe, then, you can forgive me for what is about to happen."

There was only a yard between them. He considered reaching for her; she showed no sign of fear.

"Because she's not alone," Liam said from beside him.

Mason opened his mouth to reply but forced back the words. He didn't want Priscilla to know what he lived with —what he'd *always* lived with. He felt the pressure at the back of his head—the muzzle of a gun, no doubt. "Why, my love?"

"When things draw to an end, you are best being the person who determines that ending."

"All I want is for it to end. Can it not end with us together?"

"I'm sorry, but that ending is for the delusional."

"Delusional! She's got that right," Liam said.

"Shut the fuck up," Mason said, snapping his head left. The muzzle was now pressed against the side of his forehead.

Liam, still wearing his blood-splattered army uniform, was laughing.

"Just go away, Liam. I beg of you."

"Who are you talking to?" Priscilla asked.

"Tell her, brother," Liam said. "You might as well. It'll be all over in a moment."

Mason felt his damaged eye sting as it filled with tears. "You spoiled everything. *Everything*."

"*I* spoiled everything?" Liam placed a hand to his chest. "It was almost done, brother. If you'd let me finish, you'd have had nothing to fear ever again."

"Apart from a *fucking* jailcell?"

"Brother, you were never going to jail! Look at you! You'd have seen out your days in a comfortable room on medication, watching football to your heart's content!"

"One last time, Mason, who the hell are you talking to?" Priscilla asked.

He turned toward Priscilla. The gun settled on the back of his head again. "My brother."

"There's no one there."

Liam came alongside Priscilla, and said, "He's looney, darling. Absolutely batshit crazy."

"Fuck you!" Mason said, pointing. "You're the crazy one! You killed all those people."

"How could I have?" Liam smiled. "I'm not even here."

"Stop it." Mason put his hands to his ears. "Just fucking stop."

"Listen, Mason. It was you. All you. You poisoned the cattle. You killed Henry and Bobby. You threw a dead fourteen-year-old girl into the Skweda. And tonight, you wiped out an entire family. An entire fucking family!"

Mason fell to his knees.

"And your own wife, what you did to her really is the icing on the cake."

Mason looked up at his brother as the tears washed down his face. "Lorraine?"

Liam nodded. "Yes, you raped her."

Mason shook his head despite the gun still digging into the back of his head.

"You were having a tough time, brother. You lost control. I tried to protect you. And I made you believe it was the Davis brothers."

"No, no. That's not true!"

"Have you forgotten, brother? She hardly spoke to you for the rest of her miserable life!"

"Because she was damaged by what happened. By what the Davis brothers did. What *you* did!"

Liam nodded. "She was damaged by you."

Mason lowered his head. He let the tears stream down his face. When he looked up, Liam was gone, and Priscilla was alone.

"I don't know who I am," he said.

"Seems that way," Priscilla said.

"Do it."

"Do what?"

"You know. What you came here to do."

"Ah, that." She nodded.

His final thought before his world turned black was, *Maybe there's a better world than this one.*

JAKE HAD BEEN in some impressive properties in England before but never anything like this. Money obviously went a lot further here, and if you had a great deal of money, as the Stones most certainly did, the world was your oyster in terms of land and housing.

A young servant who was suited, booted, and, undoubtedly, packing a concealed weapon, introduced himself as Simon Drake and told them Charles Stone was far too sick to receive visitors—police or otherwise.

Gabriel sneered. "I make the decisions on that, young

man. Besides, we're here to see the lady of the manor, not the dying man upstairs."

"Are the police allowed to talk like that?" Simon asked.

Jake watched in disbelief as Gabriel nodded and said, "Yep. When you're the chief, you get the monopoly on words."

"Mrs. Stone's not here."

"Okay, we can wait."

"I'd prefer it—"

"Preferences don't get a say when conducting an investigation, son."

"What exactly do you think Mrs. Stone has done?"

Gabriel eyed Jake and smiled. "Have I missed something? Does this little man think I'm in his employ?"

Jake didn't respond. This was getting far too heated for his liking.

Gabriel turned back. "Show me to your living room, son, and we'll both take coffee while we wait."

Simon frowned and stepped to one side.

"Who else is here?" Jake said.

"Just me, and Mr. Stone, upstairs, resting." Simon showed them through to a large room which opted to keep its décor to a minimum, although not its cost.

As Jake sat on a luxury designer sofa—the cost of which could take many hungry people out of poverty—he declined the coffee for fear that Simon would do something unsavory to it.

Gabriel accepted.

After Simon left them, Jake turned to Gabriel. "It's like you were born to be hostile. I've never seen anyone so good at it! Priscilla Stone might not be involved."

"I know her. I know her *well*. She's involved."

"How can you possibly be so certain?"

"She let the MSP marginalize me."

"Did she have a choice? Looking at you now, I'd have probably done the same."

"She didn't have to bend over as easily as she did. She wanted me off the investigation, and she was looking forward to it blowing over. Except ..." He narrowed his eyes. "Look what just blew into her foyer."

"Jesus. This is a mistake. Have you ever done anything calmly? Also, why has the chief selectman got bodyguards marauding as servants? Is that common practice?"

Gabriel shrugged. "I guess it depends on how important you think you are. Maybe she was expecting something like this to happen. She's certainly been living by the sword for long enough."

Jake observed Gabriel eyeing the closed door for a few minutes before suddenly standing up. "I'm going to take a piss."

Gabriel left the room and closed the door behind him.

Jake checked his cellphone and saw he had missed Lillian, so he hit Call Back. He heard a crash from the hallway and killed the call. He moved for the door, opened it, and looked out.

With his back pressed against the wall for support, Gabriel had his arm looped around Simon's neck. At their feet was a tray, a smashed cup, and a pool of coffee. Simon was tugging on Gabriel's arm, but the big chief's headlock was too powerful, and the bodyguard was starting to tire.

"Gabriel!" Jake barked.

"Come near me, Jake, and I'll break his neck."

"You're going about this all wrong, Gabriel."

Gabriel remained focused on restricting Simon's air supply. When the bodyguard fell limp in his arms, he reached around and under Simon's jacket and removed the concealed gun. Then he released the bodyguard and let him slump into the pool of coffee.

Gabriel pointed the gun at Jake. His hand shook, and his eyes darted side to side.

"What's up with you? This is more than a whiskey hangover. You're not thinking clearly."

"I've never felt clearer," Gabriel said.

"Could have fooled me! Look at you! What now?"

"Aren't you afraid I might kill you, Jake?"

"I don't think you'd be that ridiculous."

"Why is it ridiculous? You've been a thorn in my side since the day you stepped into Blue Falls."

"Yet, here I am—the only person trying to talk some fucking sense into you."

Gabriel grunted. "Anyway, you needn't worry. You're someone else's problem now."

Jake felt his blood run cold. "Whose problem? Gabriel, what have you done?"

"Nothing. Just saying your days have been numbered since you ran from something you shouldn't have. No one hides from the people they cross, as the lovely Priscilla is about to find out."

"And if she's innocent?"

"I'll get the truth first." He removed handcuffs from inside his jacket and threw them to Jake. "Go into the living room and secure yourself to something."

Jake looked at the handcuffs, then back up at Gabriel. "I'm not going to do that."

"Then you'll die now rather than later."

"You have more morals that that."

Gabriel snorted. "Have you forgotten what we did to Anthony Rogers and Jotham MacLeoid?"

"That was different. Circumstances called for it."

"And these circumstances—" Gabriel fell sideways and slammed into the wall.

Jake noticed that Simon had recovered consciousness and had reached behind to grab the chief's leg, trying to yank the big man downward.

Gabriel pointed the gun down and rewarded Simon's moment of valor with a bullet to the chest.

"Jesus!" Jake shouted.

Simon kept hold of Gabriel's leg for a moment longer until his eyes rolled back, and his arms went limp.

"You stupid, stupid man," Jake said. "What the hell have you done?"

Gabriel pointed the gun at Jake. "Shut up! This is all your fault. You should have gone in there when I told you to. Then I'd have restrained him in time." Gabriel tapped his forehead with his gun. "Shit ... shit. Let me think ... okay." He stepped backward from the body and retrained the gun on Jake. "You drag the body in there, now. They mustn't see it when they come back."

Jake pounded the wall. "When did you become such a desperate man?"

"We're all desperate. One way or another. Now, do as I say!"

Jake took a deep breath, hissed, "You fucking maniac," under his breath, stepped forward, knelt, and took the dead man's foot. As he dragged, he glared at Gabriel. "You do realize this is the end of the road for you now."

"For me or for us?"

Jake shook his head.

"We killed those men together."

"Fuck you, Gabriel. You're not going to sully the only good thing you did in your pathetic life!"

"I haven't decided yet. Keep dragging, and who knows? We both might live to fight another day."

Jake watched Gabriel pop more pills and pace around the living room.

"What are those tablets?" Jake said.

"They help me think."

"They're not working."

He stopped and stared at Jake. "Fuck you." He moved his sidearm between trembling hands, as if it was red hot.

"Killing me won't solve any of your problems. In fact"—he lifted his hand, and the handcuff rattled against the radiator pipe—"you couldn't even claim self-defense."

Gabriel paced around Simon's prone figure, as if he were a ravenous animal trying to decide the best part on which to start feasting.

Jake watched the wall clock. Ten minutes passed quickly. During that time, he tried to engage Gabriel in conversation but received little more than a few grunts in return before getting a final order to, "Shut the fuck up."

Eventually, Gabriel stopped pacing, threw back his head, and gasped. Clearly, the last handful of pills were crashing into his system, and Jake hoped for a heart attack. Gabriel lowered his head. His lips were drawn back to form an expression that couldn't be clearly linked to either pleasure or pain. He took a deep breath through his nose and said, "I've done things, Jake, things you wouldn't believe."

"Try me."

"You wouldn't understand."

"You know, I've seen some things, things that could even surprise you, Gabriel."

"Not like this. No, nothing like this."

"Come on. What have you done that's really so bad?"

"I've—"

The sound of a car outside interrupted him.

Gabriel narrowed his eyes. "If you warn them, if you shout, God help me, I will kill you, Jake, and if that's not enough of a warning, then know this; I will go and kill Piper." He retreated into the hallway.

Jake turned his attention to where he'd locked himself to the radiator. He ran his fingers over the long, copper pipe that hung from beneath the radiator. He tried pulling at it. It wasn't the sturdiest fit. He considered yanking at it, but Jake heard the front door open and opted to hold his breath instead.

Surprised voices. He heard a woman say, "... blood ..." He presumed it to be Priscilla Stones.

A loud, male voice ordered, "Get out now!"

Was it another bodyguard?

A gunshot, followed by a scream. Jake exhaled and yanked at the copper pipe.

The door burst open, and Priscilla charged in. She slipped over Simon's blood trail and went to her knees.

Gabriel followed her in, keeping his gun trained on the back of her head.

From Jake's position opposite the door, he could see the other body in the hallway. "Gabriel, you have to stop this now—"

He waved the gun in Jake's direction. "Shut the fuck up!"

Priscilla started to cry.

Gabriel slammed the door behind him and approached

Priscilla from behind. He placed the gun to the back of her head. "Stop crying, Priscilla. Crocodiles weep while they devour their prey. There's no emotion."

Priscilla looked up from the body at Jake. "Help me."

Instinctively, Jake yanked at the copper pipe.

"Stop, Jake!" Gabriel lifted the gun from her head and pointed it at Jake. "You don't have to die today. It's your choice."

Jake withdrew his hands. "Gabriel—"

"Do you know why I had to restrain your other guest, Priscilla?" Gabriel lowered the gun to her head. "Because he's a livewire. I watched him blow Jotham MacLeoid's brains out."

Priscilla murmured through her tears, "I don't need to know this."

"I'll decide what you need to know and don't! Jotham MacLeoid was on his knees, waiting for the bullet. Rather like you."

Jake shook his head. *Jesus, Gabriel, you really are going to take me down with you.*

"Oops," Gabriel said, putting a hand to his mouth. "My big mouth."

Jake leaned back and put his head against the wall, feeling condemned.

"And I killed Mason's son Anthony and your two bodyguards. Shit," Gabriel said, stamping his foot. "There I go again. Another bag, another cat. So, Priscilla, now that you kneel in a room full of killers, do you understand the gravity of your situation?"

Priscilla continued to cry.

Gabriel pushed the nuzzle of his weapon into the back of her head. "Turn off the tears. Now."

She did.

"Good. You were always the best actress. I've watched you cry in public over your husband, remember? So, do you understand the gravity of your situation?"

"What do you think, Gabriel? There are two dead bodies in my house, and you've just told me that you and this man here murdered two of our residents. I didn't get Charles and I into this position by being stupid."

Gabriel snorted. "She's back, the Priscilla we know and love."

"What do you want? It seems that if we don't come to some arrangement now, then I die, and you'll spend the rest of your life in jail, so is it not best to discuss terms? Did you forget the money I offered?"

"The only thing I want is the truth."

"The truth about …?"

"About Collette, my sister."

"What could I possibly—"

"Enough … enough!" He dug the gun in, forcing her head down. "You were in a relationship with Mason around the time my sister disappeared. If you lie to me about that now, I will end this conversation, and I will end you."

"Alright. So, I was in a relationship with Mason, and then I wasn't. That doesn't mean I killed your sister."

"You know *what* happened. The way you tried to control me, silence me. You know. I have never been so certain of anything in my life."

"You're wrong."

"Tell. Me." He pushed hard with the gun, forcing her head right down and her back into an arch.

"The truth will disappoint you."

"Let me be the judge of that."

"Loosen the gun, then. Let me back up straight."

Gabriel obliged but kept the weapon against her head.

"Our relationship lasted a few months—for me, at least. For him, it seemed to have lasted a lifetime."

"What do you mean?"

"I mean, we had some fun. He seemed to think it was something more than that. Still did, up until about half an hour ago."

"Up until? What are you talking about?"

"It seems we really are in a room full of killers, Gabriel. He's in the Skweda now."

Gabriel turned with a hand to his forehead and shuffled away.

"You killed him?" Jake asked.

"That's what I said," Priscilla said. "Well, technically, Lucas did, but on my order."

"Lucas?" Jake asked.

"The one you just shot in the hallway. Anyway, I know your secrets, and you know mine, so I guess we're all in a comfortable position?"

"Comfortable?" Gabriel turned and bared his teeth. He marched forward and put the gun to Priscilla's head again. "*Comfortable?* Mason killed my sister, and you knew about it. That makes you as far from comfortable as you can possibly be."

1990

THE HEAT PRESSED down on Priscilla Stone. As always, the sex with Mason had been intense.

While she sweated on the shop floor by the magazine rack, Mason leaned against the counter, dressing. She admired his toned body just before he concealed it behind a collared shirt and a pair of jeans. Briefly, she wondered if this affair, which had been born from lust for the local gun shop owner, was developing into something more.

"I think I'm in love with you," Mason said.

She thought about his admission, thought some more about her own developing feelings, and opted not to respond. Instead, she reached for her underwear which Mason had cast to one side during their earlier frenzy. As she slipped on her panties and fastened her bra, she settled on the safer of responses. "I need to get back before Charles returns from his council meeting."

"Can't you just tell him you're working late?"

"Quite the risktaker, aren't you? What happens if Lorraine comes back early?"

"She never gets back early when she's visiting her

mother. She'll always stay until the nurse asks her to leave. We've still got time."

Dressed only in her underwear, Priscilla slipped against him, and they kissed. When she pulled away, she said, "Do you ever wonder what'll happen to us after Lorraine's mother dies and there is no reason for her to leave your side?"

"I try not to think about it."

"It's best to be ready."

"By then, you'll be as convinced about me as I am about you."

"Even if I was in love with you, I could never leave Charles."

"There's still time for me to change your mind." Mason smiled. "Lorraine's mother is a tough old—"

The bell on the shop door tinkled.

She noticed the schoolgirl at the front of the shop—Chief Jewell's daughter, Collette. Priscilla's first thought was, *Look at the huge hole in those tights. Grab yourself another pair from one of the aisles.* Her second thought was, *Jesus, Mason, you left the shop door unlocked?* She regarded him and saw the disbelief etched on his face; to forget something so important was so unlike him. At this point, he may very well have quipped, *"Love makes you do the funniest things,"* if they hadn't been faced with the catastrophic fact that their dangerous liaison was about to become public knowledge.

Priscilla looked back and opened her mouth to speak, but nothing came out.

Collette looked as stunned as Priscilla felt, and why wouldn't she? Priscilla was a married woman in her underwear, standing close to a married man. "Sorry,"

Collette said. "I thought you were open. My dad sent me for fluid for his Zippo."

"Of course, dear," Mason said.

Was he serious? Or was he responding out of shock too?

"If it's not a good time, though ..." Collette said.

"Of course. It's fine. I was just helping Mrs. Stone with ..." He ran his gaze over her half-naked body. He didn't bother finishing the lie, because it wasn't possible to create a believable one. "Come over to the counter, dear, and I'll grab you one from the shelf."

Priscilla backed away, past the magazine rack, into one of the aisles.

Collette, pale and rigid, edged across the shopfloor to the counter.

Mason bypassed his lover and headed down the same aisle she stood in front of.

Priscilla listened to Mason fumble around for the tin on the shelf while she kept her gaze on the timid girl at the counter—the timid girl who now possessed information that could destroy everything she and Charles had worked for.

As Mason slipped past her with the tin, she gripped him. He turned his pale face to hers, and she hissed, "She can't leave."

He raised an eyebrow as if to say, *But what does that mean?*

She shrugged. "You created this mess, so you now have to fix it."

"Got it right here, dear," Mason said, approaching Collette.

"Thanks, sir," Collette murmured.

As Mason rounded the counter, he said. "Ah, darn it, it's out of date." He put it on the counter. "And I don't have any more on the shelf."

"It's okay, sir. I could take a box of matches or a disposable lighter until you have—"

"No, dear. You came here for lighter fluid, and lighter fluid you shall have. Let's head to the stock cellar."

"It's fine, sir. Honestly. Dad won't mind. As long as he gets to smoke tonight, he'll be happy. Please don't trouble yourself!"

"*Nonsense!* Come with me!" Mason came around the counter, gently put his hand on Collette's shoulder, and led her across the shop floor.

Priscilla followed at a distance so as not to make the girl more nervous than she already was.

When Mason reached the door by the shelves of liquor on the final aisle, he unlocked it, opened it, and switched on the light. He pointed down some old steps.

Collette looked up at him.

"Now, if you wait here, dear," Mason said, "I'll shoot down and grab it." Mason disappeared down the steps.

It seemed like he was gone ages. Collette tapped her foot impatiently. Even an overly polite girl like Collette would turn her back on this most awkward of situations if it didn't end anytime soon.

A crash sounded from below. "Help me!"

Collette looked back at Priscilla with wide eyes, then back at the open cellar door again.

"I'm trapped. Help me!" Mason shouted from below.

Collette responded how her policeman daddy or her elder brother wannabe policeman would probably have done. She opted to help.

Unsure of what Mason was planning exactly, Priscilla turned her back and placed a fist to her mouth and waited ...

And waited.

Eventually, she heard the door slam and turned to see Mason standing there, locking it.

He turned, out of breath, and sidestepped to lean against a shelf of beer to compose himself.

Then the thumping began. "Please! Let me out!" Collette called through the door.

Mason scrunched his face at Priscilla.

Even from this distance, she saw the tears starting in his eyes. She'd never seen him cry before. Part of the reason she'd been attracted to him—or rather, *lusted* over him—was his manliness. She'd never seen this vulnerable side before.

"Please ... *I'm scared.*" Collette said. The thumping grew louder.

Mason approached Priscilla, shaking now with tears streaking his face.

When he was close enough, she said, "Get control of yourself, Mason."

"But now what?"

"Please ... help! Daddy, help me!" Collette shouted.

"Shit," Mason said. "She's calling for her father. She's calling for the chief of police!"

Priscilla put her hands on his shoulders. "Breathe, Mason. He can't hear. No one can hear outside."

"That's not the point! The point is that I just locked the fucking chief of police's daughter in a cellar!"

"It's temporary. You've done well. You've brought us some breathing space. Don't blow it now by having a panic attack. We need a plan."

Collette's shouting continued. The door shook as she kicked it.

"Okay, okay ..." Mason said. "Money. Money solves everything. You have a lot of it, right?"

"Well, my husband does, but yes, along those lines."

"And Charles is close to Chief Jewell, isn't he?"

Priscilla nodded. "But this all depends on Charles being brought in on it. When today started, I didn't envisage confessing our antics on your shopfloor."

"How will he respond?"

"In the same way he responds to everything—with careful consideration."

Collette was shrieking.

"She's losing control," Mason said. "We need to be quick."

"He'll see the big picture. He'll want to keep this quiet. He won't want to destroy everything we've worked for. Are you ready for me to contact Charles? Can you handle that? I don't know how he'll respond ... to you."

"No. You don't understand. It'll kill Lorraine."

Collette reached new volumes.

"You have no choice though, Mason, do you? Neither of us do now."

The kicking grew louder.

Mason turned full circle. He clutched his head. "There must be some other way."

"Let me out!" Collette wailed.

"Shut up," Mason shouted back. "Just *shut up*!"

NOW

"SHE SHOULD HAVE stayed silent. Stupid girl," Priscilla said.

"Call her stupid again," Gabriel said, "and it all ends for you this moment."

"Okay, okay," Priscilla said, holding her hands in the air. "But we were so close. We had a plan. I just had to bring Mason on board. But then, it was just too late."

"Too late?"

Priscilla sighed. "Yes. And I'm sorry, Gabriel, I truly am. A day doesn't pass that I don't think about what happened next, how it could have been different. I should have put my hand on Mason's shoulder, I should have calmed him, but—"

"What happened?"

"Mason couldn't cope with her shouting and kicking the door anymore. He just lost it, marched over to the door, opened it, and shouted at her."

"Just shouted?"

"Yes, but ... but ..."

"But, what? I don't understand."

She winced as Gabriel pushed the gun harder into her head. "It scared her. She fell ... back down the stairs."

"Fell?"

"Yes. No one touched her. No one. It was an accident, Gabriel. You have to believe me."

"Did you try to help her?"

"Of course. Yes, but she was gone. It looked like a broken neck."

Gabriel backed away. Keeping hold of the gun, he pinned his wrists to his temples as if he was trying to stop his head from exploding. "You put her in that cellar though?"

"Yes. Well, Mason did; no one ever wanted to kill a little girl. It was an accident. What do you think I am, Gabriel?"

"You locked up my sister. You caused the accident, and ... and ... then you put her in a river. You threw her away. And the sightings in Portland? The witnesses who came forward to say they'd seen her with a young couple? The facial composites? You were behind all of it?"

"Charles had influence. We needed to divert attention away from Blue Falls. We had no choice. There were no other options."

"You could have told the truth." Gabriel turned in circles. "You ruined my father's life. My mother's. *Mine!*"

"If I'd gone to jail, it would have destroyed everything we were building. We wanted to improve Blue Falls. We *have* improved it. I did it for the greater good."

"Greater good? Do you have any idea what you've done to me? The things you've made me do?" He sprayed flecks of spit as he shouted.

They turned to the window when they heard another car arrive.

Ewan parked alongside Jake's beat-up rental.

Back at the burned-out store, Lillian had admitted to Ewan that she'd informed Jake of the affair. He hadn't been pleased, and most of this journey to Charles and Priscilla's house had been spent in stony silent. Having grown fond of Ewan, she was unhappy to have disappointed him, but if she had to, she'd make the same decision all over again. Jake was a valuable asset in a town with very few.

As they approached the door, they heard a gunshot and drew their weapons.

"Go to the car," Ewan said, throwing her the car keys, "and call for backup."

Lillian sprinted for Ewan's Audi, unlocking the doors with the key fob and pulling out her cellphone. She ducked into the vehicle and scrolled through her numbers until she found Lieutenant Louise Price. She looked over the dashboard as Ewan tried the front door and discovered it was unlocked.

Be careful ...

Louise answered on the second ring.

"Gunfire in Priscilla Stone's home, ma'am."

She was already aware of the location from an earlier conversation. "Stand down until backup—"

She watched Ewan disappear into the house. "Officer Taylor has gone in, ma'am."

Two more gunshots sounded in quick succession.

"Officer Sanborn!" Louise said. "Stand down. That's a direct order."

Gabriel exited the house, holding a gun.

Lillian was both surprised and relieved to see him. She stepped from the vehicle.

"All clear," Gabriel said, holstering his weapon.

She ran toward her chief. "Thank god, sir. You okay?"

He looked pale and shaken. His hair was glued to his forehead with sweat. "Yes."

"Jake? Ewan?"

"Fine, both in there. Lucky Ewan showed up when he did. Priscilla and her bodyguards turned on us." He stumbled.

Lillian took some of his weight and kept him upright.

"It was her, Lillian. She killed my sister."

"You need to sit down, sir."

"I'm fine." He stumbled again.

She pressed the car keys into his hand. "Sit in Ewan's Audi, sir."

Gabriel stroked Lillian's face. "God bless you, Lillian. I always liked you."

"Thank you, sir."

She ran toward the house and went in the front door. The first thing she saw was Ewan on the floor, clutching his throat, gurgling, and drowning in his own blood. She fell to her knees and took his hands.

He was trying to open his mouth to speak, but a bullet had also entered his cheek and ruined his jaw.

She pressed on the backs of his hands, trying to help him in stemming the flow.

He exhaled and fell still.

She heard a car starting outside.

"Lillian!" Jake said.

She looked up from Ewan's body and saw another body in the hallway. Ahead through an open door, she noticed Jake sitting at the back of a room. He seemed to be tugging on a radiator.

"Lillian, it's Gabriel. He's lost control!"

Lillian stood and ran back outside, drawing her weapon. She burst outside in time to see the back of the Audi disappear down the street. She ran back in, dodging past Ewan and the other body. She entered the living room and saw another two bodies, one she recognized as Priscilla Stone.

"Help me!" Jake said. He had his feet against the radiator and was tugging with all his might on a pipe.

She saw the handcuffs, and when she drew close, she fell to her knees and pulled a set of keys from her pocket. She fumbled through them until she found the standard key they used in the department and released Jake.

Jake stood. "I'm going after him."

"No. It's not a good idea. I'll call in the car."

"Call it in anyway." Jake ran for the door. "What car is it?"

She told him.

JAKE WAS SPEEDING down Gabriel's road when Ewan's Audi burst from his driveway. He hit the brakes. A collision would kill them both.

Gabriel turned sharply left, and Jake bashed his horn. The chief accelerated away.

"Fuck!" Fast driving was Jake's Achilles heel. He could handle many things—heights, fire, armed criminals—but stabbing an accelerator pedal and reaching ridiculous speeds was not in his repertoire. "Mike, where are you when I need you?"

His old colleague, DCI Yorke, had prided himself on a successful high-speed pursuit course. Jake had prided him on it too because it allowed him to take up the honors in situations like this.

Jake jammed the accelerator pedal, only realizing that Gabriel was about to hit a crossroads when his speedometer raced past eighty. Hopefully, Gabriel would hit the brake. Rear-ending him would be far less of a risk to Jake than a speeding vehicle T-boning him.

Gabriel cleared the crossroads.

"Christ!" Jake hit the crossroads.

He glanced left at the oncoming vehicle. His eyes were blurred from the sweat running down his forehead, so how close the vehicle was he could not ascertain. When he reached the other side, he was almost surprised he was still alive and, with that, came a burst of adrenaline and confidence. He punched the accelerator, tensed his hands on the wheel, and dinked Gabriel's bumper. "Still here, fucker."

Driving an Audi, Gabriel should really have left Jake and his Ford in the dust, but several vehicles were now in front of the chief, acting as regulators.

"Where you going to go, dickhead?" He bashed the horn again.

Jake didn't like Gabriel's answer; the bastard swerved onto the left side of the road.

Suicidal ...

Jake followed. Together they streaked around a line of cars. Jake caught a couple of surprised faces in the vehicles they overtook. He prayed to God that he wouldn't be seeing any surprised faces in any approaching vehicles, or that really would be that.

Gabriel cleared the three vehicles with ease and darted back in. The prick now had a clear run and quickly opened up some distance.

Jake was level with the third and final car. He bashed his horn, demanding the driver slow down so he could move in.

The stupid bastard shot him an angry look.

How different things would be if he were back home with flashing blue lights on the grille and a two-toned siren! He'd haul this prick over the coals for obstructing him!

He pushed the speedometer to ninety, gave the angry motorist the finger, and swept in front of them. "Shit!"

Gabriel was disappearing into the distance.

He accelerated, taking the vehicle closer to a hundred, and the Audi grew larger in his line of sight again. He could taste the contents of his stomach clawing its way up his throat and into his mouth; this was his idea of Hell.

He saw the sign for the rotary and gulped.

Gabriel entered the rotary the same way he'd taken the crossroad—recklessly. He took the second exit but clipped a biker who'd opted for the third. There was a crash as both the biker and the man danced over the concrete.

Jake was now hurtling toward the unseated biker on the rotary. "Please God, please God ..." he said as he swerved. He missed the man but caught the wheel of the upended bike. It spun like a Catherine Wheel, showering sparks.

They hit a straightaway, and, despite it being residential, Gabriel pushed the speed higher.

With a superior vehicle, Gabriel had opened a considerable distance between them, but Jake felt like he was still in it. They were approaching the bridge that crossed the Skweda and veered toward Sharon's Edge.

Jake's cell rang. He swept it up from the passenger seat, answered it, and sandwiched it between his shoulder and ear. "Yes."

Ahead, Gabriel had been forced to stop. A tractor trailer

was crossing the bridge, and a stream of traffic was coming in the opposite direction.

"Where are you, Jake?" Lillian asked in the phone.

"I'm following him. I caught him coming out of his place. I'm so close I can taste the fucker's exhaust fumes."

Jake clipped Gabriel's bumper again. The whole car shook, but he kept the cell tight against his ear. "Pull back, Jake. You have to pull back."

"No chance. After watching this bastard in action, I have a duty."

Gabriel was desperately trying to get his vehicle onto the other side of the road to evade the tractor trailer, but the traffic continued.

"I've got him trapped. Tell me that the cavalry is coming."

"Yes, but you have to stop."

"I can't."

"He could have someone in the vehicle with him," Lillian said.

"He's alone."

"*We're* at his house. Someone was in his basement. The doors were open, but he'd clearly had someone locked up down there!"

"Who?"

"I don't know. But why do you think he stopped here?"

Jake gulped.

Gabriel was forcing out the nose of the Audi now. At first break, the desperate chief would go for it. If he messed it up, he'd be wiped out.

"We think it might be a child," Lillian said. "There are children's books in the room."

Jake took his foot off the accelerator.

No one was behind him, so he let the car slow.

The tractor trailer and Gabriel drove off into the distance.

"Tell me you're going to get him," Jake said.

"Yes, major roads out are blocked. He won't be leaving the area."

He cleared the bridge and pulled to the shoulder. He bashed the wheel. "Shit."

"There's something else."

"Go on."

"Piper. She was attacked."

Jake felt his body crumbling.

"She's lost a lot of blood, but I think she'll be okay. The motel manager found her. Jake, I think—"

The cell phone slipped from his shoulder and fell to the floorboards. He didn't bother to retrieve it. Instead, he made a U-turn and headed into Blue Falls and the hospital.

AFTER ...

PETER SHEENAN STOOD by Felicity Davis's gravestone long after the service had finished. The hole was still to be filled, so he stared at the coffin. "Wherever you may be, I hope you find some peace."

"She will," Piper said.

Peter smiled down at Piper in her wheelchair, then up at the large man pushing it. "Staying with that accursed family for so long ... thinking that this was the best thing for her children ... she made a dreadful mistake."

Jake put a hand on his friend's shoulder. "We all make them."

Peter sighed and wiped away a tear. "So, how long before you are up and about, Piper?"

"Rehab's going well, but my soccer days are over. Doctor says I'll always have a limp."

"I'm sorry."

"Don't be. I always hated soccer."

Jake smiled and put his other hand on Piper's shoulder. "Shall we head to the Taps for an afternoon drink?"

"I'll pass. There's someone else I'd like to say hello to while I'm here," Peter answered.

Jake nodded. "Stay out of trouble."

Peter laughed. "Oh, the irony." Peter waited until Jake had wheeled Piper away to cross the graveyard via a path lined with blossom trees.

When he reached his destination, he opened a fold-up chair he'd left by the gravestone earlier and sat down. He stared at the fresh flowers he'd also delivered before Felicity's funeral. Then he reached into his pocket for his hip flask. After pouring some Old Crow onto the ground, he said, "There you go, old man." He took a mouthful himself. "Was at a loose end myself, and you didn't seem too busy. Going to be a clear sunset later." He pointed up at the blossom trees. "And we got the best view for it."

CROWTHER'S COFFEE shop was quieter than usual, but this just seemed to make Lillian more nervous. She quickly drank her coffee and had ordered a second before she got to the point. "I can't see you anymore."

"Oh," Jake said, opting to wash down the first coffee with water rather than order a second. "Why not?"

"Lieutenant Louise Price."

"I see. So, she can tell you who to be friends with?"

"It's more than that, Jake, and you know it."

Jake laughed. "Don't worry, Lillian. I think the world of you, you know that. If me stepping aside helps your career, just tell me how far to step."

"At least until she goes. Then we can be friends again."

"Okay. When's that likely to be then?"

"When she finds the chief and the missing child."

"Interesting how the case she turned up for closes and she sticks on for another one."

"She's like you."

"I doubt it."

"She is—obsessive, especially when it involves children."

"Aren't we all like that when it involves children?"

Lillian nodded. "I guess so. She took the death of Ewan hard too."

"As did you," Jake said, reaching to take her hand.

Lillian pulled away her hand. "I hardly knew him."

"Doesn't mean it didn't affect you."

"No. I guess you're right. You know, she's a good person, the lieutenant. You'd like her."

"I'm sure I would."

"She's had a bad life. Awful things have happened to her."

"Like what?"

Lillian opened her mouth, then closed it again. "I can't say. I really can't."

"I understand."

"She'll find them. The chief, I mean—Gabriel. And the child."

"I hope she does."

"But she doesn't want your help."

"I understand."

"She said she comes from a place where they do things properly."

"That's refreshing."

"So, you see my dilemma?"

"I don't just see it, Lillian. I *understand* it."

"She thinks he might still be in the area, in one of the adjoining towns. The main roads out were blocked. He'd been hemmed in."

Jake finished his water. "Any news on the traces of blood found in the basement?"

"I shouldn't say. I really shouldn't."

"This last question, then I'll leave you to get on with it."

"The blood belonged to Ayden MacLeoid."

"He wasn't a child."

"No."

"But his sister was."

Lillian nodded.

Jake's blood ran cold—Kayla MacLeoid, Piper's half-sister.

"You didn't hear that from me."

"Wow," Jake said.

"You need to stay out of it until she's found. Please?"

"Of course," Jake lied. "You won't hear a peep from me."

SALISBURY, ENGLAND

He ended the phone call. *It's over.* He ran a thumb and forefinger over his moustache. *Unexpected.* However, he was a man resilient to surprises, and this job itself didn't warrant emotional responses to any situation. His instructions, as always, were specific.

The target has been located. Your brief is complete. Clean. You were never there. Return the car to the address you were given. Head to the rendezvous point for your new identity.

He looked out the window to see Sheila Pettman leaving her home to take her son Frank to school. He knew her routine like clockwork. He reflected briefly on how the most important information could, in a matter of a second, become the most irrelevant. He made a mental note of the date and time, as he always did when he was about to become someone new and his target ceased to be of relevance to him.

His first instruction: *Clean.*

He heard the door open behind him.

"Stuart?" She sounded nervous.

"Yes, Mary."

"I heard you talking on the phone. I couldn't understand you."

"I was speaking Russian." He reached into his inside pocket.

"Russian? You never said you could— How do you know Russian?"

His hand closed on the garotte wire in his pocket. "Because I am Russian, Mary, and I'm afraid it is now time for me to leave."

FREE AND EXCLUSIVE READ

Delve deeper into the world of Wes Markin with the **FREE** and **EXCLUSIVE** read, ***A Lesson in Crime***

Scan the QR to READ NOW!

ALSO BY WES MARKIN
CONTINUE THE JAKE PETTMAN SERIES WITH BLUE FALLS

A preying killer. A team of bloodthirsty mercenaries. A disgraced chief of police on a trail of murder.

Following the brutal events of the past months, the Maine State Police cannot stem the rising tide of violence sweeping through Blue Falls and its neighbouring towns.

At the heart of this discontent Jake Pettman hides from men he betrayed back in England. Savage men who now know where he is.

But Jake has more pressing concerns.

Kayla MacLeoid. A kidnapped fourteen-year-old girl.

And Jake cannot turn his back on a child.

Even if it kills him.

Fire in Bone is an adrenaline-pumping crime thriller novel from the Amazon bestselling author of One Last Prayer for the Rays, and the DCI Yorke series. Perfect for fans of Chris Carter, James Patterson, Chris Brookmyre, and Stuart Macbride.

Scan the QR to READ NOW!

ALSO BY WES MARKIN
ONE LAST PRAYER

"An explosive and visceral debut with the most terrifying of killers. Wes Markin is a new name to watch out for in crime fiction, and I can't wait to see more of Detective Yorke." – *Bestselling Crime Author Stephen Booth*

The disappearance of a young boy. An investigation paved with depravity and death. Can DCI Michael Yorke survive with his body and soul intact?

With Yorke's small town in the grip of a destructive snowstorm, the relentless detective uncovers a missing boy's connection to a deranged family whose history is steeped in violence. But when all seems lost, Yorke refuses to give in, and journeys deep into the heart of this sinister family for the truth.

And what he discovers there will tear his world apart.

The Rays are here. It's time to start praying.

The shocking and exhilarating new crime thriller will have you turning the pages late into the night.

"**A pool of blood, an abduction, swirling blizzards, a haunting mystery, yes, Wes Markin's One Last Prayer for the Rays has all the makings of an absorbing thriller. I recommend that you give it a go.**" – *Alan Gibbons, Bestselling Author*

One Last Prayer is a shocking and compulsive crime thriller.

Scan the QR to READ NOW!

JOIN DCI EMMA GARDNER AS SHE RELOCATES TO KNARESBOROUGH, HARROGATE IN THE NORTH YORKSHIRE MURDERS ...

Still grieving from the tragic death of her colleague, DCI Emma Gardner continues to blame herself and is struggling to focus. So, when she is seconded to the wilds of Yorkshire, Emma hopes she'll be able to get her mind back on the job, doing what she does best - putting killers behind bars.

But when she is immediately thrown into another violent murder, Emma has no time to rest. Desperate to get answers and find the killer, Emma needs all the help she can. But her new partner, DI Paul Riddick, has demons and issues of his own.

And when this new murder reveals links to an old case Riddick was involved with, Emma fears that history might be about to repeat itself...

Don't miss the brand-new gripping crime series by bestselling British crime author Wes Markin!

What people are saying about Wes Markin…

'Cracking start to an exciting new series. Twist and turns, thrills and kills. I loved it.'

Bestselling author **Ross Greenwood**

'Markin stuns with his latest offering… Mind-bendingly dark and deep, you know it's not for the faint hearted from page one. Intricate plotting, devious twists and excellent characterisation take this tale to a whole new level. Any serious crime fan will love it!'

Bestselling author **Owen Mullen**

Scan the QR to READ NOW!

ACKNOWLEDGMENTS

Jake seems to be an unstoppable force at the moment, and it won't be long before he hits your shelves again with *Blue Falls*, but until then, I would like to deliver my gratitude to everyone who supported the production of *Fire in Bone*.

Firstly, my family, Jo, Janet, Peter, Douglas, Ian and Eileen for continuing to believe in what I am doing. My two children, Hugo and Beatrice, who are growing at a relentless rate, and so forcing us to consider moving!

Thanks, as always, to Jake, my sounding pit. Huge appreciation to Cherie Foxley who conjured up the River Skweda exactly how I imagined it!

Thank you to Jo Fletcher, Kath Middleton, Karen Ashman and Jenny Cook for getting their teeth into those earlier drafts. Thank you to all my Beta Readers who took the time to help shape my new episode in this journey – Keith, Dee. Carly, Cathy, Donna, Yvonne, Holly and Alex. Thank you to the bloggers who remain behind me – Shell, Susan, Caroline and Jason.

I hope you all join me in October for the conclusion of the trilogy when Jake's time in Blue Falls reaches its devastating conclusion...

STAY IN TOUCH

To keep up to date with new publications, tours, and promotions, or if you would like the opportunity to view pre-release novels, please contact me:

Website: www.wesmarkinauthor.com

- facebook.com/WesMarkinAuthor
- instagram.com/wesmarkinauthor
- twitter.com/markinwes
- amazon.com/Wes-Markin/e/B07MJP4FXP

REVIEW

If you enjoyed reading ***Fire in Bone***, please take a few moments to leave a review on Amazon, Goodreads or BookBub .

Printed in Great Britain
by Amazon